Kate
hersel

Then Brandi began removing pink plastic curlers from the older woman's hair and turned to Kate. "Have you met the new doctor yet?"

"He's come into the library a couple of times," Kate replied.

When it became obvious that Kate wasn't going to say any more, one of the other customers piped up. "That's not all, from what I hear." The woman practically shivered with anticipation. "I understand the two of you were together last night at the Dairy Bar."

Jean pulled her head away from Brandi and gave Kate a searching look. "Go ahead. Tell them about it."

Innuendo. Already? Kate suppressed a groan. "He was kind enough to invite me for a drink to thank me for some help I gave him."

"Careful, Katie." Grinning, Brandi shook her brush in front of Kate's nose. "That's how rumors get started."

Kate held up her hands in surrender. "Enough, please! There's plenty going on in this town without manufacturing news." And she meant every word.

Dear Reader,

We've all had experiences in our lives when the moment remembered is funnier, sweeter, more poignant or more satisfying than the event actually lived. You know, those times when we say, "We'll laugh about this later," or "This will make a good story…someday."

I rather suspect our family's minivacation in the Great Salt Plains area of Oklahoma years ago was like that—the tales we tell are more apocryphal than accurate. Boat ownership, lawn care, travel trailer maintenance, hot weather, sand flies and cramped quarters must have been frustrating, even downright unpleasant in the 1970s. But those "minor inconveniences" are not what I recall today. Lying peacefully in a hammock, allowing my mind to wander, applauding the children, as one by one, they mastered waterskiing, accompanying my daughters on their first skinny-dipping adventure, witnessing a breathtaking display of shooting stars—these are the treasured memories.

A Country Practice, set in the Great Salt Plains region, is, in part, a tribute to the hardy people of rural Oklahoma. But it was also a means for me to reconnect with a happy time in my life when getting away together as a family made a difference.

I hope you will enjoy Sam and Kate's Salt Flats neighbors and feel right at home. And maybe, just maybe, the book will call to your mind a special memory, mellowed and gilded by love and time.

Sincerely,

Laura Abbot

P.S. Write me at P.O. Box 2105, Eureka Springs, AR, 72632, e-mail me at LauraAbbot@msn.com or check the Superromance authors' Web site at www.Superauthors.com

A Country Practice
Laura Abbot

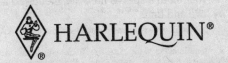

HARLEQUIN®

TORONTO • NEW YORK • LONDON
AMSTERDAM • PARIS • SYDNEY • HAMBURG
STOCKHOLM • ATHENS • TOKYO • MILAN • MADRID
PRAGUE • WARSAW • BUDAPEST • AUCKLAND

ISBN 0-373-70970-6

A COUNTRY PRACTICE

Copyright © 2001 by Laura A. Shoffner.

Visit us at www.eHarlequin.com

Printed in U.S.A.

For Betsy, Phil, Molly, Laura and Greg.

For helping create rich and lasting family memories,
for making every day Mother's Day for me,
and for the loving examples you are
to our precious grandchildren.

CHAPTER ONE

IT WAS NOW OR NEVER.

Standing outside the small brick post office in her home town of Salt Flats, Oklahoma, weighing the large padded envelope in her hand, Kate Manley fought the panic of last-minute indecision. Mailing this package could be the riskiest thing she'd ever done.

The scorching June sun warmed her back through the thin T-shirt and droplets of perspiration pooled between her breasts. She probably wouldn't be accepted anyway. Compared to so many talented others, what credentials did she possess? Even scarier, what if she *was* accepted? She'd feel like a fraud.

But she'd promised Ed. Even toward the last, when her husband had lost a third of his body weight and his skin was like crepe paper, he'd still mustered the strength to grasp her hand, fix those imploring brown eyes on her and impose his will. "You go do it, Katie. For twenty years you've sacrificed for me, for the girls, for the ranch. For every damn thing that came along. Now it's *your* turn." He'd struggled to force the words through his airway. "Don't let me down, sweetheart. And don't let yourself down." He'd brought her fingers to his cracked lips, kissed them gently, then closed his eyes, letting their clasped hands fall limply onto the hospital bed.

And so she had made him the deathbed promise.

Then, just as at this moment, fear had rampaged through her every corpuscle. Who exactly was Kate Manley without Ed? The unknown had loomed in all its terrifying unpredictability. Now, widowhood was the ever-present "known." She supposed she'd adjusted, insofar as adjustment was possible. But the loneliness was always there, lying in wait to overwhelm her.

Yet she'd emerged from the long months of mourning with renewed resolve. A great deal of life remained to be lived, and she intended to make the most of every minute.

"Toad" Portman, manager of the grain elevator and feed store, exited the post office, hitching his overalls higher on his shoulders. "You gonna stand there all day, Kate? Seems like you were waitin' out here when I went in." He glanced at her feet. "Are ya thinkin' grass is gonna grow through that concrete?" His guffaw came out high-pitched, just like his reedy voice.

Kate managed a smile. "I might wait quite a while."

"Reckon so." Toad eyed the envelope in her hand. "Mailin' a package to one of the kids?"

Kate stifled a groan. If she *was* sending something to one of her daughters, it was hardly any of Toad's business. Small towns! She loved hers, but privacy was in short supply. She had no intention of telling anyone in Salt Flats—and certainly not Toad Portman, whose wife made a vocation of gossip—the destination of this package. "No, it's just business, and if I don't get in there, I'll miss the afternoon pickup." She started up the post office steps. "Give my best to Ethel."

"Will do. Have a good 'un."

When she opened the heavy door, goose bumps pebbled her arms from a gust of cool air. Or from the realization that in a matter of seconds she would throw her future directly into the lap of the gods.

"Kate?" Minnie Odom looked up from the sorting table and approached the counter.

"I need you to weigh this parcel."

"Sure thing." The postmistress tossed the packet on the scales.

With her heart hammering, Kate slowly extracted several dollars from her billfold.

"Insurance?"

"Oh, yes. I guess." If she mailed her application and the photographs of her work, she would be committed. She could still change her mind.

"What's the value?"

Kate hesitated. How do you place value on your own creativity, talent—or lack thereof? "Fifty dollars." She paid, then watched in horrified fascination as Minnie stamped the package and handed her the insurance receipt. Childish though she knew it was, she closed her eyes as Minnie put the package in the outgoing mail bin. Gone! Her application to participate in a four-week masters' painting workshop with Lupe Santiago in Santa Fe, New Mexico. Hundreds of applicants, the brochure had stated, for only twelve positions. She must be out of her mind to think she had even the remotest chance.

As she left the post office and headed toward her Dodge pickup, she drew a deep, shuddering breath. She'd done it, actually followed through and submitted the application. Surprisingly, it felt good. Liberating, even. Maybe Ed had been right. It *was* her turn!

THE STILLNESS OF the small library, housed in a former church building and staffed by volunteers, never failed to calm Kate. Although she enjoyed working mornings when preschoolers filled the children's alcove with laughter, she preferred this Wednesday evening shift, especially during summer when the place was virtually deserted. The dying sun sent slanting rays through the narrow Gothic windows, burnishing the oak paneling to a nut-brown luster. She moved quietly among the stacks, reshelving novels. The repetitive activity was soothing in its familiarity and she found comfort in the texture, smell and heft of the books.

In the weeks following Ed's death two years ago, she'd been able to leave those awful questions at the library entrance—the future of the ranch, the intricacies of estate taxes, the complexity of insurance forms. Running her fingers down the spine of Hemingway's *A Farewell to Arms,* she smiled contemplatively, acknowledging that she'd made this place her sanctuary. Simply being here eased her fears about the momentous step she'd taken this afternoon in mailing the application.

She couldn't go on hiding from herself. Either she had talent or she didn't. Of course, Ed and her daughters, Jenny and Rachel, had bragged on her painting. The townspeople were only too happy to have her illustrate brochures, letter posters or design storefront murals. Nobody but Ed, however, took her art seriously. In fact, if anything, most acted as if her painting had little real value, viewing it as dabbling or affectation. Today's decision was the result of months of soul-searching. It boiled down to this—she had to believe in herself and step beyond her self-imposed limitations.

She shoved another book into its alphabetical resting place. So that's what she'd resolved to do. Regardless of whether Lupe Santiago accepted her, there was no reason not to exhibit her paintings at regional arts festivals. At the very least, she'd meet like-minded people and discover if her work had appeal. Let the townspeople think her peculiar. Artsy, even. She grinned, relishing the fantasy of herself in a paint-splattered smock, fuchsia leggings and a rakish beret. Salt Flats's very own bohemian!

Her daughters were on their own—Jenny, in Denver, married and the mother of a toddler, and Rachel, recently out of college and working as a flight attendant in Phoenix. All but forty acres of the pasture land had been leased, and with the insurance money she'd paid off the bank debt. Free and clear—she had nothing to lose. If she wanted, she could even move away. A heady thought, especially after a lifetime of doing the expected—marrying young, having children immediately, expending her energy as a wife, mother and helpmate.

With no one to observe her, she executed a soft-shoe shuffle. After months of seeing the world in shades of gray, colors beckoned. Rich, brilliant colors.

Humming to herself, she wheeled the book cart around the end of the shelf—directly into a man she'd never seen before. Books tumbled to the floor, echoing in the quiet. Where had he come from? She'd heard no one come in, but, then, she'd been woolgathering. "I'm so sorry," Kate mumbled. Bending to pick up the scattered volumes, she knocked foreheads with the man, intent on the same mission.

Straightening at the same time she did, he grasped her elbow. "Are you okay?"

She gazed into the most intense deep blue eyes she'd ever seen. "Y-yes. Please forgive my clumsiness." His fingers still rested on her arm.

"No harm done." His smile, full of good humor,

spread to his twinkling eyes. Slowly, almost reluctantly it seemed, he let his hand fall to his side. "In fact, perhaps you could help me."

"After barreling into you like that, it's the least I can do." Either because he was standing so close or because she was embarrassed, the man made her feel dwarflike, although she was five-foot-eight. Only when she stepped back did she notice that his dark brown hair was drawn into a ponytail. He must be a stranger here. Long-haired men didn't walk around the streets of Salt Flats without running the risk of being labeled "one of them danged hippies." But this fellow looked as if he could handle such censure. "What can I do for you?"

He eyed her up and down, in a way she could only describe as appreciative. His voice, a low murmur, competed with a strange buzzing in her head. "I'm interested in information on the history of the area."

"You've come to the right place, then. Follow me." Near the checkout desk, she showed him a shelf of books labeled The Great Salt Plains Region. Then she pointed to a large cabinet. "Over there we have a file drawer of photographs, some of them quite old. Did you know Native American tribes used to stop at the flats for their salt supply?"

"No, but I've been told the waterfowl refuge and the lake attract all kinds of birds."

"Thousands and thousands. The migrations are a sight to behold."

"Sounds like something to look forward to." He pulled several volumes from the shelf, then settled at a heavy oak library table. "These will keep me busy for a while. Thanks for your help."

"If you have any questions, let me know." She finished shelving the remaining books, then completed some routine paperwork at the desk. Out of the corner of her eye, she watched the stranger turning pages rapidly. By any standards, he could be considered rakishly good-looking. His features were pronounced, giving him a keen, hawklike visage, but his expression was more alert than threatening. She might be a fortyish widow, but she couldn't help appreciating that his body was that of a well-conditioned athlete. Overall, his appearance could best be described as unconventional. Besides the ponytail, well-groomed and clean as it was, he sported a faded Grateful Dead T-shirt, threadbare jeans and sandals. Hardly standard rural Oklahoma attire.

After half an hour, he raised his eyebrows. "Okay if I help myself to the photographs?"

"Certainly." The man had made no attempt to introduce himself. Maybe if he presented his library card, she'd discover his identity. He was either a newcomer to town or a visitor. She chuckled. The grapevine wouldn't be silent for long about a man this attractive.

Ten minutes before nine, Kate began her closing routine—adjusting the blinds, shoving in chairs, cleaning off the desk. Finally, she approached the man, hunched over a set of faded photos depicting the Land Run of 1893, which had resulted in the settlement of the Cherokee Strip and the establishment of Salt Flats. Softly she spoke. "Incredible, isn't it? All those people in buggies, on horseback, even on foot, waiting at the starting line for a signal to race across the prairie to claim government land. Their entire futures depended upon their success."

He looked up. "I suppose many folks in this area can trace their roots to those who participated."

"Absolutely. My family included."

"Really?" He began stacking the pictures.

She eased into the chair across the table. "My great-grandfather staked out a section just a little west of here."

He fixed those intense eyes on her, then smiled. "Why am I wasting my time on books? I'll bet you could give me the whole spiel, and I guarantee I'd enjoy it more coming from you."

His long, well-formed fingers played with the photographs, aligning the edges, tamping the stack against the table. She found herself reluctant to meet his eyes again—it was too easy to get lost in their depths. "I think you'll find the books more authoritative. Any history I'd give would run the risk of being folklore. Besides, it's closing time." She stood, then nodded at the volumes remaining on the table. "Would you like to check those out?"

"No, I won't have much time to read in the next few days."

She wondered why not. "Maybe another time."

He handed her the photographs, which she put into the To Be Filed tray. "Besides, I don't have a library card, yet."

"We can fix that in short order, Mr..."

"Doctor." He extended his hand. "Sam Gray."

Of course! She placed her hand in his. "Forgive me, I didn't recognize you from the picture in the *Examiner.*"

"No reason you should." He grinned. "That photo was from my yuppie period."

Eyeing him, it was hard to believe there had been a "yuppie" period. "Everyone's relieved we'll continue to have a doctor in town."

He clung to her hand and bent closer. "And you are?"

"Kate Manley."

He squeezed her fingers. "A pleasure. May I call you Kate?"

She nodded, then quickly withdrew her hand. "When did you arrive?"

"A couple of days ago. I've been setting up my office so I can see patients Monday."

"I know Dr. Floyd is pleased to have you replace him. After all these years, it's hard to believe this is his last week."

"He'll still be taking emergency calls on my days off."

She smiled. "You might not get any rest otherwise." She picked up her purse, then walked toward the door, stopping to flip off all but the night-lights.

He followed her. "May I walk you to your car?"

Kate fumbled with the lock on the library door. *Walk me to my car?* As if there was any danger in a town where the pavement rolled up at sunset. "That's not necessary, Dr. Gray."

"Hey, not so formal. Sam, please." He placed a hand under her bare elbow. "It may not be necessary, but it would be my pleasure."

She was unaccustomed to such chivalry—or to the embarrassingly welcome touch of his warm fingers. She struggled for a topic of conversation. "Have you found a place to live?"

"I've rented the Fowler house east of town near the lake. You know where it is?"

"I certainly should. Glen and Linda Fowler lived a quarter of a mile down the road from me for over twenty years."

"So not only have I met an expert on Salt Flats history, but a new neighbor. Great!"

She pointed across the street where her pickup was parked. "Thanks for the escort. And welcome to town."

He led her to the driver's side, where he put one foot on the running board while he studied her under the streetlight. "You know, Kate. I think there's going to be a lot to like about Salt Flats. A lot." He stepped back and held the door for her. "Good night."

"Good night, Dr.—er—Sam." He stood in the center of the deserted street as she edged the truck away from the curb. In the rearview mirror she saw him raise his hand and wave. For some reason, the tranquility she'd enjoyed before bumping into Sam Gray had been replaced by an unsettled, though not unpleasant feeling she couldn't quite identify, but which stirred a decidedly physical sensation in the pit of her stomach.

GNATS AND MOTHS HOVERED around the yellow light-bulb identifying Room 6 of the Shady Court Motel. The only shade Sam had experienced during his brief stay had been cast by the shadow of the portable sign beckoning travelers with its "2 for $29" sign. Despite the favorable rate and the fact it was the town's only motel, the proprietors were not overrun with business. Not surprising. Salt Flats was pretty far off the beaten track.

Sam inserted his key in the metal door. He was a long way from Oklahoma City and the comforts of hotel chains, but staying here had been his choice. Doc Floyd had offered to put him up at his home, but he was a widower and Sam hadn't wanted to impose. Besides, hadn't he always favored orange chenille bedspreads, avocado shag carpeting and pictures of flamingos?

He opened and shut the door quickly to avert an invasion of flying creatures. Fortunately he had only two more nights here before he moved into his rental house. And that wouldn't take long, considering he didn't own much. After the divorce, he'd left most of the furniture with Marcia. Since she was keeping their large home in northwest Oklahoma City, he'd wanted the twins to have as few changes as possible. He sat on the sagging mattress, then stripped off his shirt.

The twins. Just thinking about ten-year-old Bart and Blake made him grin. He glanced at the framed photograph on top of the wood-veneer dresser. They stood, arms draped around each other, mugging for the camera, their silky soccer shorts hanging Shaq-style around their knobby knees. One of the toughest things about moving would be missing their games. But even when he'd lived with them, he'd been so busy with work that he'd managed to catch only a few. Marcia had *not* been happy about that.

But she couldn't have it both ways. Because of her job as a corporate attorney, she'd insisted on moving to Oklahoma City and had nixed any thought of settling in a small town, although that had been his preference. Understanding that an urban area offered his wife the best employment opportunities, he'd compromised, vowing to give his suburban practice a chance. Besides satisfying Marcia, that decision had also pleased his father, a pediatric oncologist who had little regard for what he referred to as "country sawbones."

But no matter how hard he'd tried to arrange his schedule to accommodate Marcia's needs, she'd made it clear it wasn't enough. Arriving late to cocktail parties, having his pager sound at the symphony, taking his turn for weekend rounds at the hospital—all of it created tensions.

Her behavior baffled him. What had she expected? After all, she'd married a medical student. The twins had been born during his residency. He'd certainly been busy then. Why had she thought it would be any dif-

ferent when he joined the clinic? It wasn't as if he was
a dermatologist or something. People got sick twenty-
four hours a day.

He tossed a sandal onto the floor. Well, that part of
his life was over, and a new chapter was underway. One
that felt right. He was no country club guy and he had
never aspired to own a tuxedo for the mandatory ''black
tie'' appearances Marcia had expected of him. Ulti-
mately, they'd agreed to an amicable divorce, both of
them determined to put the boys first.

Growing his hair long had been an expression of independence, a symbol of his new beginning. It was almost funny the way Marcia couldn't look directly at
him when he picked up the boys for his weekend visitation. Even though he liked the convenience of the ponytail, he imagined he'd cut it off after he got settled.
He wasn't totally insensitive to the raised eyebrows
when he ate breakfast at the Main Street Café.

When he'd come to Salt Flats to interview, he'd been
aware he didn't exactly fit the search committee's profile—family man, rural background, fifteen years' experience, interested in people. They'd had to settle for
one out of four. He *did* like people. And apparently that
had shown. By the time they'd concluded their questioning, he'd been invited by Keith Appleby, the bank
president, to the American Legion Hall for catfish and
beer.

He stood up and shucked his pants. He'd been lucky
to get this opportunity. Ever since reading *Horse and
Buggy Doctor* as a kid, he'd dreamed of being the kind
of physician who lived among his patients and their
families, knew them and belonged to the community in
ways a specialist in a large city couldn't. The search

committee, desperate for a doctor, had taken a chance on him. He hoped to justify their confidence.

That's why he'd spent time this evening at the library. He needed to know everything he could about Salt Flats and the Great Salt Plains area. He'd committed to five years here, and he wanted the best possible start.

Kate Manley had seemed like a nice woman. And a darned attractive one. She had a gentle, graceful way of walking and speaking. Classy. She may have been a longtime Salt Flats resident, but there was nothing provincial about her looks or her mannerisms. He could swear she'd blushed when he'd helped her up from the floor. He'd noticed, too, that she'd seemed a little skittish, as if she hadn't had a man touch her in a while. Maybe she hadn't. He'd have plenty of opportunity to learn more about her when he moved nearby. A guy could do a lot worse for a neighbor.

He stretched and turned toward the bathroom. A lot worse.

"WHERE WOULD YOU LIKE me to put this, Doctor?" Nellie Forester, R.N., glanced around the bare office walls Friday morning, a curl of distaste on her lips, before lifting the framed and autographed album cover from the packing box.

"Careful with that," Sam quickly crossed the room and relieved her of the precious possession. Somehow he couldn't imagine Nurse Forester appreciating the significance of a Jerry Garcia signature, representing one of his more rash charity auction expenditures. He held the frame against the wall behind his desk. "What do you think?"

She cleared her throat, then responded dryly. "Dr.

Floyd displayed his diplomas and certificates there. Said
it inspired confidence in patients.''

He knew a suggestion when he heard one. Reluctantly,
he set down the album cover. ''Where are mine?''

''Right here.'' With smug efficiency, she handed him
his medical school diploma, certificate of residency and
membership scrolls from several professional and hon-
orary societies.

Mel Floyd had spent the earlier part of the week
showing him the inventory of supplies and acquainting
him with the clinic equipment. In addition to the office,
examining rooms and a small surgery suite, there were
two in-patient rooms, used only as a stopgap until patients could be transported to Enid, sixty miles south-
east, site of the nearest full-service hospital. With a droll
smile, Doc Floyd had also told him about Nellie Forester. ''You'll have to get used to the idea, son, that
Nellie thinks she's the doctor. She only tolerates us
medics. But she knows her stuff. And she's a helluva
hand when you have to hold down some cantankerous
farmer.'' He had taken a pull from his pipe before continuing. ''You gotta give it right back to her or she'll
browbeat you to death. But underneath? She's a damn
fine woman.''

Setting the certificates aside, he watched Nellie unpacking his medical books and neatly arranging them
in the built-in bookcase. ''You ever go to a rock concert, Nellie?''

She straightened and shot him an incredulous look.
''I beg your pardon?''

He picked up the album cover and admired it. ''You
know—Pearl Jam, Metallica—'' he searched even further back in time ''—Three Dog Night, Iron Butterfly?''

She brushed the front of her starched white uniform,

as if it was somehow contaminated. "Can't say that I have."

"Probably, then, you'd prefer some other kind of music in the clinic?" He grinned engagingly.

"Indeed. If we have to have music at all, it should be soothing, restful."

"Like?" He couldn't wait to hear what she might say.

"Mantovani, maybe." She furrowed her brow. "Or that piano player—oh, what's his name? The one with the candles."

She couldn't be serious. "Liberace?"

"That's the one."

He sighed. She'd better be one whale of a nurse. "Maybe we could compromise with George Winston and Kenny G."

"You're the doctor."

He turned and began pounding picture hangers into the wall. Between hammer blows, he said, "How are our appointments looking for Monday?"

She didn't answer. "Nellie?"

"I heard you." She crossed the room and handed him his diploma. "Try this one in that spot." She nodded her head.

"And…"

"Benjie Odom will be in for his allergy shot at ten."

"Then what?"

"That's it."

"That's *it?* Isn't the office usually busier, especially at the first of the week?"

"Yes." Instead of looking at him, she stared resolutely at his diploma from the University of Texas Medical School. "Except for Lester Jakes. He wanted to see you, but of course I told him you were all tied up."

He set the hammer on his desk. "I have only one patient Monday, but you turned another away?"

"Lester's a pest. He sees you as the new soft touch."

"Nellie, let's reach an understanding. Anyone who wants to see me gets an appointment, at least until I've determined for myself who is or is not a malingerer."

She arched an eyebrow, but when she spoke, her tone was studiously neutral. "Whatever you say, Doctor." She hooked the diploma over the hanger, then carefully aligned it. "Is there anything else you need before I leave for the day?"

"Yes. You can tell me why the usual patient load has dried up."

She pursed her lips. "They're waiting."

"Waiting?"

"Nobody wants to be the first to take a chance on a new doctor."

"I hope you'll help me change that attitude."

"That's part of my job, isn't it?"

"I'll count on you. Go on now, Nellie. Thanks for your help. Have a good evening."

"You, too, Doctor Gray." She held her ample body stiff as she skirted the packing crates and left the room.

He sank into his desk chair. Not the most auspicious of beginnings. He had one known patient, the prospect of a disturbed hypochondriac and the formidable challenge of Nellie Forester.

He'd have to give folks time. Let them get to know him. By and large, these were not patients shuttled his way through HMO bureaucracies. Although there would be numerous Medicare recipients, many rural residents saw a doctor only when absolutely necessary and then scrambled to pay cash.

Still, he wished he could shake the impression that

his inherited nurse possessed little fondness for upstart young doctors who thwarted her established order. He realized his first few weeks in Salt Flats might be lonely. Slowly but surely, though, he was getting acquainted with some pretty decent people—Millie, the waitress at the Main Street Café; Keith Appleby; Mel; and—he couldn't help smiling—Kate Manley.

That last pleasant thought was interrupted by a tap on the door, followed by Nellie's "Excuse me."

"Come in." For once she looked tentative. "Something else, Nellie?"

Gripping the doorknob, she stood just inside the office. "If I'm not overstepping my bounds, I'd like to volunteer to assist Dr. Floyd on those weekends he's covering for you." She raised one palm, apparently to stem the objections she assumed he would raise. "I wouldn't expect to be paid. I'd volunteer my time." She waited, her demeanor uncharacteristically anxious.

"That's very generous." He paused, observing her closely. He was missing something here. What? "You must think a lot of Doc Floyd."

"I do."

Was it the light? Surely Nellie Forester's suddenly mottled skin couldn't be a result of embarrassment. "I'll pass along your offer."

Only then did the tension drain from her body. "Thank you."

Sam stared at the door she'd closed behind her. What was that all about? He rolled back his chair, propped his feet on the desktop, then laced his hands behind his head. Nurse Forester's gesture seemed to have more to do with Mel Floyd than with patient care.

Then it came to him. He couldn't help himself. He laughed out loud. Maybe small-town intrigues were happening right under his nose. God, he loved this place already.

CHAPTER TWO

To BANISH from her mind the maddeningly recurring image of Sam Gray, Kate poured herself into the creation of a new painting. Wednesday afternoon she dabbed a fleck of gold onto the canvas and began texturing the tall sunflowers in the background. In the foreground an impish-looking, towheaded boy, wearing nothing but overalls, straddled a wooden fence and showed off a gap-toothed grin. The Tom Sawyer quality of the subject and the vibrancy of the colors made her smile. It was a strong painting.

A far cry from the completed work displayed on a nearby easel. An old woman, clad in a faded blue housedress and a flowered bib apron, sat on a rust-red metal porch chair, her gnarled fingers working a skein of yellow yarn with a crochet hook. Kate had started out to depict a moment of repose in a ranch wife's daily routine; instead, the woman appeared weary, resigned, inured—the crocheting a mindless distraction from hopelessness. A technically sound piece, but not a pleasant one.

In fact, the painting depressed her. She suspected the subject had been born out of that time when she'd despaired of ever again lying secure in a man's embrace.

By contrast, she was exhilarated by the nearly completed portrait of the boy—full of mischief, life, promise. She hummed along with the Creedence Clearwater

Revival CD she'd put on. Maybe, just maybe, she was healing.

With renewed enthusiasm, she settled back to the work, losing herself in the colors and textures of the oil paints. When the CD began repeating, she set down the palette, swiped her wrist across her moist forehead, then started cleaning the brushes. A familiar shave-and-a-haircut knock drew her attention. Wiping her hands on a rag, she crossed the studio and flung open the door. Charlene. Her crazy, redheaded friend with the fireplug body.

"Grab your stuff and come on," Charlene ordered as she breezed into the studio. "Roy and I are going to the lake for a long, relaxing boat ride. You're invited."

"Sounds wonderful, but tonight's my library shift."

"Blow it off. The kids will all be at the baseball field, and you don't need to stay open for Lester Jakes."

"*This* coming from the president of the library board?" Kate rested her fists on her hips as if scolding a child.

"But I'm tempting you, right?"

Charlene, Kate's oldest and dearest friend, knew her better than anyone. "Yes, you're tempting me. What could be better than a refreshing dip in the lake, a cool boat ride and a frosty beer?" She grinned. "But I'm strong enough to resist."

"Party pooper." Charlene turned to examine the painting resting on the easel. "What's with Granny Grim?"

"You don't want to buy it to hang over your mantel?" Kate teased while at the same time wondering how her friend would react if she knew about Kate's applying to the Lupe Santiago workshop.

"Only if I could view it from a dentist's chair while listening to fingernails on a blackboard."

Kate laughed. Charlene never minced words. "Do you suppose after I'm dead and gone, they'll assign it to my 'blue period'?"

Charlene tilted her head critically, still scrutinizing the painting. "It's fine, Kate, really fine. Just not very appealing."

"Point well taken. I think my next one is more up-beat." She gestured to the painting of the boy.

Charlene studied it, then turned, smiling, to Kate. "You can say that again. I really like it. And, pal, I have to say I'm relieved."

"Oh?"

"This one reflects the real Kate, the playful one I know and love." She jiggled her keys. "Sure you won't come with us to the lake?"

Kate switched off the CD player and lights, then followed Charlene to the door. "I'm sure. Besides, last Wednesday night someone else actually used the library."

"Who?"

"The new doctor."

Charlene pumped Kate's arm. "Oooh!" She wiggled her eyebrows. "What's he like up close and personal? Word has it he's one sexy-looking hunk of man-flesh."

Kate's stomach did a flip-flop. "I didn't notice."

Charlene stopped dead and pulled Kate around to face her. "Bull." Kate felt a flush creep up her face. "You noticed, all right. I've known you since kindergarten and you're a lousy liar."

Kate resumed walking toward Charlene's 4Runner, mimicking the cracked voice of an octogenarian.

"Don't you know, dearie, it isn't seemly for us widows to notice men."

Charlene hooted. "As I said before, you noticed. From the plenty I've heard, you'd have to be blind not to."

"You're not going to let me off the hook, are you?" In a nervous gesture, Kate brushed her hands through her hair. "You win. Sam Gray is tall, dark and incredibly handsome. There. Are you satisfied?"

Charlene eyed her speculatively. "And?"

"Very polite."

"Polite? *Polite?* How about charming, sexy, or, hey—*interesting?*"

"I'll grant you all of the above, but if this is going to be another of your unsolicited, unwelcome matchmaking attempts, I'm not in the market. I don't even want to think about the evening you arranged with Roy's old college buddy. Or that blind date with the attorney from Woodward."

Charlene twirled her keys from her forefinger. "You weren't ready then."

"And nothing's changed." Kate opened the driver's side door and held it for her friend, ignoring Charlene's skeptical grin. "Have a nice boat ride."

Charlene climbed behind the wheel, closed the door and rolled down the window. "You're fun and great to be around. And you've got that lovely ash-blond hair—"

"With a tress or two of gray, remember."

"Shut up, will you? As I was saying…ash-blond hair, to-die-for gray eyes and a dynamite body. You're hardly ready for the pasture. Far from it!"

Kate backed away from the vehicle, shaking her head. "Good *afternoon,* Charlene." She loved her friend, but she could be one of the most exasperating human beings on the planet.

"One last word." Charlene revved the engine, then added just before backing down the gravel drive, "Be kind to yourself. Give the good doctor some thought."

Kate felt laughter bubble up. Wouldn't Charlene be flabbergasted to know just how much thought she had already given the unforgettable Sam Gray?

Fortunately she didn't have time to dwell on that question because just then Charger, her eleven-year-old hybrid-breed hunting dog, came bounding toward her, a dead blue jay dangling from his mouth.

KATE THREW DOWN the library journal and thrummed her fingers on the checkout desk. Darn it, she was waiting for him. Hoping he would come again tonight. Was that stupid or what? It was already eight-thirty, and aside from Lester who, in between asking her the same questions over and over, had spent two hours perusing today's issue of the *Daily Oklahoman,* no library patron had darkened the door. She glanced around. The magazine shelf needed tidying.

Wearily, she went over and started in, noting the well-thumbed issues of *Time* and *Country* and the nearly pristine stack of *Harper's.* It was amazing how much could be learned about a community from the reading habits of its citizens. She felt downright voyeuristic.

Behind her, she heard the door open. Turning, she drew in a breath. There, filling the entryway and looking extremely masculine, stood Sam Gray, dressed in a red T-shirt, hip-hugging black jeans and scuffed cowboy boots. "Good," he said, smiling directly at her. "I'm glad I didn't miss you."

Before she could process the words or ponder their intent, Lester got to his feet. "Hey there, aren't you the new doc?"

"Yes. Sam Gray."

Lester pumped his hand enthusiastically. "I'm Lester."

"Lester Jakes," Kate filled in.

Lester continued treating Sam's hand like a pump handle. "Doc, I gotta, you know, I gotta talk to you. That Nellie, she don't like me. She's all the time tellin' me to quit botherin' Doc Floyd. Never mind, she says. Lester, you're just imaginin' things. But I'm not, swear to God, Doc." As he spoke, his voice grew louder and louder. "You know Aunt Julia, how she's all the time tellin' me 'Shut up, Lester, you jes crazy as a bedbug'? Well, she's after me, too. She—"

Slowly extracting his fingers from Lester's grip, Sam laid a comforting hand on his shoulder and guided him toward a seat at the library table. He settled Lester into the chair and sat down beside him. "Sounds like you need to come into the office and tell me what's bothering you."

Lester gazed around wildly, shaking his head. "No, no. Can't do that. That Nellie, she'll get me. No sir, I'd be in big trouble."

"Not if I tell her to set up an appointment."

"You'd do that, Doc?"

"Tell you what. You come to the office at one o'clock tomorrow afternoon and we'll talk."

"But what about Aunt Julia? She'll get mad."

"You leave that to me, okay?"

"Okay." Lester stood up, nearly knocking over the chair. "I gotta go home, gather all my stuff so I'll be ready. I've written it all down, Doc. A hunnert pages or more. You'll see.'' He backed away in the direction of the door. ''Evenin', Miz Manley, Doc. I'll be there.'' He fingered the misaligned buttons on his shirt. ''One o'clock, one o'clock.'' He bared his teeth in a crooked smile. ''Just tell that Nellie it's okay, please, Doc. Tell that Nellie.'' Then he scooted out the door, leaving in his wake—silence.

For a moment, Sam bent over the table, holding his forehead. Then, smiling sadly, he looked up. ''Has he always been like that?''

Kate sank into Lester's vacated chair. ''As long as I can remember. Poor Lester is a loner. It's as if he's afraid of his own shadow. Yet he's quite mechanical, almost gifted. He tinkers with everything. But he just gets more and more peculiar.''

''How old is he?''

She tried to remember how many years behind her in school Lester was. ''I'm not sure. Thirty-five or so.''

''Any violent behavior?''

''Not that I'm aware of. Everybody kind of takes Lester for granted. I guess you could say he's the town eccentric.''

''Hmmm.'' He looked thoughtful. ''Who's Aunt Julia?''

''Lester's parents were both killed in a tornado when he was a child. Julia Jakes is his father's spinster sister. She'll be the first to tell you she's done her 'Christian duty' by Lester. But, if you want my opinion, she regards him more as a cross to bear than a relative in need of help.''

''Maybe after I read his files and see him tomorrow, I'll have a better handle on the situation.'' He brightened. ''At least I'll have a patient to see.''

''Don't tell me you have open appointments?''

He spread his palms flat on the table. "Let's put it this way. I could squeeze you in."

She reached a hand toward his, then thought better of the gesture and tapped her fingers on the wooden table. "Folks'll come around eventually. It's just that people hereabouts don't adapt easily to change. Once they figure out Doc Floyd isn't there to fix them, they'll be lined up on your doorstep."

"Let's hope so."

"Did you get moved all right?"

"Managed to get everything squared away last Sunday. It's a good thing, too, because my boys are coming up to visit this weekend."

"Your boys?"

"Blake and Bart, my ten-year-old twins. They live in Oklahoma City with my ex-wife. I'm really excited about showing them the countryside."

"Do they like to fish?"

"I don't think they've ever been fishing."

"Behind my house there's a pond my husband stocked with bass and catfish."

"Do you think he'd mind if we gave it a try Saturday?"

Her voice sounded tinny in her ears. "No. He's been dead for two years." Then she smiled wistfully. "I think he'd like it if your boys fished there."

"And you?"

The way he was looking at her made it hard to concentrate on the question. "I-I'd like it, too. I'll look forward to meeting them. Come at your convenience." She made an attempt at levity. "The fish won't be going anywhere." Above the ticking of the Regulator clock, she heard the chimes from the belfry of the First Christian Church. "My goodness. It's closing time." She stood up, flustered. "I've talked too much. What did you need tonight?"

He stood, deliberately taking his time to shove the chair under the table. "Company, Kate."

"I'm glad Lester and I could oblige."

He turned toward her, his eyes capturing hers. "It wasn't Lester's I was looking for."

Her fingers fluttered nervously at her side. "Well, I—"

"It was yours."

"Oh." She scrambled for a reasonable explanation. "You want to hear the folklore version of the town's history, after all?"

"That, too." Another one of those—could she be right?—"appreciative" smiles lifted his mouth. "It's early. Care to join me for a drink at the Dairy Bar? You can give me the inside scoop on Salt Flats. How about it?"

Join him at the Dairy Bar? In full view of every Little League player and his or her parents? She would never have given his invitation a second thought before Charlene planted those suggestive seeds. Surely he was just being friendly. But if it was more? If...

Before the awkward silence lengthened, she found herself blurting out her answer. "That would be nice."

Nice. Neighborly. Friendly. Innocent. *Innocent?* Where had that come from? Of course, it would be innocent. What else could it possibly be?

KATE'S NOSTRILS PINCHED in protest as the pungent odor of permanent wave solution assaulted her when she entered the brightly lit Kwik Kurl Beautee Salon. Fanzines and styling books lay stacked haphazardly on a small table, and the babble of feminine voices overpowered the hum of hair dryers. For the umpteenth time, Kate approved her decision to wear her hair simply, occasioning infrequent trips to the beauty shop.

Jean Manley, Ed's mother, was of an entirely different persuasion, though, and never missed her Thursday morning hair-styling ritual. Jean was not only Kate's mother-in-law, but a special friend, so Kate had happily complied with Jean's request to pick her up after her appointment this morning.

"Hey, Kate." Brandi Moody, the henna-headed shop owner, waved in greeting, then continued sweeping the hair-strewn floor. "Pull up a chair. Jean'll be dry in a few minutes." On her way to the proffered seat, Kate paused at her mother-in-law's dryer and patted her on the hand. Jean lowered her issue of *People* and smiled in acknowledgment.

Kate wasn't sure how she'd have survived Ed's death without Jean and Paul Manley. Even though they, too, were devastated, they'd never wavered in their support of the girls and her. They were dear people who'd accepted her unconditionally, even years ago when her untimely pregnancy had thwarted their plans for Ed's college education. Only when she herself became the mother of teenagers had she fully appreciated the value of their blessing of their son's sudden marriage and imminent fatherhood.

Berta Jackson waved pudgy beringed fingers from the second chair where Eula Phinster was applying a blond solution to her graying locks. "Katie, you sit down right here," Berta chirped. "That way you won't miss anything." She wiggled her eyebrows, as if relishing a new audience. Berta was the mayor's wife and took her role in the community very seriously—affecting a misplaced *noblesse oblige* as she bestowed delicious tidbits of gossip.

Brandi leaned the broom against the wall, then set out combs and a curler container at her station. "Berta was just telling us that the county's going to repave the road out by your place."

"About time," Kate said, recalling with distaste the size of the potholes.

Berta pulled away from Eula, the better to see Kate. "You can thank my husband. Arnold fought for it with the county commissioners."

"Good for him," Kate murmured. Small-town politics triumph again. An unworthy thought, she acknowledged. After all, the road *did* need maintenance, but Arnold Jackson tended to take credit where none was due.

When a buzzer sounded, Brandi lifted the lid of Jean's dryer and felt her hair. "You're baked, Jean. C'mon."

Kate watched while Jean settled in the beautician's chair and Brandi began removing pink plastic curlers. Her fingers flying, Brandi launched into a stream-of-consciousness monologue. "Such pretty snow-white hair, Jean. And, for a woman of your years, your skin is in great condition. I hope I age as gracefully as you. Right now I'm doubting it, though. My feet hurt, my hands ache, my knees creak. Keepin' company with arthur-itis, I guess," she chortled.

"Maybe you should see the new doc," Eula suggested.

"I wouldn't mind *seein'* him," she raised her eyebrows suggestively, "but I don't know about any examination."

"You sick, girl?" Eula asked. "He's a heap easier on the eyes than old Doc Floyd, bless his heart."

Brandi set the curlers aside, then ran a brush through Jean's hair, relaxing the tight curls. She turned to Kate. "You met him yet?"

"Sam?"

"*Sam*, is it?" Eula's hands poised above Berta's head.

"He's come into the library a couple of times when I was on duty."

"That's not all, from what I hear." Berta practically shivered in anticipation. "I understand the two of you were together last night at the Dairy Bar."

Jean pulled her head away from Brandi, gave Kate a searching look, then winked. "Go ahead. Tell them about it."

Kate suppressed a groan. Innuendo. Already? And now this face-saving tactic by her quick-witted mother-in-law, who knew nothing about her conversations with the new doctor. "He was kind enough to invite me for a cold drink in thanks for helping him locate some resources."

"Careful, Katie." Grinning, Brandi shook the brush in front of her nose. "That's how rumors get started."

Kate laughed and held up her hands in surrender. "Please, ladies. There's plenty going on in this town without manufacturing news."

"Still," Berta breathed huskily, "Dr. Gray is one fine-looking fellow."

"Fellow's one thing," Brandi said, "but doctor? I dunno. I gotta tell ya, I don't want any hippie examining *my* privates!"

"What's with the ponytail, you reckon?" Eula asked. While theories were bandied about, Kate sat back and closed her eyes. Poor Sam. A new arrival, particularly one with a high profile, was fair game for this kind of scrutiny and dissection. Nobody intended ill will. Such speculation was merely a sign of the boredom of small-town life.

Brandi whisked the plastic cape off Jean's shoulders and shook it out. "Aren't I gorgeous?" Jean admired the back of her head with the hand-held mirror.

"Yes, you are," Kate answered sincerely, for Jean's beauty had far more to do with a quality of heart than with her coiffure or slim, well-preserved figure.

Brandi beamed. "Jean says that every week. Makes me feel like a million bucks."

As the two started for the door, Berta called after them. "'Bye now. And, Kate, stay out of those dangerous Dairy Bars." The woman's smug laughter followed Kate and Jean outside. God help any woman in this town, Kate thought, who fixes her sights on Dr. Gray.

"Would you have time to run me by the pharmacy on the way home?" Jean asked.

"Sure." She helped Jean into the truck. Then as they headed down Main Street, Kate glanced worriedly at her mother-in-law. "Anything wrong?"

"Wrong?"

"You know...the pharmacy."

Jean laughed. "Mercy, no. Just need to renew my angina prescription. I had Doc Floyd write me a new one last week."

"Dr. Gray could write you one, too."

"I know." She sighed. "I suppose one day he'll have to, but after all these years I'm not that comfortable thinking about going to a different doctor."

"Sam Gray seems very nice," Kate said noncommittally.

"Oh, I'm sure he is. But it's going to be hard for us old-timers to adjust."

Therein lay the crux of Sam's problem. The fear of change. Distrust. If someone as open-minded as Jean was leery, then others would be as well. She hoped Sam was a patient man. *Sam?* She realized she'd have to get over that habit. *Dr. Gray.* There, that was better.

"By the way, how *was* your cool drink with the new doctor?" Jean was gazing at her with an inscrutable expression.

"Refreshing."

"Is that all?"

Kate clenched the steering wheel, knowing full well she couldn't tell Ed's mother how lighthearted, how lovely Sam had made her feel—emotions she hadn't experienced for far too long. "Jean, I don't know what to say except I found Dr. Gray very pleasant."

"Hmm." Jean was silent for the next block, then murmured, "That's nice."

Kate pulled into a parking space in front of the pharmacy and waited while Jean went inside for her prescription, relieved she'd been spared from going into detail. An innocent limeade. So why had her friends' gentle teasing and Jean's question made her feel— what?—guilty? Embarrassed?

She didn't have time to pursue that disturbing thought because Jean returned then, bearing a small sack containing her medication. On the way to the Manleys' house, there was no further mention of Sam. When Kate pulled into the driveway of the trim white bungalow, Jean hesitated before getting out of the truck. "Have you heard from Jenny lately?"

Something in her mother-in-law's voice alerted her. Her older daughter and Jean had a special bond. In some ways Kate envied the older woman the closeness she herself rarely enjoyed with Jenny. "We talked on the phone about a week ago."

"Was she all right?"

"Why wouldn't she be?"

Jean ran her hands over the surface of her handbag. "No reason, except…"

Kate waited, tiny alarm bells ringing in her brain. Her headstrong older daughter had always kept her guessing. Her insistence on leaving Salt Flats after only two years of college and her impetuous marriage to Todd Lanagan, whom she'd met at Oklahoma State, had been typical Jenny behavior. But she seemed to have settled down now that she was a mother. "Except?"

Jean waved her hand dismissively. "It's probably nothing more than an old lady's overactive imagination."

"Is something wrong?"

"It's just that her last letter seemed, I don't know, strained. After she wrote about Parker's antics, she didn't have much else to say. Nothing at all about Todd."

"She was probably in a hurry."

Jean grabbed the handle and opened the door. "Of course, you're right. I ought to be grateful she writes her old granny at all." Jean smiled, then, gripping the handhold, stepped out. "Thanks for the ride. I hope I didn't inconvenience you. But Paul really needed to go to Enid this morning."

"Not at all. My pleasure."

Driving to the ranch, Kate felt grateful for the air-conditioning. The day promised to be another scorcher. She worried her lip. Jenny. With her, there was always something. She hadn't been a difficult child, exactly, just an independent, restless one. From puberty on, she'd vowed to get out of Salt Flats—as quickly as she could. And she'd made good on her promise. But Kate couldn't help wishing she'd found a better reason to leave than Todd. She couldn't put her finger on anything specific, but the young man had always struck her as...well, shallow.

How different her girls had been—Jenny who couldn't wait to escape to the big city and Rachel who longed to settle here in Salt Flats but presently led the nomadic existence of a flight attendant.

Swerving to avoid one of the potholes Berta claimed would soon be a thing of the past, Kate couldn't help wondering if the day ever came when parents could quit worrying about their kids.

Deep in her heart, though, she knew the answer. Absolutely not.

SAM CLOSED THE LAST FOLDER in the stack of patient files, shoved away from the desk and rested his head against the back of the office chair. So much to learn about so many people. Unfortunately, it appeared few residents of the county put emphasis on preventive medicine. According to Mel Floyd's charts, although there were the usual patients checking in periodically as a result of chronic conditions, most waited until the acute stage before entrusting their symptoms to a physician. Worse yet, an astonishing number had no health insurance. He closed his eyes briefly, then stood and paced to the window.

He grinned self-consciously when he realized he was scanning the sidewalk for potential customers. So far, except for the usual emergencies—an infant running a high fever, a teenager needing stitches and an elderly woman suffering from shortness of breath—he'd had few patients. He corrected himself. Make that three walk-ins, each of whom had seemed more curious than ill.

He'd anticipated a more leisurely pace in a small town, but not *this* leisurely. He checked his watch. Nearly time for Lester Jakes's appointment. Although Nellie had sucked in her cheeks when he'd mentioned asking Lester to stop by, she hadn't commented. She didn't need to. He read her disapproval loud and clear.

Restless, he returned to the desk and reviewed Lester's file. Nothing too unusual. A bout with pneumonia, a burn incident and periodic notations about Lester's manic talkativeness. At one point, Mel Floyd had prescribed an anti-depressant, but the chart showed that Lester often failed to take his medication. He was reading a scrawled notation concerning Lester's Aunt Julia and her uncooperative attitude, when Nellie ushered Lester in.

His ball cap shaded his eyes. His shoulders jerked nervously before he balanced tentatively on the edge of a chair. Sam noticed him moistening his lips.

"Thank you, Nellie. That will be all," Sam said, leaning across the desk to shake Lester's hand. "Afternoon, Lester."

Lester nodded his head. "Doc."

Folding his arms across his chest, Sam smiled. "I have a pretty open schedule, so why don't you tell me what I can do for you."

"You sure that Nellie's not mad at me?" Lester eyed the door.

"I'm sure, but let's concentrate on you."

Lester dug in the pocket of his oil-stained jeans and pulled out a bundle of notebook paper, folded in quarters. "It's this stuff, Doc. I been keepin' track." He handed Sam the thick wad.

Sam unfolded the papers, noting that Lester's large block printing covered both sides of each sheet as well as much of the margins. By conservative estimate, there were at least forty pages. Sam scanned the first few sentences, then looked up. "To save time, Lester, why don't you tell me about all of this."

"You won't show Aunt Julia, will you? Or that Nellie?"

"Our session is strictly confidential."

Lester's eyes darted about the room and he began pulling on each finger, cracking each individual knuckle. "Okay, Doc. Besides headaches, I'm all the time worried 'cuz somebody's stealing my tools. They hate me, so they sneak in my barn and take stuff."

"Like what?"

"Drill bits, washers, screws, pliers, planes—"

Sam recognized the compulsive list-making and interrupted. "Who takes things?"

Lester shifted in the chair, then leaned forward and whispered. "Everybody. Toad Portman, Mayor Jackson, mean kids, that Jensen at the bus depot—"

"Why would they do something like that?"

"They hate me 'cuz they think I'm stupid. I'm not, you know. I can fix anything. Radios, toasters, carburetors, you name it." He nodded his head enthusiastically. "Yessir, I can fix it."

"You're definitely not stupid."

Lester snugged his cap down over his ears. "They call me names like 'loony' and 'weirdo.'"

It wasn't hard to imagine that Lester drew his share of insults, but more disturbing were his symptoms of genuine paranoia. Changing the subject, Sam inquired about Lester's aunt.

"Aunt Julia? She don't hold much with doctors. She says I'm jus' wastin' time and botherin' folks. Doctors are highfalutin she says and never cured nobody, else so many people wouldn't die in the hospital. She'll not be happy, no sir, if she ever finds out I come to see you."

"Tell me about the medicine Dr. Floyd prescribed for you."

"Didn't do no good, so I quit takin' it."

"How do you know it didn't do any good?"

"People still called me bad things. And Aunt Julia, she said I was wastin' her money."

"I see." Sam placed the papers on his desktop, then stood, lounging against the desk. "Have you ever been seen by a psychiatrist?"

"A shrink, you mean?"

"Yes."

Lester bolted out of his chair and began pacing. "You think I'm crazy, too. Everybody thinks Lester is crazy. But he's not. He's a genius. He can fix complicated motors and electronic stuff—"

"'Crazy' is a dangerous and misleading word. I don't think you're crazy, but we need to explore why you feel so uncomfortable with people. Why your head hurts sometimes."

Lester stopped in his tracks and stared at Sam. "Can I have some medicine for my head?"

"Not before I run some tests."

"Tests? Oh, no, Doc. Aunt Julia'll never let me do that." He shook his head emphatically. "No sir. Not Aunt Julia!"

"What if I speak with her?"

"Won't do no good."

Sam noted the furtive searching gestures Lester was making with his fingers, as if trying to find a safe place to put his hands. Sam rounded the desk and took the other man gently by the shoulders. "It can't hurt for me to try. Okay?"

Lester avoided meeting his eyes. "Won't do no good." He stepped back and took hold of the doorknob. "But I guess you can try."

"Thanks, Lester. I will. Remember, I'm here to help."

"Ain't nobody helped Lester," the man said as he scuttled from the room, leaving the door ajar.

Sam leaned against his desk, lost in thought. There was more here than met the eye. He needed to talk with Mel before he approached the formidable Aunt Julia. Not a pleasant prospect, but wasn't that why he'd chosen this career path? So he could help people like Lester?

He flipped on his radio and tuned in a classic rock station, feeling the tension in his shoulders ease as he listened to Jefferson Airplane's rendition of "Somebody to Love." He sat down and leaned back, closing his eyes.

When he opened them, he blinked twice, but Nellie was still there, a disapproving frown on her face.

"Not crazy about Jefferson Airplane, huh?" he said, struggling to an upright position.

"That caterwauling is hardly 'therapeutic,' Doctor."

"Oh, Nellie. Give it a few months. You just might develop a taste for it."

She sniffed, then looked pointedly at him. "That's not likely to happen." She crossed the room and set a file in front of him. "Berta Jackson is in the waiting room. She's complaining of 'female problems'."

"I'll be with her in a moment." He opened the file and glanced at Doc Floyd's latest notation. "And, Nellie, I'll need you to stand by."

He thought he detected a flicker of approval in her eyes. "A prudent plan," she said cryptically as she departed from the office.

MOONLIGHT STREAMED through the bedroom window Friday evening and made the double bed a luminescent island in the sea of shadows. Kate enjoyed sleeping with the windows open to the gentle night breezes, lulled by the reassuring sounds of June bugs thumping against the screen and the sporadic lowing of cattle. She'd grown up with these nocturnal country sounds and with the earthy fragrances of loam and freshly baled hay. She'd never envied city dwellers whose lullabies, if you could call them that, consisted of barking dogs, the screech of automobile brakes and occasional wailing sirens.

But sleep eluded her, as it often did when the moon was bright. On these nights more than on others, Kate found herself unconsciously smoothing the sheet beside her, letting her fingers linger over the folds as if, against all reason, she'd encounter Ed's hand, warm and alive, or hear the gentle exhalations of his breath. Countless times she'd come awake groping for his body, only to encounter the flat, empty expanse of sheet. Even after two years, she slept on *her* side of the bed—as if moving toward the center would be a corroboration of Ed's absence.

Wide-awake, she threw her forearm over her eyes to blot out the moonlight—illumination that once had perfected their nakedness, airbrushing away the flaws. She had loved lying in the curve of Ed's body, feeling his work-roughened fingertips gently arousing her to heights of passion that sometimes, when reflected upon in the light of day, embarrassed her.

She bit back a sob. God, she had loved him! He had been a man who let actions speak for him. But he'd given her the words, too—things like "my Kate" and the "love you, babe."

Desperate to stifle the instinctive throbbing of her body, to ignore the reality that fulfillment might never come again, she rolled onto her stomach, pressing the pillow against her hot, moist cheeks.

It was easier in the daytime. Easier to fool herself that nothing significant had happened. Her house was comfortingly familiar, the daily chores went on as usual, the friends of a lifetime remained changeless—their idiosyncrasies as predictable as their routines. There were even hours at a time that she could almost forget about Ed. But something would always remind her that her life, unlike the others', *had* changed. Irrevocably.

In the distance she heard the plaintive hoot of an owl and, for some reason, thought of Poe's raven and the mockingly appropriate, "Nevermore."

Unless…

CHAPTER THREE

KATE WOKE WITH A START, sunlight momentarily blinding her. She struggled to sit up, then threw back the sheet wadded around her legs and stared at the clock in disbelief. Eight? A ranch wife is up at dawn—a habit Kate hadn't even tried to break. She loved dew-fresh mornings, and, weather permitting, had her first cup of coffee on the back porch watching the rising sun transform the prairie horizon from blue-violet to molten orange.

Yawning, she ran her fingers through her hair. Then, with a sharp pang, the demons of the night returned, reminding her of the reason for her insomnia. Ed. *Damn you. When will it ever end—this sudden onslaught of loss?*

She immediately censored herself. Lord knew Ed hadn't deliberately set out to get cancer, hadn't chosen to leave her. Sometimes, though, anger was the only antidote to need.

Drawing on her cotton robe, she walked barefoot into the kitchen where she spooned coffee into the pot and switched it on. The butter-yellow room with its ivy-green countertops and glossy oak cabinets was Kate's pride and joy—the last major renovation project she and Ed had undertaken before...before he got sick. She'd made do for years with cracked linoleum and peeling wallpaper. There had always been other more pressing financial drains—tractors to repair, acres to purchase, barns to reroof. It had taken Ed the better part of one winter to tear out the old cabinets and replace them, but he'd done it for her.

Good memories. Lots of them. She was luckier than many because she knew she'd been loved.

She poured a cup of coffee, unlatched the screen door and stepped onto the back porch. Charger roused himself from his nest in the corner by the lawn chairs. She set the mug on the railing and hunkered beside the dog, scratching his ears. "Good morning, fuzzy thing. Were you wondering where I was?" The dog made a soft *grrr* of pure contentment.

She rose, picked up her mug, then settled at the top of the porch steps, gazing at the familiar scene. The gambrel-roofed red barn, the adjacent corral, the equipment shed, her studio and the detached double garage sheltering her pickup and car. Multi-colored zinnias lined the fence separating the yard from the work areas. Close to the house, two hardy elms cast the only shade. Off in the distance, she could just make out the silver expanse of the Great Salt Plains Reservoir. Charger settled beside her, resting his head in her lap. A faithful dog, a sunny morning, brisk coffee. What could be better? Gradually optimism displaced her nighttime thoughts.

She found her glance drawn repeatedly to the pasture gate, its crisscrossing metal slats reflecting the sunlight. Hollyhocks on either side of the gate masked the fencing. She blinked her eyes. For one brief moment, she thought she'd seen…no, that was ridiculous. Then she looked again. No one.

Yet in her mind's eye, with startling clarity, she'd seen Ed—pictured his gloved hand resting on the gate, the familiar faded denim shirt tightening across his muscular chest, his straw hat pulled low over his forehead, shielding his eyes from the glare. Then he'd looked directly at her. For a brief instant, the image had been so real Kate was convinced she had only to cross the lawn to reach out and touch him.

Never taking her eyes from the gate, she slowly sipped from the mug, the fingers of one hand idly stroking Charger. The void where the living, breathing Ed had stood, taunted her. She could have sworn...

Finally, she stood and, trailed by Charger, went into the kitchen. The dog ran expectantly to his food dish. Kate poured some chow, then popped a piece of raisin bread in the toaster.

Sitting at the table a few minutes later, nibbling on the toast and fingering her orange juice glass, she still couldn't shake the certainty that for that millisecond, Ed *had* been there. Had not only been there, but was getting ready to tell her something. Something important. What?

As she went about her morning chores, Ed's image went with her. Finally, standing in the shower, lukewarm water sluicing down her body, she knew what she had to do. She couldn't wait. She quickly finished bathing, toweled off, drew her hair up in a careless ponytail, threw on an old sleeveless cotton T-shirt and shorts and went straight to her studio.

The impulse to draw was at its peak. She pulled out her pad and pencils and began sketching the lines, planes and shadows of her husband's hardened body— a firm shoulder, a gloved hand, a muscled, denim-covered thigh.

She'd worked for several minutes before the full implication of this spate of creativity hit her—she was supposed to paint Ed, exactly as she'd seen him this morning. With that realization came a peace she had not known for many months.

"DAD, HOW BIG'S YOUR HOUSE? You got a Ping-Pong table?"

"Can we go to the movies tonight?"

The twins had peppered Sam with questions all the way from Enid to the outskirts of Salt Flats. He had to give them credit. They'd tried manfully to hide their disappointment upon learning there were no Ping-Pong tables nor movie theaters and only one fast-food franchise restaurant.

Perspiration dampened the back of Sam's shirt. He had a lot riding on the boys' reaction to his new surroundings. Marcia had graciously agreed to drive Bart and Blake halfway to meet him for their every-other-weekend visitations. But what if the boys didn't like Salt Flats? Didn't want to come again?

On the horizon loomed the grain elevator and the water tower welcoming them to Salt Flats, Home of the Cougars. He'd been so sure this move was right, but now, with Bart and Blake staring bug-eyed out the window at the treeless expanse of pastures and fields, he was less confident.

"Dad, what's that white stuff in that field over there?" Blake pointed out the passenger window.

"That's the salt plains I told you about, where the Indians used to stop to replenish their salt supply."

Bart leaned forward from the back seat. "You mean where the weird rock thingies are?"

"Selenite crystals." Sam was glad he'd boned up at the library. "Believe it or not, you're looking at the only place in the world where this particular geological formation can be found.''

"You mean it's famous?'' Blake asked.

"Certainly among geologists and rock collectors.''

"That's kinda cool,'' Bart grudgingly admitted.

"Maybe on one of your visits, we can try our luck at digging,'' Sam suggested.

"Digging?'' both boys said at once.

Sam laughed. "You don't think those crystals are just lying around, do you?'' He went on to explain the careful rinsing process involved in unearthing the crystals. "They're very fragile.''

"Is that Salt Flats?'' Blake, sounding unimpressed, nodded his head toward the town.

"Yes.''

"You mean that's all?'' Bart's disappointment was evident.

"I told you it wasn't very big.''

"Yeah, but—''

Blake interrupted his brother. "I thought you said we'd have lots of fun here.''

Sam felt a tug of irritation with the boys' growing skepticism. He needed a home run on this first visit, not a puny bunt. "We will. Just a different kind of fun.'' He turned onto the country road leading to his house. "In fact, this afternoon I'm taking you fishing.''

"*Fishing?*'' Blake's tone indicated fishing ranked right up there with tiddlywinks as a worthwhile pastime.

"I don't know how to fish,'' Bart said sullenly.

Sam sighed. Even a skittering bunt was looking good right now. "Nothing's more fun than landing a big old catfish.''

"Catfish?''

"Cool,'' Blake said. "You know 'bout them, Bart.

They're those ugly suckers with whiskers. Real gross! Dad, you think we'll see one?''

"Maybe. But you'll have to wet a line first.''

Bart seemed to be mulling over the idea. "Do you know how to fish, Dad?''

"When I was a kid, I was pretty good at it.''

"So you could teach us maybe?'' Blake seemed minimally interested.

"This afternoon.'' Sam said, breathing easier. But he wouldn't feel really good until at least one of his sons had landed a fish. Unfortunately, there was no guarantee of that.

To THE STRAINS of a familiar rock tune blaring from the radio, Kate boogied around the kitchen, knowing full well that making homemade ice cream was pure self-indulgence. But the fresh strawberries had looked so inviting. Carefully she poured ice, rock salt and water between the barrel and the tin can. Once the electric ice-cream maker was humming steadily, she rinsed her hands and whistled for Charger to accompany her on the walk down the lane to the mailbox.

The merciless sun had wilted her by the time she collected the few magazines, flyers and bills. Yet despite the heat, as she retraced her steps, she felt energized, purposeful. The morning in the studio had gone well, and although she was eager to start the painting itself, she wanted to take the time to nail down each detail, each nuance. She had a huge stake in capturing Ed's likeness exactly.

Preoccupied, she nearly tripped over Charger, who'd stopped in his tracks, ears cocked. She shaded her eyes and watched a white Suburban turn up her drive. At the same time she recognized the driver, she felt the flutters in her chest. Sam Gray.

The vehicle stopped beside her and Sam rolled down his window. "I tried to call you earlier, but couldn't rouse anybody."

"Oh." She sounded flustered, even to herself. "I often turn off the phone when I'm in the studio."

"Studio? Are you an artist?"

"I dabble. Painting, mostly." Hah! That evasion showed exactly why she'd been a fool to send her application to Lupe Santiago. She couldn't even call herself an artist.

"Bart likes art, don't you, son?" A black-haired freckle-faced kid with the wildest cowlick she'd ever seen nodded from the passenger seat, while another boy, identical except for his glasses, stared from the seat behind Sam. "Boys, this is Mrs. Manley and—" he floundered, nodding at the dog.

"Charger."

"Cool dog," Bart said.

"I was wondering about the fishing. You remember the other night, you offered—"

"Fishing! Of course. Park by the barn and I'll direct you to the pond."

"Can we give you a lift?"

"Thanks, but I'll walk." Sam nodded, then pulled slowly ahead. Just as well. She needed a minute to compose herself. If that was possible. She'd forgotten how his eyes pierced you with their warmth. She found herself wishing she'd changed her shirt, now sporting unsightly cream splatters. Undoing the rubber band containing her hair, she snugged up her ponytail and hoped she didn't look too frazzled.

At the barn, the twins had jumped from the Suburban

and were climbing on the corral fence. Sam lounged against his vehicle, watching her approach. "Nice place you have here," he said, indicating the house and outbuildings.

"I like it. But it's a lot of work."

"You have help?"

"The neighbor who rents my pastureland feeds my few head of cattle and handles the big chores. But I do most of the work myself."

"Did you grow up on a ranch?"

"My parents had a small farm on the other side of town. You?"

"I'm a city boy. Dallas. But I spent summers with my grandparents on their spread in West Texas." He glanced toward the boys, now sprawled on the grass playing with Charger. "I better be getting them out of your hair. Directions to the pond?"

She pointed to the pasture gate. "Follow that fence line till you come to another gate. Then catercorner to that you'll find the pond."

"I really appreciate this, Kate."

Kate. The way he said her name made her feel like the only person in the world. He must have a wonderful bedside manner if he made his patients feel this important. With a tiny grin, she acknowledged she wouldn't mind finding out firsthand about a certain kind of bedside manner.

When she questioned him about his fishing gear, he mentioned he didn't have a net. "If you land Mudman, you'll need one. I'll get ours out of the shed."

"Wait." He took hold of her arm, his fingers on her bare skin sparking prickles of pure sensation. "Who's Mudman?"

"Mudman?" She gathered herself. "Our version of

the Loch Ness Monster. Ed and my daughter Jenny both claim to have seen him. This long.'' She stretched her arms as far apart as she could.

''Wow. Wouldn't that be a thrill for the boys?''

''Mudman's very slippery. He's wise to the tricks of mere mortals.''

Sam beckoned to his sons. ''We're no mere mortals, right guys? We're mighty men.'' Teasingly, he flexed his muscles. The boys clambered into the Suburban.

''Good luck,'' she said.

Sam laid a hand on her shoulder. ''We'll be sure to leave everything just as we found it.'' He got into the driver's seat.

Then she surprised herself by saying, ''When you're finished, would you like to stay for supper?'' He opened his mouth to speak, but she hurried on. ''We could grill some hamburgers—the boys would probably like that—and just this morning I picked some fresh tomatoes. For dessert there's homemade strawberry ice cream and—''

He grinned lazily. ''When you started that list, I wasn't sure I should accept, but when you said 'homemade strawberry ice cream,' that did it.'' He swung his head around to the back seat. ''You game, boys?''

When their heads bobbed up and down, Sam winked. ''Looks like you have three dinner guests.''

Kate stood watching the Suburban bump over the rough ground and disappear on the other side of the rise. Only then did she realize they'd be in big trouble if, by some miracle, they hooked Mudman. Lost in the pleasure of Sam's company, she'd forgotten all about getting them the net. And, for some reason, so had he.

''LOOK, MIZ MANLEY! I caught one!'' Blake ran toward the back porch, a six-inch catfish dangling from his stringer.

"Good for you!" Kate held out her hand to examine his catch. Sam observed she'd changed out of shorts and into one of those long gauzy skirts and a pink scoop-necked sweater that defined all too tantalizingly her nicely rounded breasts. She looked as if she'd smell good, like flowers maybe, and he was definitely interested in getting close enough to find out.

Bart swaggered behind him. "His is little. I had a *big* one on my line, but he got away."

Blake glared at his brother. "The ones that get away don't count, dummy."

"Bo-oys." Sam held up his hand in warning. He leaned against the porch railing and watched while Kate admired the fish.

"Any sign of Mudman?" she asked.

"Maybe," Blake said. "This one time there was a big swirl in the water."

"That was only an old turtle."

Sam smiled to himself. In one afternoon Bart had turned into a self-proclaimed fishing expert.

Blake looked hopefully at Kate. "Could we cook my fish?"

"He's pretty small, but—"

Sam pushed off the railing. "Remember, son, we talked about throwing him back."

"Do I hafta?"

"Who wants to keep that pitiful fish, anyway?" Bart challenged.

Kate slipped her arm around Blake's shoulder and drew him close. "I know you'd like to keep him. Catching your first fish is a very big deal." Blake, his lower lip thrust out, nodded solemnly. "But if you put him back, he'll grow. Then next time you catch him, he'll be huge.''

"Really?" Blake asked dubiously.

"No doubt about it.''

"Let's do it, then, fellas.'' Over the boys' heads Sam mouthed his thanks to Kate.

"Dinner will be ready in about forty minutes.''

"Will you at least let me cook the hamburgers?" Sam asked.

"I was counting on it.'' She smiled, and his heart swelled with an unnamed feeling.

"What're we gonna do after dinner?" Blake asked.

"Can we go to the arcade? Please, please!'' Bart was practically jumping up and down.

"Sorry, guys. No arcade, either.'' Sam's stomach began churning again.

"No arcade!''

"Bummer.''

Kate strolled between the boys toward the Suburban. "But we have other attractions here in Salt Flats.''

Sam trailed the trio, straining to hear.

"Like what?" Bart eyed her skeptically.

"Hmm. Like licking dashers.''

"Licking dashers?" Blake rolled his eyes, clearly confused by the unfamiliar term.

"And capturing lightning bugs.''

"That could be cool,'' Bart said.

"And stargazing, and—''

Blake scuffed his toe in the dirt. "Stars are no big deal.''

They'd reached the truck and Kate turned to face the boys. "No big deal? Not in the city, maybe. But here? Spectacular is the only word for it.'' The boys eyed her doubtfully. "But watching the stars would mean being up way past your bedtime."

"We can stay awake, honest."

"Please, Dad, say we can stay up late. This is our first night here, remember?"

Sam was impressed. Kate had maneuvered them exactly where she wanted them—and where he had hoped they would be. At least willing to give Salt Flats a chance. Maybe, thanks to her, they wouldn't reject this place—or him—after all.

She was quite a woman, he reflected as they headed toward the pond. Independent, hospitable, fun. And apparently talented. He hadn't missed the self-deprecating flush that came to her cheeks when she'd mentioned her painting. And it sure didn't hurt that she could qualify as a child psychologist.

And to top it off, she was sexy as hell.

WHEN KATE LIFTED the lid off the ice-cream maker, the twins' heads nearly obscured her view of the tin. "Stand back while I pull out the dasher." She was amused by their interest. Apparently they had assumed all ice cream came from the store. More than miles separated Oklahoma City from Salt Flats.

She put the dasher in a large mixing bowl and handed the boys each a spoon. "Can you take care of cleaning this up?"

Bart, his mouth already full, managed to mumble, "No problem," while Blake held up his spoon and grinned.

Kate winked at Sam, then tamped down the remaining ice cream, covered it and set it in the freezer. "We'll have ours after the sun goes down."

Later after they moved to the front yard to watch the

sunset, Kate sank gratefully into a chaise. "This is one time I'm glad we have so few trees." She pointed to where wisps of vermilion and purple-gray clouds framed the central attraction—a coppery sun resting on the horizon.

"Pretty spectacular," Sam agreed from the weathered Adirondack chair beside her.

They sat quietly watching the twins throwing a stick for Charger to retrieve. Kate stifled a small sigh. Tonight was a bittersweet reminder of how much she missed all the rituals of family—the laughter of children, the give and take of dinnertime conversation, even the stack of dirty dishes. But most importantly, male companionship. Guiltily she realized her thoughts had strayed from generalized "male companionship" to the very specific Sam Gray. She focused on the horizon where the sun had slipped into the pocket of the earth. In the western sky the evening star twinkled gaudily.

"That was a terrific meal, Kate." Sam stretched out his legs and folded his hands across his stomach.

"You deserve credit for the tasty burgers. I appreciated the help. Ed always used to do the barbecuing." For an instant, Ed's name stung her, as if he had suddenly intruded on the evening. Intruded? A strange and unworthy thought. She hurried on. "I'm glad you stayed." She gestured toward the boys. "Those little guys are pretty special."

"Yeah, they are." Sam sounded wistful.

"You miss them a lot, don't you?"

"Like the very devil." He sat up straighter. "I see them every other weekend. Mel Floyd covers for me then." He paused. "I hope they'll look forward to their visits."

"Why wouldn't they? They're obviously crazy about you."

"I know, but they're just kids. Kids used to pretty sophisticated entertainment. That's why I'm grateful to you."

She turned to look at him. *"Me?"*

"Yeah, *you.*" He reached out and, just for a moment, gently stroked her forearm. "I was scared spitless they wouldn't like it here. That they'd be bored." He shrugged. "But you've singlehandedly made this first day for all of us."

She was grateful for the deepening dusk that hid the faint flush of pleasure. "I was just being neighborly."

"It was more than that. You made this strange new world exciting for them." His smile melted away her self-doubt. "And for me," he added softly.

Over the pounding of her heart, she managed a response. "It must be a strange new world for you, too." When she said the words, the truth of them hit her. What had he given up to come to Salt Flats?

He studied the horizon before speaking. "In some ways, it's what I expected. Wanted." In the pause before he went on, she sensed his underlying reservations. She waited. "But the long-standing relationships here, the whole way of life. It's…different. Somehow I'd thought…"

"That you'd be immediately welcomed as the savior of medical services?"

Chuckling, he turned and studied her. "Pretty perceptive, aren't you?"

Flattered that he'd been able to trust her with his vulnerability, she considered his situation. "I've been lucky never to be a newcomer to Salt Flats. But that hasn't kept me from observing that the residents are slow to form attachments. But when they do, they're forever."

He looked intently at her, as if trying to convey something significant. "I'm counting on it," he said quietly.

Suddenly uncomfortable with the intimacy of his gaze, with the implied promise she couldn't deal with just then, she eased out of the chaise. "Hey, if I'm not mistaken, there's our first lightning bug sighting." She nodded across the yard where Blake had triumphantly captured an insect in his cupped hands.

"Dad, I got him! Look."

When the boys came to show Sam their prisoner, Kate walked toward the house, calling over her shoulder. "I'll be back with the Mason jars."

She collected two jars and a couple of quilts for stargazing, then hurried back outside where she joined the others in the heady chase.

An hour later there were sixteen flickering bodies in jars, which, with solemn ceremony, the boys liberated, watching while the insects flitted into the shadows. Kate searched the sky. Almost perfect, but not quite. "How about some ice cream? By the time we finish, the heavens should be on full display."

The boys scampered ahead. Companionably, Sam fell in beside her. "You know, if we stick around you long enough, the boys and I will learn lots about the fun of simple things."

Kate warmed to his words. With his pleasant, easy manner, he was a potent reminder of a kind of joy she hadn't experienced in a long time. Somehow she resisted the impulse to reach out and squeeze his hand in…gratitude.

The boys had turned on the kitchen lights and stood

waiting. "Can I have two scoops, Miz Manley?" Blake asked.

Kate turned to Sam and raised her eyebrows. "Dad?"

"A guy couldn't survive on any less."

"All *right*!" Bart and Blake each claimed a dish from the counter and waited while Kate retrieved the ice cream from the freezer.

"If you're going to eat my ice cream and watch my private star show, it's time you called me Kate. What do you think?"

"Kate." Bart paused as if listening to the sound of the word. "Yep. I can do that."

Blake edged closer to her. "I like that name," he said softly.

Kate treasured the moment, at least until Bart poked his brother in the side. "Yeah, Blakey, you like that name. That's because your *girl*-friend's named Kate." Bart danced around the room singing, "Blakey's gotta girlfriend, Blakey's gotta girlfriend."

Sam threw her a what-are-you-gonna-do? look, then snapped his fingers. "Whoa, guys. I don't know about you two, but I'm ready to eat."

Just as Kate finished her ice cream, the phone rang. "Excuse me, please." She patted her mouth with a paper napkin and picked up the portable phone.

"Mom? Where have you been?"

Jenny wasn't much for amenities. She always jumped into the middle of a conversation. "Right here. Did you try to call earlier?"

"Two or three times."

"I've been outside."

"*Outside?* It's nine-thirty your time."

Kate turned her back on Sam and the boys. "I know." Since Ed's death, Jenny, the typical older child, had treated her as if widowhood had suddenly rendered her incapable of rational behavior.

"What in the world were you doing outside?"

Kate strolled into the hallway between the kitchen and the living room. "Catching lightning bugs."

"I beg your pardon?"

Kate bit her lip to keep from laughing. "And now I'm going to stargaze."

"*Stargaze?* Mother, are you all right?"

"I'm having a ball. Just another exciting night in beautiful Salt Flats."

"Give me a break. There's nothing exciting in that hick town."

There it was again. That attitude. "It all depends on your perspective," Kate answered dryly.

"Well, a scorching summer evening in Oklahoma isn't my idea of fun. But that's not really why I called."

"Oh?" In the background, she could hear Bart and Blake rehashing their fishing outing.

"What can I substitute for unsweetened chocolate in a recipe? I thought I had a box, but I can't find it anywhere."

"Aren't your Denver stores open all night? Why don't you send Todd to get some?"

"I would...if he were here. But I can't leave the baby." Kate thought she detected a tightening of Jenny's voice.

"Is Todd working late?"

"You could say that." Her daughter's breath caught. "But, Mom, I'm in the middle of this recipe. Can you help me?"

"Yes. Substitute cocoa and vegetable oil. Wait a minute and I'll tell you the proportions." Kate returned to the kitchen and grabbed a dog-eared copy of *The Joy of Cooking* and gave Jenny the information.

"Thanks. And, Mom...why don't you consider staying in the house and locking the doors? Charger isn't that great a guard dog."

"Jenny," she strained for patience, "you've lived in the big city too long." At that moment, Blake made a face at his brother who erupted in giggles.

"What's that noise?"

"The Gray boys."

"The Gray boys? Who's that? Are you baby-sitting?"

"The new doctor's sons, and, no, I'm not baby-sitting."

"Is *he* there?"

"Who?"

"The new doctor."

"Yes."

"Mo-ther! I've heard about him. What's going on?"

"I'm being a good neighbor." Kate smiled at Sam.

"Well, you be careful just how 'neighborly' you get."

Kate bristled. Did her daughter suppose she was having some kind of rendezvous with Sam? "Is that all, Jenny?"

"I guess. You'd better get back to your...company."

"Good night, honey." As Kate cradled the receiver, she couldn't help thinking that although Jenny had left Salt Flats, she hadn't left behind the small-town dwellers' predisposition to jump to conclusions. Kate scolded herself. She'd done the very same thing by assuming something wasn't right with Todd and Jenny. But why hadn't Jenny volunteered more information about her husband's whereabouts? Was Jean on to something?

She was aware of a sudden silence in the kitchen. Three pairs of eyes studied her. She laughed dismissively. "My daughter in Denver. She can't believe we're going to stargaze." Flicking off the lights, she moved toward the door. "Some people just don't appreciate miracles."

The boys ran on, but Sam lingered, his face only dimly visible. He touched her lightly on the shoulder. "But *we* do, Kate." His voice was low, intimate, questioning.

Rattled, she looked up at him. Finally she spoke, the words sounding momentous. "I hope so."

JENNY HUNG UP the phone, then checked on Parker, asleep in his crib, before starting in on the cake she was making for the neighborhood potluck dinner tomorrow evening. She hoped Todd would come home in time to help her put forth the illusion of a family. She was tired of having to come up with excuses and evasions, tired of pretending things were fine, tired of wondering what she'd done wrong. But damned if she was ready to tell anybody about her hurt and frustration. Even though her parents had married young, theirs had been a happy marriage. Why couldn't hers be, too? Abruptly she stopped sifting the dry ingredients, remembering how her friends still living in Salt Flats had described the new doctor. He was hot! What in hell was her mother doing chasing lightning bugs and stargazing with him? And what about that coquettish lilt in her voice that sounded nothing like anyone's mother, for cripe's sake, let alone hers!

She stared out the kitchen window at the blanket of lights that was Denver. This was what she'd always wanted, wasn't it? She was out of two-bit, windblown, dusty Salt Flats. She had her life in the big city. Just the ticket, right?

Adding eggs to the creamed sugar and butter, she beat the mixture with a fury out of all proportion to the requirements of the recipe. Damn it, she wasn't born yesterday. How could Todd do this to her? The evening sales calls, the cell phone that beeped late at night, the times too numerous to count when the golf round, the Nuggets' game or the softball tournament took precedence over any family plans had led her to the inescapable conclusion—the least of her husband's priorities was their marriage.

The first time she had admitted to herself there were cracks in their relationship was when Todd refused to cancel a guys-only ski trip to go back to Oklahoma for her father's funeral. She'd covered for him, pleading business obligations. Her mother had been too distraught to question her explanation, but Rachel had looked at her searchingly and Grandma Manley had sighed, then pursed her lips. Neither of them had pressed her, thank goodness, because then she might have blurted out the truth. But she couldn't. Even if she'd wanted to unburden herself, she'd just learned she was pregnant, so it had been easier to rationalize that impending fatherhood would force Todd to get his act together.

How stupid could she be? This was Todd of the charming smile and the glib explanations. The Todd who was somehow able to twist events and words to make her responsible for the flaws in their marriage.

She swiped the back of her hand across her cheek, hoping that a few salty tears wouldn't mar the flavor of the cake. If it weren't for Parker, she'd...

But she wouldn't trade Parker for anything, and he

needed a daddy, even an unreliable one. She could always hope maybe one day Todd would grow up and assume his family obligations.

When hell freezes over.

SPRAWLED WITH BART on one of the quilts, Sam locked his arms under his head and gazed at the breathtaking array of stars—stunning in number and brilliance. Veiled by the city lights, they hadn't awed him in quite this way. But, then, as an adult, when had he ever taken the time to lie on his back studying them?

Blake, already asleep, nestled on a quilt with Kate, his arm flung around a dozing Charger, and beside Sam, Bart's eyes were drooping. It was after midnight, yet he was loath to disturb them, to break the spell cast by the hum of locusts, the fragrance of mown grass and the soft light of heavenly bodies. They'd watched shooting stars too numerous to count, spotted satellites etching their orbits in the night sky and laughingly identified the Big Dipper and Orion. Blake had even said, "This is way better than the planetarium."

Kate deserved much of the credit for making the boys' first day in Salt Flats memorable. But for him it had been more than that. Much more. His throat closed as he tried to put a label to what he was feeling. Being with her, he hadn't felt, even once, that he had to try to be something or someone he was not.

He turned his head and took in her profile. Her fingers were laced across her chest and her breathing was slow, shallow. As if sensing his scrutiny, she turned, a lazy smile on her lips. "Awesome, huh?"

Awesome, all right. And not just the stars. Kate. Beside him Bart snored softly. Sam rolled on his side and propped himself on one elbow. "I can't thank you enough. This is an evening neither the boys nor I will soon forget.''

She playfully swiped at his arm. "It's no big deal.''

Heart thudding, he captured her fingers in midair. ''It is to me.'' He rolled over on his back again, aware he was still clutching her hand, reluctant to release it. "Tell me about your children.''

She was silent for a while, her fingers limp. But she hadn't withdrawn them. He could barely hear her. "Jenny is the older of our two daughters.'' At the word "our,'' she slowly pulled her hand away from his. He watched a rueful smile cross her face. "She wouldn't appreciate an evening like this. She's no small-town girl. For her the greener grass was always the city.''

"Did she succeed in finding what she wanted?''

"I'm not sure. She married after her second year at Oklahoma State, moved to Denver and has a twenty-month-old son. I suppose she's happy.''

Sam heard the doubt in her voice. "You don't sound convinced.''

"Only time will tell.'' She was silent for several seconds. "My other daughter, Rachel, recently finished college and is a flight attendant based in Phoenix.''

He turned to study her again. Her lips were parted and her long lashes concealed her eyes. "It's hard to believe you have grown daughters.''

Her eyes popped open and she gave a short laugh. "You can. But understand I was a child bride.''

"You must've been.'' He covered her hand with his. "How old were you?''

"When I married? Eighteen.''

He tried to imagine her as a teenager. She couldn't have been any more lovely—or lively—than she was at this moment. "Let me tell you what I see when I look at you now."

She gazed at him, her large, gray eyes wary. "Please, Sam, I..."

"Shh. I want you to know. I see a beautiful—" she started to raise up in protest, but he stopped her "—caring woman who also knows how to play." He twined his fingers with hers. "You have no idea how rare a combination that is."

"Sam, please." She moved gently so as not to disturb Blake and sat up, pulling her hand from his grasp. "I'm not sure I'm comfortable with this conversation."

He, too, sat, legs crossed, facing her. "Why not?"

"Aren't we being a little too personal?"

"I didn't mean to make this awkward for you."

"It's probably just the moonlight."

He reached for her hand, rose, assisted her to her feet, then reluctantly relinquished his grasp. Although he stood close, he didn't touch her again, even though he desperately wanted to. She trembled like a wild bird poised for flight. "Believe me, it's not the moonlight."

She averted her face, then slowly turned back to look at him. "I'd like to be your friend, Sam." Her warning was implicit.

"That's a start." He swallowed. "May I see you again?"

"What do you mean?"

"I want to get to know you better." He sensed her distress. "No big deal, Kate, just slow and easy."

"But—" she stammered "—I'm older than you."

Smiling into her eyes, filled with uncertainty, he ran his hands down her arms and captured her hands. "That's weak, Kate. You'll have to come up with a better excuse."

"Sam, I don't know—"

"Please. Think about it." He leaned closer and grazed her forehead with his lips. He had just registered her breathless little sigh when he became aware that Bart was sitting up and rubbing his eyes.

"Dad, I'm thirsty."

Kate abruptly pulled away. Turning her back, she knelt beside his son. "Come with me to the house and I'll fix you a drink."

Sam gazed at the bone-white moon, wondering if he'd overstepped a boundary. He hoped not. A woman like Kate was worth every shred of patience he could muster.

KATE STOOD ON THE BACK PORCH, watching the tail-lights of Sam's Suburban grow fainter and hugging herself against a chill that had nothing to do with the soft night breeze ruffling the leaves of the elm trees. During the twins' preparations for departure, a breathless self-consciousness had seized her. Thinking about it now, she couldn't even remember what she'd said, only that her tongue had seemed immobile, her thoughts incoherent.

"Sam." She repeated his name softly, and her nipples peaked in betrayal. She was only dimly aware of Charger, sitting beside her, his fur brushing her bare legs. She caught her breath, her thoughts whirling chaotically. It couldn't be. It *shouldn't* be. But the ache deep inside her told her it was. Sam had aroused her. And if laced hands, a gentle brush of warm lips and a pair of intense eyes could have such an effect, how could she face him again?

What insane urge had caused her to invite him and

the boys to dinner? How could what had begun as a neighborly gesture have spun out of her control?

She rubbed her hands up and down her arms. ''C'mon, boy, time for bed.'' Charger trailed her to the screen door. In spite of herself, Kate paused, inhaling the faint fragrance of the honeysuckle bordering the porch and entertaining a remarkably embarrassing fantasy.

Then, as if summoned by her conscience, Ed's face filled her mind, creating a chasm in her heart. She swiped at her eyes, opened the door and rushed blindly to the bedroom where she flipped on the light, grabbed their wedding portrait from the dresser and clutched it, like a security blanket, to her breast. How could she, even for a moment, have considered Sam as anything but a neighbor? Much less have loosed this uncharacteristic wildness?

Moving toward the nightstand, she tenderly fingered the youthful bride and groom frozen beneath the glass, then set down the photograph. For several minutes she stared at it, willing it to save her.

It was only much later lying on her bed in the dark that she acknowledged the truth. She should be shamed by her wanton longing. She should be labeling herself unfaithful to Ed, to his memory. Yet despite all that, the fact remained. She was alive. Alive in a way she hadn't been for many months. For all its disturbing implications, tonight had shown her she was still very much a woman.

And for that, she had Sam to thank.

CHAPTER FOUR

HE SHOULD HAVE SEEN IT COMING. One ideal day did not acceptance make. Slumped on the sofa, Sam mindlessly channel-surfed through the Sunday evening programs, but neither the frenzied sports announcers nor the screech of police vehicles drowned out the judgments his sons had laid on him throughout this long day. "There's nothing to do here, Dad." "It's *boring!*"

Finally settling on a European soccer match, Sam flung down the remote and leaned his head back. Man, what he wouldn't give for a beer! But Mel Floyd's weekend coverage had ended at six, and Sam made a point of never drinking when he was on call. Had Bart and Blake simply been bored or were they punishing him for moving? Probably a bit of both. He hadn't thought the drive to inspect the dam or this afternoon's Monopoly marathon had been so bad, but the boys' good humor had revived only when they'd climbed into the Suburban for the trip to Enid to meet their mother.

When his stomach growled, he lumbered to his feet, ransacked the kitchen and finally came up with a few crumbled tortilla chips and a nearly empty bottle of salsa. He opened a cold Dr. Pepper and settled at the kitchen table. Without Kate, the entire weekend would have been a disaster. She'd succeeded in making the simple act of licking a dasher seem like an event. What might *she* be able to do with a Monopoly game?

He paused, a chip halfway to his mouth. Kate was something else. In one fell swoop enchanting young boys and charming the hell out of one grown man. But it was both selfish and unrealistic to expect her to help sell the boys on Salt Flats. But just until they adapted, maybe he could prevail on her. At least for the crystal digging excursion and...

Gray, you jerk! Admit it. There's more to this than Bart and Blake and Salt Flats, Oklahoma. You can't stop thinking about Kate. You want to be with her again. With or without the boys. Smiling thoughtfully, he popped the chip into his mouth.

She'd looked startled, tentative, when he'd told her he hoped to see her again. The last thing he wanted to do was scare her off. Yet in her own way, he could swear she'd been receptive to him. He wondered if she'd dated since her husband's death. That would be a difficult step for anybody. Divorce was tough enough. How much harder would it be if you'd really loved your mate? And it was evident Kate had.

He folded the empty chip sack and tossed it toward the nearly full trash can. Chugging down the rest of his soft drink, he checked the clock and made a decision. Maybe it wasn't too late to call. To thank her. To suggest...what? Hell, simply to hear her voice.

Before he could reach for the phone, the darn thing rang as if some malevolent force was at work. The 911 dispatcher's voice was businesslike. "Dr. Gray, we have an emergency coming in to the clinic. An eleven-year-old girl with a possible skull fracture, broken leg and contusions."

Instantly alert, Sam leaped to his feet, grabbing his

keys off the wall hook. "I'll be right there. Put the helicopter service on standby."

He turned off the TV and lights and strode to his truck. This didn't sound pretty. His mind racing over possible diagnoses and procedures, he forgot all about Kate until, as he sped down the road, he noticed the lights still on at her farmhouse.

She'd been awake. He could've called. And he would. Another time. Soon.

KATE PAUSED in the doorway of the clinic waiting room. Nighttime lent it an eerie quality—the fluorescent lights too bright, the quiet too intense, the sense of crisis imminent. When Charlene spotted her, she threw herself into her friend's arms. Roy, his face a stoic mask, shrugged helplessly, then turned to stare in the direction of the examining room. Kate smoothed a wayward curl back from Charlene's forehead and led her to a seat. "I came as fast as I could after you called. What's going on?"

Charlene collapsed into a chair, then began to speak, so quietly Kate had to lean forward to grasp the words. "Amanda fell down the cellar stairs. They're so dangerous. We've been meaning to fix them." Roy flinched at his wife's implied accusation. Massaging Charlene's back, Kate pictured in her mind the ancient, dark basement stairwell of the Klingers' ninety-year-old farmhouse.

"Don't blame yourself. Accidents happen."

"I sent her to fetch some pickled peaches from the storage room. I should have gone myself. She's so clumsy."

Not surprising. Charlene's eleven-year-old daughter

had, overnight, become all arms and legs. "How is she?"

Charlene smoothed her hands over her jean-clad thighs. "We don't know yet. The ambulance arrived ahead of us, and we've only seen Dr. Gray briefly. He thinks she has a badly broken leg and a possible skull fracture. She...she hit the floor with her head." Charlene swallowed back a sob. "Oh, God, Kate, I'm so worried."

"Of course you are. You're her mother, but Sam will know what to do." The "Sam" escaped from Kate's mouth, but fortunately Charlene didn't catch the slip.

Roy suddenly stiffened. "Char, Doc's comin'."

Charlene went to her husband, who hugged her to him, as if for dear life. Kate gripped the arms of her chair, hoping that Sam's news would be good. But her first glimpse of his face caused her heart to sink. His features were drawn, his eyes compassionate. "Mr. and Mrs. Klinger, with time Amanda should be fine—" Charlene laid her head on her husband's shoulder "—but she's had a nasty fall. We've treated her for shock and stabilized her. I need to send her to the hospital in Enid. I've called for the helicopter, which should be here soon. She needs a CAT scan to determine the extent of her head injury and I'd like an orthopedist to set that leg of hers, so I'll be referring her case to staff doctors there. I'm sorry, but regulations prohibit family from flying with patients. Can you meet her at the hospital?"

"Whatever you say, Doc." Roy ran a hand over his balding head.

Charlene's voice broke. "Can...can we see her?"

"Of course. She's scared but trying to be brave. A paramedic's with her. Go on back. First room on the

left. I'll call the hospital and get the paperwork underway.''

The anxious parents nodded, then disappeared down
the hall.

Kate approached the counter where Sam was thumb-
ing through files. ''Is there anything I can do to help?''

He looked up, the lines of his face softening. ''Here.''
He thrust a questionnaire at her. ''Fill out whatever personal information you know about Amanda. We'll get
the rest from her parents.'' He picked up the phone and
punched in some numbers. ''Friends of yours?'' he
mouthed over the receiver.

''The best,'' Kate responded simply.

''Lucky them.'' His eyes captured hers in a manner
that caught her off guard and caused a brief cessation
of her breathing. Then his attention shifted and, suddenly alert, he spoke into the phone. ''This is Dr. Gray
in Salt Flats.''

As Kate filled in what she could on the form, she half
heard Sam's precise, authoritative orders for the admitting personnel in Enid.

Even though Charlene emerged a few moments later
to tell her to go on home, Kate waited while the transfer
arrangements were finalized. Charlene planned to spend
the night and next day at the hospital and would need
a vehicle, but Roy had to be back home by early morning to feed his stock. Without a second thought, Kate
pulled out her keys, insisting that Roy take her car. Only
then did the realization set in—there was only one logical way to get home. Before she could consider back-
pedaling, Sam intervened. ''Kate lives just down the
road. I'll give her a lift.''

Charlene had sufficiently recovered to shoot Kate an
''atta-girl'' look. Kate busied herself straightening the

waiting room, hoping that neither Charlene nor Sam had read a hidden agenda into her offer. Certainly none had been intended.

Nevertheless, she was uncomfortably aware of a sense of giddy anticipation.

IT WAS AFTER MIDNIGHT when the helicopter lifted off and Charlene and Roy departed. That left just her and Sam. It would be a simple matter, Kate reassured herself. A brief, uneventful ride home, hurried thanks and a blessed escape. *Escape?* She corralled her runaway thoughts. She wasn't looking for anything from Sam. He had merely been friendly, appreciative of her help with Blake and Bart. Her reawakened hormones were working overtime, that was all.

"Ready?" Sam stood poised at the bank of light switches. When she nodded, he flipped them and, for a moment, blackness overwhelmed her. Then she felt his sure fingers on her arm guiding her toward the door. Slowly her eyes grew accustomed to the dark, but all her other senses centered on Sam—the warmth of his hand, a faint whiff of antiseptic, the deep rumble of his voice.

When she stumbled in the parking lot, he steadied her, then helped her into the passenger seat. He climbed behind the wheel and started driving slowly through the town, lifeless except for the occasional stray cat or barking dog. The scene was fraught with expectation, like one of those Sci-fi movies. Any minute now a band of aliens could land on the deserted pavement.

Sam seemed lost in thought. Finally he spoke. "Amanda will be all right...eventually. It could've been a lot worse."

"She was lucky to have you here."

His hands lay lightly on the wheel. "I'm the lucky one. Being a small-town doc has been a dream of mine."

"Why? I would've thought the goal of most doctors is specialization."

"That's certainly where the big bucks are. But there's more to it than that. At least for me."

She waited, aware of his fingers tightening on the steering wheel. She felt as if he was on the verge of a confession. "And the 'something more' is...?"

He hesitated. "I suppose *involvement* is as good a word as any. Patients have to matter. Believe me, I've seen clinical objectivity taken to the extreme. No way could I refer to a human being as 'the gallbladder' or 'the appendectomy.' The day came when I knew I had to get away from my big-city clinic. When I had to find my own practice. In a place where I'd know the Amandas and Benjies and Lesters."

His voice rang with passion and commitment. And something else. Caring. "But your decision came with a price, didn't it?"

He sighed. "Yeah. Bart and Blake."

"Give them time, Sam. Kids are flexible. You're doing what fulfills you. That's a fine example for your sons."

"God, I hope so." After a pause, he turned and smiled gently. "I didn't mean to get on my soapbox."

"Well, for what it's worth, I was impressed tonight. You were very professional."

"We can hope I did no harm."

"Amanda's tough. She'll bounce back."

"Once she came to she was pretty alert." He chuckled. "She kept calling me 'Tonto.'"

"Let me guess. The ponytail?"

He nodded. "I suppose I asked for it. What do you think? Is it too much?"

"Let's just say it's challenging Salt Flats's cultural norms."

"Some of us wait until we're adults to express adolescent rebellion." He quirked his mouth, but the half smile never reached his eyes. "It'll have to go soon."

She thought better of pursuing the topic. They rode quietly until Sam turned off the highway onto their country road. He hesitated, then laid a hand on her shoulder. "I don't want to impose, Kate, but would you be willing to help me with the boys when they come again in two weeks? Maybe do a salt crystal dig?"

She studied him curiously. Where had his confidence gone? "You don't need me."

He let out a disgruntled snort. "Oh, but I do. Today was a disaster."

"What do you mean?"

"The boys thought everything we did was incredibly dull. They spent the better part of the day complaining."

"Patience. Salt Flats will take a bit of getting used to."

"But what if they don't want to come anymore?"

She searched for some way to reassure him. "Don't give them the option. You have visitation rights, don't you?"

"Yes." He sounded dubious.

"They're kids. They'll adjust. Besides, they love you." She paused. "But you could sweeten the kitty."

"How?"

"For starters, introduce them to some boys their own age. Charlene could help. Amanda must know a bunch of kids."

"Okay. What else?"

"Ever think about horses or a boat?"

He smacked the wheel with the flat of his palm. "You're a genius. A boat. That makes a lot of sense. The boys love the water."

"See? That wasn't so hard."

He slowed the vehicle, drew to a stop at her back fence but made no move to get out. Clearly his primary interest in her involved his sons. Nothing more. She let out a breath, aware that although she was relieved, she was also disappointed.

She clutched the door handle, then paused. "Thanks for the lift. And go with the boat. The boys'll love it."

"Wait." He bounded out of the truck, circled the vehicle and opened her door. He held out his hand. Ed hadn't been much on formalities. Sam's gesture made her feel special. Gingerly, she grasped his fingers and slid to the ground. He was standing close, too close, his chest blocking the yard light, his slow, steady breathing making her pulse thrum. He didn't move. She avoided looking at him and, instead, edged around him until finally he dropped her hand and stepped back.

Had she misread him after all? Imagined that if she had stood still, raised her face, sought his eyes, he might have kissed her?

Charger chose that moment to set up a howl. "Quiet, boy." Followed by Sam, she hurried up the walk and onto the porch.

"Good guard dog." Lounging against the door frame, his hands stuffed in his pockets, Sam didn't look as if he were leaving any time soon.

"He tries. Good night, Sam. Thanks again."

He reached out and captured her elbow. "Whoa. Before you go in, I need to get something off my chest."

He straightened up. "Remember when I said I wanted to see you again?"

She lowered her eyes. "Yes."

"I want you to understand this is not only about the boys. That's important and I'm grateful for your help, but there's more to it. Much more."

Willing her knees to support her, she looked up at him. "There is?"

"It's you, Kate. I want to get to know *you*."

"But I'm—"

"What? Older than I am? A widow? That's what you were going to say, wasn't it?"

Helpless, she nodded.

"I respect the fact you loved your husband and that maybe this is awkward for you. I'm asking you to trust me."

He placed one warm finger under her chin and slowly tilted her head up so she couldn't avert her eyes. "What is it you're afraid of?"

She was incapable of uttering a sound.

"That I don't know my own mind? That I'm using you? That other people won't understand?" He sighed heavily and his voice became intense. "Give me a chance, Kate. I'd never knowingly hurt you. But—" he cleared his throat "—you make me feel good. Happy." He continued haltingly. "It's been a long time since I could say that."

He dropped his hand and stood waiting for a response. What kind of answer could she give? Her fantasy stood before her. Not a ghost, nor a figment of her imagination, but a living, breathing, all-too-tempting man. She was flattered, even wildly hopeful, but at the same time she realized she had the capacity to hurt him. And that she herself was especially vulnerable.

To keep from reaching out to him as every nerve in her body urged her to do, she folded her arms across her chest. "I don't know if I'm ready—"

He ran his knuckles gently down her cheek. "Is anyone ever ready? It just happens, Kate."

She was helpless against the tears threatening to flow. With a shudder, she swallowed them back, then found her voice. "This is a small town. You have your reputation to consider, just as I do. And that's not even taking into account how your boys will feel, or my daughters, for that matter." She was rambling. This was so awkward. She'd forgotten everything she ever knew about—what should she call it?—dating?

A tender smile played around his mouth. "I can live with all the obstacles if you can." His eyes never left hers.

With difficulty, she drew a breath. "Could I sleep on it?"

"Sure. But please come up with the right answer." And just as he had the previous night, ever so lightly, he brushed his lips across her forehead, only this time she couldn't rationalize her reaction. Her flesh prickled with desire and her pulse quickened.

He backed down the porch steps. "Good night, Kate."

"Good night." She eased open the door, shaking her head uncertainly like someone with a very special, but potentially explosive secret.

"MOM, IT'S ME."

Rachel's voice, calm and melodious, filled the bedroom from the answering machine and, as always, warmed Kate's heart. She missed Rachel. Unlike Jenny, her younger daughter had always been easy, as if she had been born with an "old soul." And she could read Kate's moods like a book. "Give me a call when you get a minute. I had a chat with Jenny earlier. She didn't sound like herself. I'm concerned. Do you have any clue what's going on?"

Kate slumped into the rocking chair. First Jean and now Rachel. Not to mention her own unsettling suspicions. But, as usual, Jenny wasn't reaching out or confiding. From babyhood on, her cry, in one form or another, had been, "I'll do it *myself!*"

Lost in her concern, Kate hardly heard the end of Rachel's message. But what she did catch caused her to hit Play again. This time, as she concentrated on her daughter's words, she felt a blush, unsuitable for somebody's mother, spread across her chest, neck and face.

"Where were you tonight? It's late your time. Jenny says you got all evasive when you told her about the new doctor in town. About—" she paused, her voice filled with glee "—stargazing. Are you two getting friendly?" The innuendo was unmistakable. "Want my advice? Go for it, Mom!"

Kate gripped the sides of her chair. Nothing had happened—except in her imagination—yet her own daughters were already making her and Sam an item. If they'd do that from a distance, and based on so little evidence, how in the world would people like Berta Jackson, Brandi Moody and Ethel Portman, who lived right here, react? Or, most important, Jean and Paul?

She winced. She didn't even want to think about it.

ON THE SHORT DRIVE HOME, Sam realized he'd unwittingly bared his soul to Kate. He'd told her she made him happy. But he hadn't told her why. Hadn't told her he could be himself with her. That insight shouldn't have seemed so earth-shattering. But it definitely did.

He'd spent his life trying to please others. His mother, who'd stressed good manners and for whom his well-connected friends, high grades and membership in the best fraternity were measures of his success. And hers. His father, who'd groomed him from childhood for a high-powered medical career. When his older brother, the golden boy, had developed a major cocaine habit in college, disappointing his parents, the mantle had fallen to Sam. Perfection was a pretty high standard. But, God knows, he'd tried.

Then there was Marcia. He supposed, at first, they'd been the typical power couple—privileged, professional, promising. But somewhere along the line the overwhelming weight of expectation had suffocated him. He could never earn enough, do enough, be enough.

The day came when he simply couldn't take it any longer. He needed *his* space, *his* aspirations, *his* future. Marcia hadn't understood.

She'd tried. They'd tried. It hadn't worked.

And now? Though he was still struggling to establish a practice in Salt Flats, every day was better than the one before.

He pulled to a stop next to his house and sat unmoving, letting the night sounds lull him. Odd how you could feel so free when you'd just given away your heart.

THE NEXT MORNING Kate waited only until the dew dried to fire up the power mower and attack the overgrown grass in the yard. After a restless night, she knew she needed exercise—lots of it—to banish the conflicting emotions plaguing her. Sam Gray touched something deep and primitive in her, and she seemed helpless to control the strong emotions he brought to the surface. Emotions she'd thought had died with Ed. It wasn't just a physical attraction, although that was part of it, it was something more subtle, and even more dangerous.

Damn, she had to get a grip. She pushed until perspiration dampened the bandana she'd tied around her hair, but she couldn't mow fast enough to rid herself of the terrifying—and, at the same time, delicious—possibility that she might not be able to resist Sam.

Concentrating on subduing a stubborn patch of crabgrass, she didn't hear the truck drive up. Or see her father-in-law climb out and stand at the fence, studying her, a weathered straw hat dangling from his hands. It was only when Charger ran in front of her barking excitedly that she idled the mower and looked up. "Paul?" She cut off the motor and wiped her moist hands on her shorts. "What a nice surprise!"

He shook his head wonderingly. "Gal, I never saw anyone attack a lawn like that. It's enough to give a body heatstroke just watching."

"I'm not much for finesse, I guess. Ed was the perfectionist." She pulled the bandana from her head and used it to wipe her face.

Paul surveyed the yard, then the outbuildings. "He kept things in apple-pie order, all right. Wish I was younger and could help you." He leaned on the fence post, his sad eyes fixed on her. "That's a man's job. You shouldn't have to be doing these things." He worked his gnarled hands together. "I still can't believe my boy's gone."

Neither could she, but there was no point dwelling

on that. "Come on up to the porch. I'll get you a glass of iced tea."

"Thanks, but I've just come from a church committee meeting at Fannels' ranch. I'm full to the gills."

"You're sure?"

"Yep. Fact of the matter, sometimes I just need to see this place. Kinda puts me in touch with Ed, know what I mean?"

"I do." Paul's drawn expression had been a standard fixture since his son's death, as if he thought it should have been him and not Ed who'd gone. "You're welcome anytime."

"I know that." A wan smile creased his tanned skin. "Ed couldn't have had a better wife. He always knew you were devoted to him. Devoted." He seemed lost in his thoughts. "I hate it that you're alone here. That you have to do chores like mowing. But that's life, isn't it? I guess you're getting used to it."

As if she'd ever get used to it. "I suppose."

He slammed the straw hat back on his head. "You were the light of Ed's life. Jean and I have been so grateful you're the kind of woman you are. Loyal. Committed." He pushed off the fence post, then nodded at the mower. "Ed'd be proud of the job you're doing here."

Despite the heat, Kate felt an icicle forming in her throat. Paul was giving her too much credit. Especially after last night. Loyal? Guilt racked her. She forced a "Thank you" out of her mouth and was limp with relief when Paul, in his usual reserved manner, simply tipped his hat, uttered a "See you" and drove off.

With a vicious pull, she started the mower and headed off again. The damn grass hadn't seen anything yet! Hell, yes, she needed a man around the place. But how would that ever happen? How could it? Tears mingled with the sweat streaming down her cheeks. People expected her to be the contented widow, to deny her needs, to be, God help her, good old Kate.

But could she resist the pull Sam exerted? If only she could cut him out of her heart as effectively as she mowed down the intruding crabgrass.

"DR. GRAY, I TRIED to stop her, I really did, but Julia Jakes insists on seeing you." Nellie, her mouth pursed, stood in the door of Sam's office. "Honestly. I knew this would happen."

Wearily, Sam set down the insurance form he was signing and, not for the first time in their brief acquaintance, wondered if Nellie had ever considered a career as a fortune-teller. "I told you so" screamed from every inch of her adequately padded frame. He'd had a surprisingly busy week, including two trips to Enid to check on the Klinger girl. He might as well see the Jakes woman, with or without an appointment.

"Doctor?" Nellie's old-fashioned uniform practically rustled.

"Sorry, send Ms. Jakes in." Sam didn't have long to wait. An angular woman, with a faded print dress, orthopedic shoes and a face that looked forbiddingly like the Wicked Witch of the West brushed past Nellie and planted herself squarely in his line of vision.

"What're you doin', foolin' with my Lester? Ain't no cause to meddle, no cause at all."

So much for pleasantries. Rising to his feet, he gestured to a chair. "Please have a seat, Miss, er, Mrs. Jakes?"

"'Miss' and darned glad of it." She waited until he sat back down before settling herself.

"I'm pleased you came by. I need to get some history on Lester. I'd like to help him."

"Help Lester?" The idea clearly struck her as preposterous. "I came to tell you to leave that boy be. Ain't nobody helped Lester yet, so I don't reckon some long-haired doctor who don't know nothin' about us is of any use. 'Cept to get that boy all worked up." She clutched her wooden-handled cloth purse in a death grip.

"Hear me out, Miss—"

"No." Her chin shook. "You listen to me. You ain't been the one takin' care of that boy, you ain't seen what's he like when he gets hisself all worked up, you ain't—"

"No, I haven't. But that's what I'm trying to learn. If you'll help me identify symptoms, there may well be a treatment that will help him."

"No. And that's final. We're not travelin' that road again."

"You're telling me you're unwilling to assist me with Lester's history? There have been many recent break-throughs—"

"Stop." Pointing a bony finger at him, she rasped, "You leave Lester alone. Hear?"

Biting his lip to keep from losing his temper, Sam slowly rose to his feet. "Lester is a grown man. Shouldn't we respect his wishes in the matter?"

"Grown man?" She stood and advanced a step toward him. "He don't have the sense God gave a duck. He don't know what he wants. I'm tellin' you one thing. Back off."

"I can't do that. I respect the fact you're his aunt, but Lester has asked for my help."

Her eyes turned to slits. "I'm warning you." With

those words, she turned and, spine straight as a rake, walked out of the room.

Oh, boy. Lester had problems beyond his condition, but meeting Aunt Julia had confirmed one thing. Sam was more determined than ever to help the man.

He flicked on the intercom. "Nellie, could you step in here?"

When his nurse appeared, Sam calmed himself. "Bring me every file you have on Lester Jakes, then call Dr. Floyd and set up a time for me to talk with him."

She eyed him speculatively. "You're taking Lester as a patient."

"The man has asked for help. I will do everything in my power to see he gets some." A slight twitch of Nellie's mouth led him to the improbable conclusion that she approved his decision. He reached for a slip of paper on his desk. "Here are the results of Berta Jackson's tests—all negative. Could you notify her?"

"Right away, Dr. Gray." She took the test results, turned to leave, then paused before pivoting to face him again. "If you'll pardon my saying so, Berta didn't need any tests. She was checking you out."

"Checking me out?"

"Yes. And from her comments in the waiting room after her examination, I'd say you're the one who passed the test."

Unbelievably, Nellie's face was about to crack into a grin. "What are you talking about?"

"She said you live up to your billing as—" Nellie's brow furrowed in concentration "—'a *hot* number.'" Before he could figure out how he was supposed to respond, Nellie added, "Julia isn't the only woman in this town who's capable of giving you fits." And then, Nellie Forester, R.N., by God winked!

After she left the room, Sam slumped back in his chair and expelled a huge sigh. Julia Jakes had declared war, Berta Jackson considered doctor's visits entertainment, and Nellie Forester read minds. Women! He was in deep trouble. If that wasn't enough, his nurse's words taunted him. Julia, sure enough, *wasn't* the only woman in Salt Flats to tie him in knots.

He closed his eyes and conjured up the image he couldn't get out of his mind. Kate, drenched in moonlight and crying out, whether she knew it or not, to be kissed—long, hard, passionately.

TO THE STRAINS OF SANTANA, Kate cocked her head and studied the sketch. She tapped her drawing pencil on the drafting table. Still not right. Something about the fullness of the cheeks…or, no…maybe the way the torso appeared foreshortened. She threw down the pencil and stood, working the kinks out of her back. She'd spent most of the week on renderings of Ed's portrait, wanting to get it exactly right before she started on the canvas. For whatever reasons, though, it wasn't coming. Early this morning she'd sat on the back porch, willing Ed to reappear at the pasture gate. Needing him, not only as a model for this painting, but to ground her, to dispel, once and for all, her wayward and baffling flights of fancy.

She walked to the battered old desk and stared at the vase of fully opened pink roses. On the scarred surface lay several fallen petals. She fingered them, registering their velvety softness even as she recalled the card that had accompanied the floral delivery Monday. "Thanks for helping with the boys. You made quite a conquest of them. And of me. Hoping for a 'right answer.' Sam.''

Scooping the petals into her palm, she crossed to the trash can and watched them flutter into the depths. Sam had called twice this week and, against her better judgment, she'd agreed to accompany him to the other side of the lake to look at a boat advertised in the paper. Who would see them there? She chewed on her lip, recalling all too clearly Paul's visit. Why did she regard a simple drive with a friend as clandestine? Whose life was it, anyway?

She sat back down at the drafting table, picked up the eraser, smudged Ed's cheek line, then redrew it. No wonder she couldn't get him right. Not with Sam's roses in her peripheral vision. She'd been in the studio when Red Carpet Floral had delivered the flowers. At the time, it had seemed a good idea to leave them here where she wouldn't be tempted to look at them morning, noon and night.

She slipped from the stool, picked up the vase and marched to the house. Charger's tail thumped a welcome when she entered the kitchen and set the roses in the middle of the table. In another day or so she could throw them away. But tomorrow was Saturday. The day of the outing. Sam might wonder if he didn't see them.

For the umpteenth time this week she thought about the Lupe Santiago workshop, a lifeline in her sea of uncertainties. Getting away would cool things with Sam. Provide objectivity, a fresh perspective. She should be hearing soon. And the irony was that instead of feeling insecure about the workshop, she was now cautiously expectant.

"Charger, I'm nuts." She hunkered beside the dog and smoothed his shaggy coat. "Running away isn't the answer, is it?'' As if in agreement, the dog turned his head and licked her hand. "I can make a mature decision. This thing with Sam doesn't have to get out of hand, attraction or not."

She paused, gave Charger's ears a final scratch, then stood. The dog followed her with his eyes while she went on talking. Saying the words aloud drove the points home in a way mere thinking didn't. "For the first time in my life I'm on my own. I can go where I want, do what I please. I can sleep late or stay up all night working in the studio. I don't have to answer to anyone." A slow grin spread across her face. The declaration of independence felt good.

Then she glanced at the flowers. She sank into a chair, pulling the vase close and burying her nose in the blossoms, still redolent with a faint, evocative fragrance.

Sam. How could such an unexpected, unlikely temptation have been placed in her path?

Slowly, like the approach of a spring rain, the truth pierced her heart. She wasn't ready to give up the stirrings, honey-sweet yet achingly wild, that Sam kindled in her.

JEAN MANLEY, standing over a sink full of soapy dishes, handed Kate a clean tea towel. "You know you don't have to help. Now that there's just us, it doesn't take me long."

Kate recognized the wistfulness in her mother-in-law's voice. The traditional Sunday dinners continued, but with three glaringly empty spaces. No Ed, no Jenny, no Rachel. Sometimes Kate wished she could go straight home from church and do something decadent like work the Sunday crossword puzzle or take Charger for a long walk in the pasture. But the family rhythms were set, and there was a kind of comfort in their repetition.

"I'm glad to help. I always look forward to our chats." And it was true. Through the years some of the best communication with Ed's mother had come amid the clank of silverware and the swish of dishwater.

Jean removed her wristwatch and set it on the window ledge above the sink, then began immersing goblets in the sudsy water. "I do, too. Have you heard from the girls lately?"

"Rachel called last week. She didn't have much news. I think she was really checking on me."

"And how *are* you?" Jean looked at her, her brow slightly drawn as if she was fearful of prying.

Kate removed a goblet from the rinse water and slowly began wiping it. "I'm fine. Every day gets a little easier. Not that Ed is ever far from my mind, but I'm learning, day by day, to be my own person." She felt a sudden urge to confide. "In fact, I've applied for an art program in Santa Fe."

Jean stopped working on the plate in her hand and turned toward Kate, a smile spreading across her face. "That's wonderful. Ed so wanted you to pursue your painting. When will you go?"

Her mother-in-law's approval meant more than she'd realized. "Don't get too excited yet. I haven't been accepted." She spoke more quietly. "It's very competitive."

"If they know talent when they see it, you don't have to worry."

Kate smiled. "I appreciate the vote of confidence, but let's wait and see." It was nice to know at least one person in Salt Flats supported her artistic endeavors. Until now, she hadn't realized quite how nervously she'd been anticipating people's reactions. Then, in response to a question from Jean, Kate elaborated for several minutes about Lupe Santiago.

After a pause, Jean spoke. "And what do you hear from Jenny?"

Was it her imagination or was Jean's tone deliberately neutral. "Not too much."

"Nor have I." Jean scrubbed a casserole dish longer than was necessary, repeatedly running the dishcloth around the rim. "That's not like her."

"She's probably been busy. We'll hear soon." Kate wished she felt as confident as she sounded.

"Did you have a good time yesterday with Dr. Gray?"

"Wh-what?" Could she have heard accurately? She hadn't told anyone she was going boat shopping with Sam. How could Jean possibly know?

"Mel Floyd told me Dr. Gray had asked him to cover his calls yesterday so he could locate a boat. Then Ethel Portman mentioned at church that she and Toad had seen you in the doctor's car."

Kate sighed. "Sam and I are neighbors, and he asked me to ride along."

"You could use some diversion. I hope you had a nice time."

Was her mother-in-law fishing? "I did, Jean, thank you." Kate prayed the matter would lapse before she was tempted to tell Jean what a very good time she had had and just how fraught with overtones the word "diversion" was. But how could Jean ever understand? The mere thought of confiding to her mother-in-law caused her hands to tremble. With lightning reflexes, she caught the casserole lid just before it threatened to slip from her hands and crash to the floor.

Ed's family was a major reason it was foolish to entertain unrealistic notions about Sam. The sun had risen and set on Ed. Paul, especially, had doted on him. She could only imagine how the Manleys would react to gossip—unfounded or not—about Kate and another man.

If she permitted her relationship with Sam to go any further, she could be risking much more than her reputation.

Jean pulled the plug and let the dirty dishwater gurgle down the drain. "You're an adult, after all," she said. "But, dear, you can't be too careful."

"Jean—"

"'Nuff said." The older woman patted her arm. "Let's join Paul on the porch."

When Kate opened the door and stepped outside, she felt stifled, not so much by the overbearing heat and humidity as by an uneasy sense of entrapment.

CHAPTER FIVE

LATE TUESDAY AFTERNOON Kate tucked the packages under her arm and walked briskly toward the Klingers' back door. She hoped Amanda would like the Maud Lovelace books and 'N Sync poster. Charlene ushered her into the roomy, remodeled kitchen decorated with a cheery apple motif. "Boy, am I glad to see you."

"What's up?" Kate set her packages on the counter, then plucked a cookie from the platter Charlene kept perpetually filled.

"Amanda. Ever since we brought her home from the hospital, she's been a pill. I know this wasn't how she expected to spend her summer, but I wish she'd lighten up. At least a little."

Kate studied the shadows under her friend's eyes. "How much sleep are you getting?"

Charlene shrugged. "Not a lot. I know, I know, worrying won't solve anything. But that break was serious, and the way she's behaving, I'm not sure how cooperative she'll be with the physical therapist."

Kate took a bite of the chocolate-chip cookie, then regarded Charlene thoughtfully. "Aren't you borrowing trouble?"

"It's hard not to. I'm a mother."

Kate cringed, thinking guiltily about Jenny and making a mental note to call her. "Maybe what Amanda needs are some new faces." She nodded toward the packages. "I'll deliver these and see if I can cheer her up."

She found Amanda in the den, ensconced on the sofa watching TV, her fractured leg resting on an ottoman, her glazed eyes fixed on a *Brady Bunch* rerun. "Hi, honey. How're you doing?"

Amanda, her freckles standing out in relief against her pale skin, glanced up and gave a wan smile. "Not so good."

Kate laid the packages on the end table, then settled on the sofa where she could look at Amanda. "I'm sorry to hear that. What's the absolute worst thing about the accident?"

The girl muted the TV, then mumbled, "Missing baseball season. I was gonna be the pitcher."

"That's a bummer," Kate agreed.

"Most of my friends are doin' fun stuff. And me? I hafta go to dumb ole therapy soon."

"Don't you want your leg to get stronger?"

"Yeah, but it's gonna hurt."

"Yes, honey, I expect it will. But you know what athletes say? 'No pain, no gain.'"

Amanda apparently didn't want to discuss the unpleasant subject further, because she waved a hand toward the table. "Are those for me?"

Kate winked. "What do you think?"

"Can I open them?"

"Sure."

Kate watched Amanda remove the wrapping paper. She seemed ecstatic about the poster, but only minimally enthused about the books. "The characters in those books—Betsy, Tacy and Tib—were my favorites when I was your age."

"Really?" Amanda sounded cautiously interested.

"Give them a try."

"Okay." Amanda tried a pale imitation of a smile, then, with a sigh, ran her hand down her encased thigh.

Hearing voices, they both glanced toward the kitchen. "More company?" Kate inquired.

Amanda, her eyes never leaving the door, sat up straighter. "I hope it's Dr. Sam. He said he'd come by today."

Kate hadn't seen Sam since their trip to look at the used boat, which he'd bought and left with the owner for servicing. Numerous times since she'd relived their time together. It had been a day of spontaneous laughter, easy conversation—and confused emotions.

When Charlene and Sam entered the room, Charlene gestured toward Kate. "You remember my friend Kate Manley?" There was definite mischief in her tone.

A flicker of amusement glinted in Sam's eyes. "Of course I remember. Good to see you again." Then, to Kate's relief, he turned to Amanda. "Glad to be home?"

He sat on the coffee table, his hands dangling between his legs, and studied his patient.

"Mom, do you hafta stand there? Me and Dr. Sam have things to discuss. After all, it is *my* leg."

Charlene's jaw dropped.

Sam grinned reassuringly. "It's okay, Mom. I'll fill you in later."

Kate rose to her feet. "A glass of milk would sure go well with another cookie. How about it, Charlene?"

As they left, Amanda called to her. "Thanks, Kate, for the presents."

Charlene opened the refrigerator, picked up a half-gallon of milk, then slammed the door. "What do you make of that?'' she asked indignantly. ''The child's got a mind of her own.''

From her perch on a kitchen stool, Kate nibbled on another cookie. ''Your daughter must've inherited some of your genes.''

Throwing her an exasperated look, Charlene handed her a glass of milk. ''Sometimes friends can be so annoying,'' she said as she grabbed a cookie and sank down beside Kate. ''You can't slip anything past 'em.''

Kate felt another twinge of guilt. She hadn't told Charlene anything about Sam. Why not? The answers to that question, she realized, all had to do with self-protection, pure and simple. ''You wouldn't want a passive Amanda. The fact she seems to like Sam should help. She's coming to that age where parents are the last people she'll talk to.''

''I know you're right, but it's hard.''

Kate patted her friend's hand. ''Everything will be okay. Give it time.''

''Thanks, Kate.'' Charlene toyed with her cookie, then glanced up, a smile quirking her mouth. ''Gawd, it makes me wonder what you and I must've put our mothers through.'' She shuddered. ''I better not even go there.''

''If you think what's going on now is bad, wait until Amanda's a teenager.''

Charlene rolled her eyes and poked Kate good-naturedly. ''Gee, thanks a bunch. I feel *so* much better.''

Sam's cheerful whistling preceded him into the room. ''Charlene, that's quite a gal you've got there.'' He lounged against the counter, his arms folded over his chest. ''She's going to be fine.''

Charlene stood. "I'm relieved to hear it. I just wish she wouldn't act so moody."

"At the moment she's justifiably discouraged," Sam said. "But that's temporary. She'll feel better when she gets into therapy and can actually measure progress."

Charlene wrinkled her brow. "I hope she'll cooperate. She can be pretty stubborn." She pointedly ignored Kate's grin and, picking up the platter, offered Sam a cookie.

"Thanks," he said, taking one. "I don't think you have to worry about Amanda, though. She'll tear into her therapy program."

Charlene stopped in the middle of the kitchen floor, still holding the platter. "How can you be sure?"

Sam headed for the door. "Let's just say she and I have a little wager."

"But—"

Grinning enigmatically, he waved the cookie toward her. "I can't say any more. Amanda made me promise not to tell."

He opened the door, paused, then turned back. "I have an idea. That is, if it's not too presumptuous. Maybe Amanda would enjoy it if I brought my boys over to see her. They're about the same age and they play a mean Monopoly game."

Charlene beamed. "Would you mind?"

"Not at all. You'd be doing me the favor. I'll call you."

Kate watched the exchange, marvelling at Sam's ability to charm Amanda, comfort Charlene and arouse libidinous thoughts in her.

After he was gone, Charlene turned, cocked her head and studied her. "When are you going to tell me?"

Kate busied herself scooping crumbs to the edge of

the counter, then swallowed the bit of cookie clogging her throat. "What?"

"About the flowers."

"What flowers?"

"You know damn well what flowers. The roses from…Sam."

"I didn't want to bother you. You've been busy with Amanda."

"Not *that* busy." Charlene sat back down beside her. "Have you been holding out on me?"

"He sent them to thank me for helping with his boys."

"And?" Charlene drummed her fingers on the countertop.

"Wait." Kate struggled to extricate herself from what she anticipated would be a grilling worthy of *NYPD Blue.* "How did you know about the flowers?"

"Get real, girlfriend. He ordered them locally. It didn't take Mavis Hortell at the flower shop long to spread the word. Then when I saw Jean at the grocery store yesterday, she mentioned your Saturday boat-hunting excursion."

Kate groaned. "Is nothing sacred in this town?"

"Nope," Charlene responded cheerfully. "So out with it. What's going on with you and our handsome new doctor?"

Kate gave her the bare-bones version, ending with the caveat "We're just friends."

Charlene bit back a skeptical smile. "Okay. I'll buy 'just friends.' For now."

"Mom!" There was urgency in Amanda's voice.

Charlene leaped to her feet. "No telling if this is the real thing or the girl who cried 'Wolf.'"

Kate waved her out of the room. "Go tend to her.

I'll see myself out.'' Amanda's bid for her mother's attention couldn't have been more timely. It circumvented Kate's need to tell Charlene the truth about Sam. About his humor, his gentleness, the way he made her feel special.

About her disturbingly strong reactions to him and, worse, the very real temptation he posed.

THE MAIN STREET CAFÉ was packed at six-thirty Wednesday morning with ranchers and farmers speculating on cattle and wheat prices, deliverymen with company logos stenciled on their pockets, and merchants and professionals identifiable by their pressed pants, short-sleeved dress shirts and ties. Even this early the overhead fans labored to dispel the heat.

Millie glanced up from behind the serving counter to say, ''Mornin', Doc,'' but few others acknowledged Sam's presence, even though he'd made it a habit to begin every day with breakfast here. He wondered how long it would take to be accepted as a fixture. He rather suspected it might be years.

He slid into a booth across from Mel Floyd, already nursing a cup of coffee. ''Thanks for meeting me.''

''It does me good to get stirring early. Warms up my hips and knees,'' the older man said, laying aside the limp vinyl-bound menu.

''Arthritis?''

''Been bothering me for a good long while, but it's worse lately. That's one reason I retired when I did.''

''Who're you seeing about it?''

Mel wiped a hand across his balding pate, then fiddled with his silverware. ''Nobody.''

Sam knew the drill. Physicians were notorious for

thinking they could heal themselves. "Don't you think it's time?"

"You sound just like Nellie."

Sam hid a grin. "Is she on your case, too?"

"On my case? The woman never stops harping on the subject. Called last night, in fact. Wants me to see a doctor in Enid."

"Nellie can be determined, all right."

"Determined! Once she gets hold of something, she quivers like a bird dog on point."

Millie set a cup of black coffee in front of Sam. "The usual?" she asked. He nodded. "What about you, Doc Floyd?"

"I'll have tomato juice and the short stack, hold the bacon."

Sam blew on his coffee before taking a swig. "You have any notion why Nellie's so hell-bent on getting you to a specialist?"

Mel leaned his elbows on the table. "Pure cussedness, that's what."

"I'm not so sure."

"What's that supposed to mean?"

Sam stretched, resting his arms along the back of the booth. "She's no longer your nurse, yet she wants to help on the weekends you cover for me. And I hear tell that ever since you've been batching it, she occasionally brings you a casserole. Today you're telling me she still has more than a passing interest in your health." He waved his hand airily. "Doesn't all of that suggest something to you?"

"I haven't the foggiest notion where you're going with—" Mel's chin fell to his chest and he stared incredulously at Sam. In the distance a persistent dinging signalled "order up" and voices swirled around them.

After several seconds, Mel picked up a fork and jabbed it in Sam's direction. *"Nellie? Me?* Wait just a minute."

Sam smiled benignly. "Stranger things have happened."

Mel dropped the fork and slumped back. "Well, I'll be damned."

Although the older man appeared befuddled, he didn't look entirely unhappy. *You owe me one, Nellie,* Sam thought to himself.

Millie slapped down their plates. "Eat it while it's hot, gents," she said, tucking a hank of dyed blond hair behind her ear.

Sam attacked his oatmeal while Mel slathered his pancakes with butter and maple syrup. When Sam had first started eating here, Millie had teased him about not having a farmer's breakfast. "You one of them cholesterol freaks?" she'd asked. But she'd never tried to sell him on the merits of the eggs, sausage, cream gravy and yeasty cinnamon buns favored by the regulars. Fat consumption had never been out of vogue in Salt Flats.

Mel took a bite, chewed thoughtfully, then fixed his gaze on Sam. "Somehow, son, I don't think you invited me here to talk about Nellie Forester."

Sam grinned. "No, that was an aside." He wiped his mouth carefully, then launched into the subject he'd come to discuss.

"I have some further thoughts about Lester Jakes."

"I'm interested in hearing them. As you know from what I told you last week, he's difficult to diagnose. At first I suspected schizophrenia, but he didn't appear to have hallucinations or any other manifestations of that condition, except, of course, for the paranoia. He wouldn't take the medications we tried, and Julia Jakes was no help at all. I suppose he could have paranoid personality disorder.'' Mel picked up a forkful of pancake. ''I never could get to the bottom of it, especially when Lester wouldn't go to Enid for evaluation. After a while, although I'm not proud to say it, I came to treat him as a nuisance.''

''Looking over the files, I'd say you did everything anyone would've done. Is there any possibility there's a situational cause for his paranoia?''

Mel chewed as if ruminating. ''What are you getting at?''

''Suppose something happened to him as a child, something that Julia or others keep reinforcing.''

''You're suggesting his behavior could be justified?''

Sam set down his fork. ''Bear with me. By anyone's standards, Lester is eccentric and believes himself to be persecuted. But he showed no distrust of me whatsoever, and I'm a stranger, ordinarily an automatic target of suspicion. He showed me a list he'd kept of wrongs done him. Frankly, Mel, the more I look at it, the more I'm open to the possibility he's not so much sick as legitimately victimized.''

Mel had stopped eating and was regarding him with interest. ''Go on.''

''We assume life with his aunt has been a sterile existence at best, and we know he is the subject of ridicule, even debasement, by some in the community. Is it possible others have directly and indirectly contributed to his sense of persecution?''

''Given the fact I've considered everything else, it's certainly a viable hypothesis. What do you intend to do about it?''

''I don't know yet. Mainly I wondered if you feel the scenario I've laid out is possible.''

Mel shook his head resignedly. "Lord knows I couldn't help him. Far be it from me to discourage you, son."

"What do you know about his parents' deaths?"

Shoving his empty plate aside and rubbing his stomach contentedly, Mel seemed lost in thought. "Lord, that was years ago. Lester wasn't but a little bit of a fella. Fierce tornado came through. Julia was visiting at the time and she and Lester made it to the storm cellar, but Lester's folks didn't. They were killed. Their barn flat disappeared. The boy was never the same afterward. Kept to himself. Scared of his own shadow."

"Hmm." Sam shifted in his seat. Here was a clue to pursue.

Mel continued, "I don't know what would've happened to Lester if Julia hadn't inherited the farm and taken him in. She was his only surviving relative."

"So she's legally responsible for him?"

"Not now that he's an adult, but he's always been very dependent on her."

Sam ran his forefinger around the rim of his mug, pondering the implications of Mel's words. "He tells me he's good with appliances, machines. Any truth to that?"

"Sure is. I can't tell you how often he's resurrected my lawn mower when I was ready to junk it." Mel chuckled. "Strange as it may seem, the man has an eerie kind of genius."

Millie materialized at Sam's elbow. "Anything else I can get you gents?"

Sam noticed the café had cleared out as customers left to begin their workday. "Just the check."

The waitress dug in her apron pocket and produced it. "You eat like a bird, Dr. Gray. Saving up for the pie-eating contest?" She cocked one hip and eyed him with amusement.

"Pie-eating contest?"

Mel pointed a finger at him. "I think she's got your number, son."

"Fourth of July competition. I can sign you up right here." Millie pointed to a poster hanging behind the cash register.

"Are you trying to talk yourself out of a tip?"

"No, sirree. I'm trying to find worthy competition for Kenny Smutz. He always wins."

Sam slipped a couple of bills under his plate, then stood, towering over the diminutive waitress. "I think I'll be an observer this year."

Millie grinned. "Well, you can't blame a gal for tryin'."

As they strolled out onto the sidewalk, Sam paused. "Fourth of July's a pretty big deal around here, huh?"

"Yes, indeed. There's a parade in the morning, featuring the high-school marching band, a fire truck, floats, even a queen. In the afternoon, there's a bike-decorating contest, games and competitions of all sorts. After dark the fireworks display draws folks from all over."

"I'm sorry my boys will miss it," Sam said. "They'll be here the weekend before, though."

"I know." Mel clapped him on the shoulder. "I'm covering for you, remember?"

"You and Nellie." Sam couldn't resist the good-natured gibe.

"Slow down there, boy. Don't you go making us a twosome. Speaking of twosomes, though, I understand you and Kate Manley have been seeing something of one another." He winked.

The mere mention of Kate's name lightened Sam's mood. "I like her," he said.

"She's a fine woman, one of the best." Mel's voice lost some of its playfulness. "But take it easy there."

"What do you mean?"

Mel kept walking, nodding occasionally to people they passed. "Folks think mighty highly of Kate just like they did of her husband. Nobody'd want to see her get hurt. You're trying to establish yourself here. Build trust. Get people to accept you. There's those that wouldn't take kindly to your coming on too strong, if you catch my drift."

You wanted a small town, Gray. Now you've got one. The hell of it was that at the same time he saw the common sense in Mel's word of caution, he bemoaned the need to go slowly with her. And he resented the fact it was anybody's damn business but his and Kate's. "Thanks, Mel. I appreciate your concern, but I'll handle it my way."

They'd reached Mel's car. The older man paused and looked him over appraisingly. "Wouldn't be much of a man if you didn't."

After Mel drove off, Sam walked briskly in the direction of the clinic, pondering his future in Salt Flats and where Kate fit. Because regardless of Mel's well-intentioned warning, he couldn't stop thinking about her.

And hurting her was the last thing he had in mind.

THE MORNING CHORES had taken longer than Kate had anticipated, interrupted as they were by a visit from the rancher who rented her pastureland, and it was nearly noon before she could think about going to the studio. She'd had an inspiration in the night about the back-

ground for Ed's portrait and she itched to get to her
sketch pad. But she knew if she postponed the phone
call to Jenny, she'd be preoccupied all afternoon. She
didn't want to pry into her daughter's life, but something was definitely amiss. Maybe Jenny would welcome the opportunity to talk about whatever it was.

Kate settled at the kitchen table, the portable phone
cupped against her ear. It took five rings before Jenny
answered. "Hi, Mom."

"How'd you know it was me?"

"We have caller ID now."

Kate wasn't surprised. Todd was a gadget buff.
"Screens out telemarketers, right?"

"Right." Jenny's voice sounded tight.

"Did I catch you at a bad time?"

"No, this is fine. The baby's napping."

"How is he?" Jenny spent several minutes filling
Kate in on Parker's latest achievements—counting,
watching Barney, using his spoon. When she finished
the catalogue, Kate waded into the topic at hand. "It
doesn't sound as if you and Todd have much time for
yourselves. Do you get out often?"

"Baby-sitters are hard to find."

"It's important, though, for husbands and wives to
spend time away from children."

"Mo-ther, I don't need a lecture. Like I said, baby-
sitters are scarce. They're also expensive."

"I'm sorry, honey. Are finances a problem? Maybe
I could send you a little treat money."

"Look, Mom, I know you mean well. But just forget
it, okay?"

Kate pinched her nose between her thumb and index
finger, fighting off the headache gathering behind her

eyes. "Jenny, I'm worried about you. Are you and Todd getting along all right?"

Jenny laughed hollowly. "'Getting along'? That's difficult when I scarcely see him."

"Is he working that hard?"

"So he says."

The brittle quality of the words brought Kate up short. Jenny could be impatient, even demanding, but she wasn't ordinarily sarcastic. Since the beginning of the conversation, Kate had had the distinct impression of…bitterness, hurt. "Do you have reason to doubt him?"

"Oh, Mom." From Jenny's tone of voice, Kate could imagine her daughter crumpling into a chair. "He's in sales, for heaven's sake. Who's to know if fishing trips to Gunnison or dinners at the Broadmoor are business or not."

"So you're alone a lot?"

"I've got Parker."

"That's not what I meant." Concern and impatience washed over her. There was too much Jenny wasn't saying. "Is there something you need to talk about?"

"No."

Before Kate could press further, Jenny went on. "This is my business, Mother. When there's something to talk about, I'll tell you. Meanwhile, could we just drop it?"

Kate had the sense Jenny was holding herself together by force of will. Saying any more would threaten her daughter's precarious control. "For now. But I'm always here if you need me."

"I know. Mom…" Jenny's voice trailed off. "I miss Daddy."

The anguish in her daughter's voice splintered Kate's

heart. "So do I, honey. So do I." Yet in that moment, if her life had depended upon picturing Ed's face or recapturing the sound of his voice, she couldn't have.

Silence resonated between them. Finally Jenny said, "I've gotta go, Mom. The baby's waking up."

"Give him a hug for me." Kate hesitated, all her maternal instincts attuned to the careful way Jenny was ending the conversation.

"I will. Gotta run. And don't worry about me, Mother. I'll be fine." And she hung up.

Kate sat, staring at the receiver, replaying Jenny's last words in her mind. Not "I'm fine," but "I'll *be* fine."

Something was very, very wrong.

FEW OTHER CRYSTAL DIGGERS were on the Salt Plains. The flat, chalky surface glinted in the morning sun and crunched underfoot.

"Over here, boys!" Kate gestured to the twins who were running on the walkway, their faces set determinedly, their tanned legs churning. She planted a lopsided beach umbrella in the crusty earth and began dividing up the gear—empty coffee cans, trowels, shovels.

Sam, lugging a large ice chest and beach towels, approached, grinning. "You didn't tell me you'd need a pack mule."

She tilted back the brim of her straw hat and set her mouth in imitation of an exacting scientist. "This is a geological dig, so we require lots of equipment." She studied the layout in front of her. "Looks like we have everything." Bart and Blake, panting for air, flopped down beside her. She looked from one to the other. "Who won?"

"I did," they both said.

Before they could dispute one another, she tossed each of them a tube of sunscreen. "Lather up."

Blake made a face. "Lather?"

"The sun is fierce, and the salt plain acts like a giant mirror. Even though we have an unusually breezy morning, sunburn is a real danger."

"And don't forget to wear your caps," Sam said.

"So when can we start digging?" Bart asked, smearing sunblock on his arms.

"Anytime." Kate gestured to the coffee tins. "Help yourselves. But when you start digging and rinsing, remember how fragile these salt crystals are. The slightest jarring can shatter them."

"So how come the ones at your house are hard?"

"After they've been in the air awhile, they harden."

"Oh," Blake said. He glanced at Bart. "Betcha I get the first crystal."

"Not if I can help it." Bart threw down the sunscreen, picked up a trowel and set off toward a spot nearer the reservoir. Blake wasn't far behind, a coffee can clasped against his chest.

Kate glanced up at Sam, who was shading his eyes with one hand to watch his sons. With his lean physique, ponytail and rugged profile, he resembled a frontier sentry. "You ready to get down and dirty, Doctor?"

"What do you have in mind?" A hint of amusement colored his voice.

His sunglasses shielded his eyes and she couldn't tell if he'd intended the double entendre. But who was she to talk? What, after all, was in *her* thoughts? Summoning equanimity, she explained that digging in the salt and sand was filthy business.

He squatted beside her. "Like making mud pies?"

His breadth blotted out the sun and Kate wondered

whether the heat she felt was generated by his body or by her reaction to his proximity. "Exactly."

He pulled a pail close, then shoved the glasses up on his head. He studied her and she felt prickles work their way down her spine. Finally he stood, pulling her up by the elbow. "Then pick a spot, madam. Let's dig."

Two hours later, her jeans soiled with briny mud, her hands and forearms caked with sand and perspiration dripping from her nose, Kate scooped up a small amount of water from that pooling in the bottom of the excavation and carefully poured it over a projection arising from the hole. Beside her Sam observed intently. Bart and Blake, who had joined their father to watch Kate work, stood behind her, holding their breath as slowly, cup by cup, a complex crystal form emerged. Using a small paintbrush, Kate gently dusted away some grains of sand.

It struck her that this painstaking exposure of layers, the rinsing away of detritus and the baring of the fragile treasure hidden in the earth were not dissimilar from the process of unleashing the soul of a painting. Nor, she realized with sudden self-insight, from her attempts to recover the Kate buried under the protective layers of numbness, solitude and grief.

She sat back on her haunches, studying the selenite crystal. "Now it has to dry in the sun. Then we can excavate further and take it home."

"Yours is a lot bigger than the ones we found earlier," Blake said, his voice awed.

"We're fortunate," Kate said. "This is one of the largest I've ever uncovered."

The boys scampered off to try their luck further. Sam moved the umbrella and cooler nearer the site of Kate's find. He held up a bottled water. "Thirsty?"

"Very." She sat propped against the cooler. He handed her the bottle, which she upended, gulping the refreshing liquid. "That's hot work."

"It's hot, period," he said, tossing a damp towel toward her.

After she wiped her face and neck, she leaned back, closed her eyes and let the breeze ruffle her hair. The animated voices of children, the thrum of a fishing boat motor and the buzz of nearby sand flies lulled her into a contented stupor. Yet even behind her closed lids, she was aware of Sam's presence. The cocoa-tang of his sunscreen, the faint gurgle of water sluicing down his throat, a sense of his body so close to hers it would take only the least movement of her hand to come in contact with his thigh. She imagined running her fingers over his leg, dusted with hair, striated with muscle, warm and firm beneath her touch. Imagined leaning into him, permitting her lips to find the tender, vulnerable spot at the base of his neck. Fantasized how it would throb to the rhythm of his heartbeat, how his sun-warmed skin would taste salty on her tongue.

Slowly, as if in a dream, she became aware he had moved closer and was caressing her hand. She kept her eyes closed, concentrating on the way he picked up each finger, stroked it, explored it, then laid it down, before moving on to another. These tiny gestures paradoxically created in her a spasm of longing so intense she held her breath. If he could arouse her this way with so innocent a gesture, what response would he excite if he kissed her? Made love to her?

He laid her hand back in her lap. The absence of his touch felt like abandonment. Then he started smoothing the worry lines between her brows. "Why so serious?" he asked, his voice low, intense.

Her eyes fluttered open and before she could consider her response, she blurted, "That felt so good."

His face hovered just above hers, his eyes searching as if for permission. "I'm glad. Maybe this will, too."

There was no time for reason or protest because now his lips were on hers—testing, sipping, pressing, tasting—and she was lost in a sensation so powerful that she was helpless to stifle a tiny, strangled moan before clutching his shoulders as if his solidity would somehow save her from drowning.

He continued kissing her in a way that removed any doubt this was an accident. In her heart Kate knew this moment had been destined since she first met Sam. But never in her romantic fantasies had a mere kiss approached the wild sweetness of his lips exploring hers.

With an effort of will, she placed her hands against his shoulders and pulled away, her emotions chaotic. All at once objections stormed within her—what about the twins? Other onlookers? Her daughters? Paul and Jean?

As if reading her confusion, Sam cupped her chin, then whispered, "It's okay, Kate. We didn't do anything wrong." He chuckled throatily. "In fact, I'd say we did something very right. At least it felt that way to me. What about you?"

She bit her lower lip and briefly considered lying. But she couldn't, not when he was looking at her with such candor, such warmth. "You almost make me forget who I am."

"Or maybe discover who you are."

She blushed under the intensity of his gaze, admitting to the duality in which she'd been living—clinging for safety to the good, old Kate who did what everyone expected and longing to risk becoming the new Kate

who might shock or surprise others but desperately
needed to be true to herself. "We shouldn't be starting
this," she finally managed to say.

"Give me one valid reason why not."

"The boys, the—"

He placed his fingers gently over her mouth. "One
valid reason, Kate. Other people, even those close to us,
are just that. Other people. This is about you and me."
His fingertips soothed her sun-chapped lips. "It's not
selfish to want something for yourself, and those who
truly love you would understand and want you to be
happy."

"You make it sound so simple."

"Trust me. It is." At a shout, he glanced over her
head. "But speaking of other people, here come the
wild Indians."

She looked over her shoulder to see Bart and Blake
heading toward them. "Is it time, Dad?" Blake yelled.

"You said early afternoon," Bart added. The boys
stopped on the other side of the cooler.

Sam patted Kate's shoulder, then stood. "Nearly.
Why don't you help gather up the beach towels and the
umbrella. Then we'll finish extricating Kate's salt crystal from the ground." Sam smiled down at Kate.
"We're picking up the boat for the maiden voyage later
this afternoon. Will you come?"

She rose to her feet, brushing the salt and sand off
her jeans. "Thanks, but I don't think so.

He looked disappointed. "You're sure?"

"Positive." She nodded toward the boys who were
returning from their trek to the van. "Your time with
them is limited. Your first boat ride should be a special
father-son time."

He shrugged in acquiescence. "You're right, but—"

"Stop there. I'm right." She waved at Bart and Blake as they approached, then pointed to the excavation in the sand. "Now comes the fun part. Bringing that salt crystal up into the light of day."

Sam glanced at the twins and smiled mischievously. "Without breaking it."

"Without breaking it," she echoed, thinking not of the brittle geological formation, but of her own fragile heart.

CHAPTER SIX

"DID YOU BRUSH YOUR TEETH?" Sam stood in the doorway of the boys' bedroom, watching them pull on their shorty pajama bottoms, their knobby knees out of proportion to their skinny legs.

"Da-ad!" Bart threw him a long-suffering look. "You always ask that."

Sam sauntered toward them. "Maybe that's because you sometimes forget."

"We're not babies, you know," Blake said.

Gathering them to him in a playful headlock, Sam continued. "I've noticed. I don't think I could have gotten the boat launched today without your help."

Bart squirmed out of his grip. "The boat's way cool, Dad. Next time can we water-ski?"

"I'll have to buy some skis and rig a tow rope."

"You've got two weeks till we come again," Blake said, his voice muffled by the pajama top he was pulling over his head.

Sam studied his sons' exposed reddened skin. "How about the aloe vera? Did you remember that?"

"It feels good even if it's squishy," Bart said. "Blakey's more burned than I am."

"Am not," Blake mumbled, throwing his brother a disgusted look.

"Are, too," Bart challenged.

Sam stepped between them. "Hey, fellas. Calm down. Time to turn in."

The boys jumped into their beds, Bart sprawled on his back, Blake huddled on his side, his legs drawn up to his chest. Sam pulled the sheet up over Bart. "Good night, buddy." He smoothed back Bart's hair and squeezed his shoulder before perching on the edge of Blake's bed. "You've been awfully quiet this evening. Everything okay?"

By way of answer, Blake pulled his legs tighter against his chest and burrowed his chin in the pillow.

Sam's stomach turned over. Bart was an open book; Blake was more sensitive, introspective. "Son?" He placed a hand on the boy's hip.

"Leave me alone, okay?" Blake mumbled.

"He's just in a dorky Blake mood," Bart offered, his tone condescending.

"Shut up, Bart!" Blake rasped, on the edge of tears.

Sam moved to sit closer to Blake. "If something's bothering you, we need to talk about it. Maybe I can help."

"No." He made a production of closing his eyes. "I'm going to sleep."

Sam slumped, defeated by his son's intransigence. He rubbed his hand over Blake's tense back, then tousled his hair before saying, "I love you, guys. Sleep tight." He flipped off the bedside lamp and turned to go.

"He doesn't like it that Kate's your girlfriend," Bart volunteered into the darkness.

"Girlfriend?" Sam was momentarily at a loss for words. "Kate and I are good friends. I thought you both liked her."

"Yuck!" Blake sputtered.

Sam shook his head. "Look, fellas, I don't know

where this is coming from. Kate's been great. She let you fish at her pond, made you ice cream, showed you the stars, and found you a fantastic salt crystal.''

In a sing-songy voice, Bart said, ''And that's not all she did.''

''Shut up,'' Blake repeated, his words laced with venom.

Sam took a step back toward the twin beds. ''What are you guys talking about?''

''I saw you,'' Bart said, his bravado tempered with uncertainty.

''Saw me?''

''The two of you,'' Bart mumbled. ''Kissing.''

Blake sat up in bed, glaring at his brother. ''Did *not!*''

''Did, too, dork. How many times do I have to tell you? I know kissing when I see it.''

''Whoa, gentlemen.'' Sam sank to the floor between the beds, one hand on each boy. ''Sounds like I have some explaining to do.''

Blake flopped back down on his pillow. ''I told you I'm going to sleep now.'' From the light cast from the hallway, Sam saw him make a show of closing his eyes.

''You were kissing her, right, Dad?'' Bart was not to be deterred. ''It looked kinda like in the movies.''

''Gross.'' Clearly, Blake had not been successful in drifting off.

Sam struggled to find the words to explain his adult feelings to two vulnerable boys. ''I like Kate a lot.''

''Yeah, but that doesn't mean you have to—'' Blake choked out the word ''—kiss her.''

''First of all, I'm sorry if my kissing Kate upset you. I thought it was a private moment.''

''Jeez, Dad, there were other people there, too. What

if they saw you?'' Blake obviously had a highly developed sense of propriety.

Sam knew if he wasn't careful he'd come across as defensive. And the boys had a point—the Great Salt Plains wasn't the most isolated place in the county, although he'd been certain at the time that they'd been unobserved. But he hadn't counted on Bart's hawklike interest in all things adult. He certainly couldn't expect the boys to understand that he'd been overwhelmed by Kate's rosy cheeks, smudged with mud, by her eyes alive with excitement and her moist lips parted in appeal. So, okay, it was an impulse, but one he hadn't regretted. Until now.

He cleared his throat. ''What if Kate *were* my girlfriend?''

''You can't have any girlfriend but Mom,'' Blake blurted.

''You are *so* dumb!'' Bart sat up in the middle of his bed and crossed his legs. ''Mom's not Dad's girlfriend. Not anymore.''

''Well, she should be,'' Blake said, not looking at Sam.

''You boys know that your mother and I love you a great deal, and we've explained that we can no longer live together as a family.''

''You coulda tried!'' Blake's voice broke around a swallowed sob.

Sam joined him on his bed, feeling his son jerk away when he touched him. ''We did, Blake. For a long time. Sometimes grown-up relationships are hard to understand.''

A slight breeze ruffled the shades at the window. A car rattled past the front of the house. Bart scratched a bite on his leg.

Blake finally spoke. "So are you gonna marry her?"

"You're getting way ahead of me here."

"But you kissed her."

Sam sighed. "Yes, I did. And I'm not sorry. I think Kate is a lovely, good woman, and I have feelings for her." He paused, aware both boys were looking at him wide-eyed. "I'd like for you to get to know her better."

Neither twin said a word. Recognizing the conversation was at an impasse, Sam stood and leaned over first one and then the other to kiss them on the forehead. "For now, though, why don't we all sleep on it. Remember, you've got a big day tomorrow."

Bart fell over sideways against his pillow in mock defeat. "Yeah, big day. Monopoly with a gi-rl." He made the word sound like a synonym for *cootie*.

"You'll like Amanda," Sam assured him.

"That's *all* we're doin' in this stupid town. Giving girls a chance. I hate it!" Blake abruptly turned his back to Sam and pulled the sheet over his head.

Dejected as Sam felt, he couldn't help counting the months until puberty set in. Then Blake would be giving all kinds of girls a chance and hoping against hope that they'd return the favor.

Sam left the room, then paused in the doorway looking back at them. He owed his sons more than a voyeur's view of stolen kisses. And he owed Kate more, too.

DRIVING HOME early Sunday evening after taking the boys to meet Marcia in Enid, Sam reflected on the generosity of folks in Salt Flats. Slowly he was beginning to feel accepted. At least by some. On her way to church, Minnie Odom had dropped off warm, home-made crullers for their breakfast, and Charlene Klinger had thoughtfully rounded up a couple of neighbor boys to join the afternoon Monopoly game, which had turned out to be a "blast," at least according to Bart. Who knew about Blake? He'd continued his punishing silence throughout the day.

And therein lay a problem. He couldn't expect his sons to see Kate through his eyes or accept his interest in her right off the bat. Nor fall in love with her at first sight, as he could finally admit he had done.

He hadn't gone looking for it. And he certainly hadn't expected it to happen. But it had. Right from that first night in the library. With time, surely the boys would come around. They had to. Because, for him, there was no turning back.

He hoped he was right that Kate reciprocated his feelings. Her eyes said she did. So did her response to the kiss. Yet she still seemed skittish. Tentative. He supposed her behavior was understandable. Maybe she hadn't expected to find love again, or perhaps she was more concerned than he realized about the few years' difference in their ages.

Almost mechanically, he pulled out to pass a slow-moving pickup, grateful for the level, traffic-free expanse of highway ahead. He shifted in his seat, impatient with the distance that kept him from Kate. She had no idea how important she was becoming to him. Through her eyes he saw and understood Salt Flats more clearly. She made him laugh. She was the friend he could trust, the lover he wanted by his side. Always.

He needed to be with her, to hold her, to tell her. Tonight. Outside, the telephone poles seemed to creep by, even at sixty miles per hour. He could no more stay away than fly.

AFTER SUPPER Kate moved restlessly through the house, straightening towels in the bathroom, swiping at specks of dust, smoothing the guest-room bedspread, unused since Rachel's last trip home in the spring. Yesterday afternoon she'd thrown herself into making jar after jar of peach preserves, hoping the activity would drive Sam's kiss from her mind. Yet even now, as she paused in the upstairs hallway, her finger found its way to her lips as if testing whether they still smoldered from the heat of his mouth. There was no escaping the reality that his had not been just any kiss. Nor any denying she had crossed a dangerous threshold.

This morning at church and afterward at Jean and Paul's for Sunday dinner, she had kept a low profile, wondering if the change in her was obvious, speculating what the reaction would be if they could look into her heart. She knew what they would find. An upsurge of hope, the reawakening of feelings she thought she'd left far behind and an excitement powerfully and elementally sexual.

And, undeniably, guilt.

She sank onto the top step of the stairs, dimly aware of Charger nudging her arm seeking attention. Darn it, anyway! Why should she feel guilty? She ticked off the rationalizations she'd catalogued during the long night. She was an adult fully capable of making her own decisions. She had been a good and faithful wife to Ed, a man she'd loved with all her heart. But he was gone. She had years in front of her that could either stretch out long and lonely or be filled with meaningful activity and love. Everyone deserved love. What, then, was making her feel ashamed?

She buried her head in her hands. Several minutes passed before she acknowledged the answer to the ques-

tion—the complex expectations of those close to her.
Especially Jean and Paul, who would be devastated if
they knew what she was considering.

Feeling suddenly claustrophobic, she hurried down
the stairs, grabbed a quilt and a couple of pillows, then
marched outside. Whose life was it anyway? Hers. Only
hers. She didn't want to hurt anyone. But neither did
she want to be alone.

She spread the quilt, fluffed the pillows and lay down,
letting the twilight soothe her with its comforting
sounds of doves cooing, katydids thrumming and small
gusts of wind sighing through the branches of the protective elms.

She closed her eyes, willing herself to think about
something other than Sam. Dear God, it was nearly time
to hear from Lupe Santiago. At the thought, her stomach
turned to mush. Not being accepted to the workshop
would be a more crushing blow than she'd been willing
to admit. Being accepted, though, meant subjecting her
work—and herself—to painful criticism.

She seized on a thread of hope. Acceptance would
take any decision about Sam out of her hands. Surely
distance would prove that their flirtation had merely
been a fleeting infatuation. A kind of summer madness.

She squelched the accusation of her conscience that
flirtation didn't begin to cover what she was starting to
feel for the man.

Slipping off her sandals, she wiggled her toes, then
stretched luxuriously, her arms spread at her sides. As
the sky darkened, the stars appeared, one by one, awakening memories of lying here beside Sam. She stirred
fitfully, caught up in an intense longing.

Suddenly she heard a car, and shortly headlights
pierced the darkness, blinding her. She wasn't expecting

company. She stood, tucking her scoop-necked, sleeveless T-shirt into her shorts, and walked, barefooted, to the gate. But long before the Suburban pulled alongside the fence, she knew, as if she'd subconsciously willed it, who was arriving.

Sam stepped from the vehicle, his yellow polo shirt outlining his lean, athlete's torso, his jeans riding low on his hips. A sudden warmth oozed through her.

"Sam, what are you doing here?"

He said nothing, just walked slowly to her, his eyes fixed on hers. He stopped in front of her, resting his hands on her shoulders. "We need to talk, but first—"

Before she could react, he pulled her to him, rendering her breathless from the shock of his warm body electrifying hers. His strong arms enfolded her, and she had only long enough to gasp his name before his mouth closed on hers in a kiss, at first tender, questioning. Then, as if neither had a choice, their joining became endless and needful—lip to lip, tongue to tongue, breath to breath. Something deep inside her convulsed and she found herself unable to let go as he walked her backward until they sank onto the quilt, still clinging to each other.

She collapsed onto her back, regretting the momentary loss of his body against hers. As he stretched beside her, his intense eyes blocking the night sky, she heard him say, "I can't stop thinking about you." He ran a hand from her shoulder down her arm, then along the curve of her hip, exciting nerves that led straight to her womb.

"I know the feeling," she managed. "But—"

The words died in her throat when he sought her mouth again, this time gently, wonderingly. When he released her, he spoke again, punctuating his remarks with tiny kisses, first on her forehead, then her temple and finally on her cheek. "After I left the boys in Enid, all I could think about was getting here—to you."

"Sam, I—"

"You don't have any idea how important you are to me, do you?"

"I—"

"Because I haven't told you. Not the way I want to."

She placed two fingers across his lips. "Maybe it's best not to say it."

He rolled on his side, propping his chin in his hand, but so close she couldn't escape his gaze. "Kate, please. Hear me out."

Even in the dim light she couldn't mistake the set of his jaw, the need in his eyes. She gave a small shuddering sigh. "Okay."

"I think it's obvious I'm very attracted to you. But there's much more to it." He trailed his thumb along her collarbone. "You're the woman I want to be with, share confidences with, grow old with—"

"Shh." She squirmed away from him, knowing that a mere touch of his flesh against hers could drive away all reason.

He grasped her gently by the shoulder. "Kate, don't pull away. I'd never hurt you."

"It's not that," she murmured, aware that what she feared most—and craved—was losing control.

Then he embraced her, cradling her as if she was precious to him. "I'm falling in love with you, Kate."

A spasm of desire shook her, making it hard to think. To respond. This couldn't be. "Sam, I don't know what to say. This is all happening so fast."

"Does it feel as right to you as it does to me?"

"It can't be just about feelings."

He nuzzled her ear. "Why not? What else is there when you care about someone?"

And she had no answer. All the logic in the world served no purpose when her body was trembling, her heart overflowing.

"But that's not all." His voice grew husky.

She knew what he meant, what he was too gentlemanly to suggest. And, heaven help her, she wanted it, too. Not someday when all the stars were in alignment. Now. "I know," she managed to moan before she found herself shamelessly tugging his shirt out of his pants. Then, as if with a life of its own, her hand moved up his chest, exploring his rib cage, the plane of his breastbone, the taut nipples nested in coarse, curly hair.

He gave a low moan. "You're something else, Kate." As he kissed her, she felt his hand slide beneath her shirt and, helpless to resist, she found herself moving to make access easier for him. Every nerve screamed for him to touch her—there, everywhere—each caress reminding her once more how potent desire can be.

He fingered the hook at the front of her bra, then freed her breasts. He paused, his eyes finding hers. "Do you want me to stop?" In urgent response, she shook her head and clung to his shoulders, waiting with indrawn breath as he lifted her T-shirt, gently shoved the undergarment aside, then lowered his head to suckle first one rosy nipple, then the other.

She felt an unaccustomed, terrifyingly welcome clenching deep within her that wouldn't be stilled until... "Don't stop," she whispered.

He nudged against her, his thickening pressing against her abdomen, and suddenly she pictured in her mind that other Kate, the levelheaded, sensible one she seemed to have lost in the heat of the moment. "We can't," she managed to gasp.

He rolled onto one elbow. "What's wrong?"

"I'm not—" She fumbled for words, all the time aware of the pad of his finger resting on her jawbone. "I don't know if I'm ready."

He kissed one eyelid, then the next. With a tenderness that melted her, he said, "How long has it been, Kate?"

Misgivings—cold and real—surfaced. She was long out of practice. He was a doctor, for heaven's sake. Would the act seem clinical? Would her body, stretch marks and all, please him? Could she live up to his expectations? "A very long time." Yet the tormented aching of her body cried out for release. "I...I'm nervous, Sam."

His hand moved caressingly up her bare thigh to the vee of her shorts. "I think it'll all come back to you."

She felt herself slipping into a half world of sensations, dimly aware he was unzipping her shorts, easing them down her legs, tossing them to one side. Now. She could still summon reason. Still conjure...and then his lips were on her abdomen, his fingers inching down her briefs. She grabbed the jersey of his shirt, pulling it off. She wanted to feel his skin on hers.

Breathing heavily, he stood, stripped off his jeans, fumbled in the pocket, then stepped out of his shorts before he lowered himself to her. As she felt the warm flesh of his chest tease her nipples, she squirmed, wrapping her legs around him. "Now, Sam!" she heard herself crying out.

"Just a minute." He moved away. She heard him rip open a foil packet, then sheathe himself. When he returned to her, he held himself, muscles quivering, poised above her. "You're sure?"

"I'm sure." And, triumphantly, she knew she was.

"You're so beautiful," Sam murmured, just before lowering himself to her.

"So are you," she whispered, his initial thrust drawing from her a rush of desire so intense the stars she saw were not in the night sky but imprinted against her eyelids. Then she spiraled up, up, up, pulling him closer, closer until, with a tiny cry, she shuddered with the welcome release. Tears she could not blink back trickled down her cheeks.

When Sam finally collapsed against her, she knew she was lost. Lost in a world of sensation and wonder. She ran her hands up and down his back, damp with perspiration, then loosened his ponytail, an act that freed something savage, primitive within her. Unbelievably, she was ready again. This soon.

Sam kissed away a tear poised in the corner of her eye. "Did I hurt you?"

"Oh, no," she said lifting his hand to her mouth, suckling his fingers. "The tears? They're for joy."

"Tell me about it," he agreed, rolling over on his back and pulling her toward him, settling her head in the crook of his neck.

She snuggled against him, slowly becoming aware of the breeze cooling her skin, of the half moon pinned against the velvet sky, of the wonder of his virile body stretched unashamedly beside her.

Had it ever been like this with Ed? She tried to think. She remembered the first, awkward experimentations when their intimacy was guided more by hormones than expertise. Then, later, there had been the cozy, often comfortingly predictable lovemaking. The will-the-kids-hear-us? did-you-lock-the-door? variety.

But *this?* Skyrockets illuminating the horizon, a brilliant palette bursting with color, immense waterfalls cascading into deep, frothy pools—none of the comparisons even came close.

She shuddered, her body convulsing with the thought. "Sam?" she whispered tentatively.

"Yeah?"

"I was wondering—well, whether—"

He took a nipple in his warm mouth, his tongue flicking the nub before he looked up and grinned. "If we need a little more practice?"

Suddenly shy, she nodded.

Chuckling, he positioned her on top of him. "That, my dear, is not a problem."

As he proceeded to demonstrate just how exciting an encore could be, her inner voice spoke with conviction. She'd been transported far beyond mere flirtation.

LONG AFTER Sam had left, Kate, with the quilt snug around her, sat on the back porch with Charger for company, alternately marveling and wondering if she'd opened Pandora's box. For heaven's sake, they'd lain together under the stars as if they were the only inhabitants of a private Eden. She wrapped herself more tightly. Anyone could've come along.

As an excuse, that's weak, Kate. She couldn't recall the last time a vehicle of any sort had turned up her lane at night. "I'm kidding myself, aren't I?" she said, scratching Charger between the ears. It didn't help that her faithful pet turned reproachful eyes on her. "I've been waiting for this to happen, hoping for it to." She sighed in admission of her own responsibility. She could've halted the lovemaking at any point. Sam was a fair man. He'd offered her an out. Twice. The truth was, she hadn't wanted one. The truth was…it had been wonderful.

The musky scent of his body clung to the quilt and she buried her nose in the fabric, unable even now to stem the tide of emotion that had sent her helplessly spiraling over the edge. She was tinglingly alive, her carefully woven cocoon of disengagement shattered. How could she regret what had felt so good, so right?

Yet when Charger rose and bounded off the porch in pursuit of some nameless night creature, Kate let the whole weight of her actions settle around her. Such behavior was out of character. A clandestine love affair was not in her nature. She closed her eyes picturing the reactions of her family and friends if they knew. And Sam? He had a great deal to lose—the trust of an entire community.

The whole affair was insane.

She buried her head in her hands. *Affair?* Why that word with all its judgmental associations? Their love-making hadn't felt like something sordid, back-street. It had felt like…like…love. But commitment? She shivered. His words haunted her. *You're the woman I want to grow old with. I'm falling in love with you.*

Charger returned, planting himself in front of her, insinuating his nose under her clasped hands, his doggie breath hot on her cheeks. She hugged him fiercely. "Oh, what am I going to do?"

By way of answer, he licked her fingers, then settled back on his haunches with his head cocked, as if studying her. She and Sam had been borne along by passion, their bodies blending as if each had been made for the other. Had it been too much to ask? This one night under the stars?

She gathered the blanket, then stood, looking once

more at the night sky. "Thank you, dear Sam," she whispered, before entering the house where she knew she'd lie sleepless in her bed, awaiting the light of morning when common sense and a kind of shame would overtake her.

For now, though, she'd treasure Sam's parting words to her. "This is about much more than sex, Kate. It's about you and me and how we're meant to be together."

Throw caution to the wind? Follow destiny? It had all seemed plausible in the darkness, but tomorrow the sun would beat down, illuminating the truth—compared to the real world of Salt Flats, Oklahoma, "destiny" was ephemeral.

MONDAY MORNING Sam didn't mind being a loner in the Main Street Café. He needed to sort himself out. Talk eddied around him, odors of fried food rose from the grill, jukebox music jangled in the background. He sat, staring into the depths of his coffee cup as if hidden beneath the liquid surface would be the answer he sought. How to convince Kate he wanted to share a lifetime of days—and nights—with her?

He'd been totally blown away by the abandon of their lovemaking. She had given herself completely in a way that flat-out humbled him—as if she caught fire every time he touched her. Surprisingly, there had been none of the holding back he might have expected. Instead, an implicit trust that had aroused him even further.

Yet he knew the arguments she would marshall. Their children. Her husband's family. The community repercussions. The slight age difference she clung to and which didn't matter a damn to him. All he knew was that her presence energized him like a breath of fresh air.

He picked up his cup, gently swirling the coffee before taking the first welcome sip. It wouldn't do to discount the obstacles in their path, but he was nothing if not stubborn. Or to put a different spin on it—patient. He'd play his cards however she needed him to play them, but he wouldn't give up.

"Hey, Doc, what'll it be?" Millie stood at his elbow, her all-knowing smile seeming to probe his innermost thoughts.

"How long have you been standing there?"

"Long enough to know you're someplace other than this dinky café. Daydreamin', are ya?"

"Guilty as charged, ma'am," he responded, grateful as hell that Millie lacked psychic powers.

She raised her order pad. "So?"

"The usual, please."

"Figgered as much. But one day maybe you'll surprise me and order an omelet and sausage."

"Maybe. One day." He grinned up at her. "When I have something to celebrate."

He made quick work of his fruit and cereal, turned his thoughts to the day's scheduled appointments and did his best to put thoughts of Kate aside. As he left the café, he made a mental note to check the clinic inventory of burn supplies. Tomorrow was the Fourth of July and accidents happened.

As he crossed the street, he heard a panting behind him. "Doc. Doc. Wait up." Lester Jakes caught up with him and skittered along beside him, walking first forward, then backward so he could observe Sam. "I gotta tell ya 'bout somethin'. There's a bunch of fellas," his head swiveled as if his eyes were searching out potential hiding places, "say they're gonna scare the pee outta me tomorrow with firecrackers. Lester don't like that, no sir. Loud noises, explosions. It's like the time that—" He stopped dead in his tracks, shook his head violently, then muttered under his breath, "Can't talk about it, can't talk about it."

Sam, laying a hand on Lester's shoulder, propelled him on down the sidewalk. "Can't talk about what?"

Lester, his head down, carefully avoided stepping on cracks in the pavement. "Can't tell you. No. Aunt Julia would be mad."

"I'm here to help you."

"I'm scared. Them fireworks is frightful."

"Maybe you could just stay home." Sam suggested.

"But I like the fire trucks and the parade and the watermelon and—"

"Tell you what, Lester. Why don't you come sit at the clinic during the fireworks? I'll be on duty just in case something happens and I could use the company."

Lester's face lit up. "You'd let me do that, Doc?"

"Sure. See you about eight-thirty just before dark, okay?"

"Lester'll be there. You wait and see." He grabbed Sam by the arm. "You won't forget, will you? People are always makin' promises. But they don't keep them."

"No, Lester, I won't forget," Sam assured him before turning and entering the clinic.

Nellie, dressed as usual in starched whites, looked up from the reception desk. "Good morning."

He nodded. "Nellie."

"You're late. Bud Hargis is waiting in examining room one."

Sam gritted his teeth. Nellie's rigid standards allowed

little margin for error. A good trait in many circumstances. But this morning he could do without her criticism. "Give me a minute." He walked toward his office, removing his summer-weight sport coat as he went. Business was picking up little by little, and this Monday sandwiched between a weekend and a holiday would probably be busy. He hung the jacket in his office closet, washed his hands, donned a fresh scrub coat, draped his stethoscope around his neck and started toward the examining room promising himself to call Kate between patients.

He imagined she'd need some reassurance after last night. He had plenty of that—and more—to give. He banished the sudden memory of her body, bathed in moonlight, and tried to concentrate on his next patient's diverticulitis.

But it wasn't easy.

CHAPTER SEVEN

THIS FOURTH OF JULY promised to be a scorcher, Kate thought as she carefully pulled the box of homemade pies from her car and headed for the library where members of Book Keepers, the library auxiliary, were setting up a bake sale. American flags flew from every lamppost along Main Street, and the red, white and blue bunting draped over the library entrance added an additional patriotic touch. Charlene and a couple of other women were spreading red paper cloths on card tables set up near the sidewalk.

Spotting Kate, Charlene jerked her head in the direction of the building. "Take those on in. We need to keep stuff cool until after the parade. Berta and Ethel are inside."

Kate hurried toward the door, not daring to stop to visit with Charlene. Ever since Sunday night she'd been convinced that something about her demeanor would scream out, "Hey, everybody, look at me. I've been loved." She knew that was silly, yet she felt different and couldn't help wondering if it showed. Did she still look like good old, everyday Kate? Or was there an aura about her, obvious even to the least observant?

Balancing the box on her hip, she eased open the heavy door, grateful for the cool quiet of the library itself. As usual, a long table was set up in the children's area to receive the assorted cakes, cookies and pies.

Before she could announce her arrival, she was stopped
in her tracks by Ethel's voice drifting over the top of
the stacks. "...so, do you think he's like that Dr.
Fleischman fellow on *Northern Exposure?*"

"Who?" Kate recognized Berta's voice.

"Dr. Gray." There was no mistaking Ethel's triumphant tone. "Don't you remember? Joel was stuck in
Alaska working to pay off his medical school loans.
That's the only reason any self-respecting doctor goes
to a burg like that—or this. But our Dr. Gray's no green
kid fresh out of med school. So what do you suppose
his story is?"

"All I can think is that he has something to hide."
The spitefulness in Berta's voice chilled Kate's blood.

"Maybe malpractice," Ethel hissed. "I'll bet that's
it."

"I don't know, but something's fishy about his being
here."

Kate's heart sank. "Anybody here?" She clomped
across the floor and set down the cherry pies.

Berta poked her head around the corner of the bookshelf. "Kate, we didn't hear you come in."

I'll just bet you didn't. "I'm delivering my pies."

Ethel hove into view, tugging her navy and white
striped T-shirt down over her ample pedal-pusher-clad
hips. "Cherry crumble again this year?"

"Yes." Kate eyed the two and decided to take the
bull by the horns. "I couldn't help overhearing your
conversation."

"You mean about 'Sam'?" Berta asked, her persim-
mon-tart smile a giveaway that the use of the first name
was no accident.

"If he'd had something to hide, the search committee
would've discovered that."

"Maybe, maybe not." Berta stood her ground, while Ethel hastily busied herself rearranging items on the table.

"Charlene says Dr. Gray's been wonderful with Amanda, and I've heard other good things. Idle speculation serves no useful purpose and might lead to unfortunate misunderstandings." Damn. Even to herself she sounded sanctimonious.

Ethel paused uncertainly, then lifted her chin and looked straight at Kate. "It just don't make sense. But you're right. We're stuck with him and may as well make the best of it."

"Oh, I think Kate *is* making the best of it," Berta said airily, her contrived expression the picture of innocence.

Kate felt her fingers curling into her palms, but she was determined not to let Berta goad her. "I have no idea what you're talking about."

"It's not what I'm talking about, dear. It's what everyone is talking about." The woman practically gloated.

"And what might that be?"

"You're a single woman. Dr. Gray is a single man. This is a small town, if you catch my drift."

"I'm not sure I like what you're implying."

"Like it or not, if I were you, I'd watch my p's and q's."

Blood pumped in gushers through Kate's veins, undoubtedly mottling her fair skin. "Thank you, Berta. Ethel." She nodded toward the older woman, who was removing foil from a platter of brownies. "Your solicitousness on my behalf is touching, but I assure you, unnecessary." With that, she turned and walked steadily toward the exit.

She hadn't quite reached the door when she heard Ethel's sibilant whisper. "Did you see that, Berta? You're right. There's definitely something going on between those two."

Kate stepped outside and stood on the steps trembling. How dare they? First, they were impugning Sam's professionalism. Not content with that, they were determined to pin a scarlet A on her chest. What she and Sam did together was nobody's business, least of all theirs.

But that was wishful thinking, wasn't it? Salt Flats thrived on gossip, and it couldn't always center on someone else.

Engrossed in thought, she didn't realize Charlene was speaking to her until her friend laid a hand on her shoulder. "Are you okay? You look like you could throttle somebody."

"Two somebodies." Kate felt the breath she'd been holding whoosh out of her.

Charlene raised an eyebrow. "Ethel and Berta?"

Kate nodded. "They're impossible."

"Sam?"

She blinked. "Yes. How did you know?"

"It figures. What else is going on around here? A handsome new doctor. Flowers. Boat buying. Honey, you weren't born yesterday. You know how rumors get started."

"Exactly what *are* the rumors?"

Charlene shrugged. "Depends on who you're talking to. Either that opportunistic Dr. Sam is taking advantage of a lonely widow or that the sex-starved widow is on the prowl."

Kate choked. "That's so...so despicable."

Charlene put her arm around Kate's shoulder and

started walking her toward the flower garden on the far side of the building. "Forget about it. You know how Berta and Ethel are. Grasping at straws."

Kate stopped. "Charlene, they aren't straws."

Charlene's eyebrows peaked. "They're not?" Recovering herself, she hugged Kate. "Honey, that's great!"

"I'm not so sure."

"Why not?"

They walked in silence for several paces before Kate answered. "There are so many obstacles. So many other people to consider. Then there's Sam's professional reputation."

"Set all that aside for a minute. What about you? Your feelings? What do *you* want?"

Kate shook her head wearily. "If only it could be that simple." This wasn't just about her and Sam. Other people mattered. All those dear to her—Jenny, Rachel, Paul, Jean—who wouldn't understand. And who could be hurt.

"It could be," Charlene insisted.

Kate sank onto a concrete bench, then whispered, "I don't think so." But, oh, in her heart, how she wished Charlene was right.

SAM LOUNGED AGAINST THE PLANTER at the corner of Main and Cypress, origin point for the parade. Children clustered in groups, looking eagerly up the street. Under every available shade tree, senior citizens had set up camp with their folding lawn chairs and coolers. A block farther down, two enterprising youngsters manned a lemonade stand, and making his way along the route was a bespectacled politician in a wilted dress shirt shaking hands and distributing campaign literature.

Sam spotted Lester in the vicinity of the 4-H float

where a flustered woman gestured helplessly as she addressed a group of disappointed teenagers. When Lester sidled closer, the woman turned abruptly, made shooing motions, then raised her voice. "Go on, Lester. We've got enough trouble without you."

Lester hung his head and began slinking off. Sam moved through the onlookers toward the scene. "What seems to be the problem?" he asked the woman. Out of the corner of his eye, he saw Lester pause.

"We can't get the engine started on our float. The boys and girls have worked so hard." She flapped her arms. "I can't believe this is happening." Behind her the youngsters clustered in groups of twos and threes, shaking their heads in discouragement. "The parade is about ready to start. We don't have time to do anything."

Plunging his hands in his pocket, Sam spoke with studied nonchalance. "Could I make a suggestion?"

"Any suggestion is more than welcome."

"Let Lester take a look."

Heads jerked up and the woman drew in a breath. "Lester Jakes?"

"He's a genius with motors, I'm told."

The woman's mouth gaped. "I've heard that, but I never believed Lester could—"

"What have you got to lose?" Sam continued.

She fixed her eyes on Lester, considering. Finally she responded. "Uh...nothing, I guess."

"Lester?" Sam beckoned to the man, who cautiously edged forward. "The lady needs some help here." Sam eyed the woman expectantly.

"Er, Lester, our float motor won't start. You probably can't do anything, but...well, go ahead."

Lester turned to Sam for reassurance that this wasn't

yet another joke at his expense. "Go on, Lester. It can't hurt to give it a shot."

Darting a scared-rabbit look at the assembled 4-Hers, Lester approached the float, then stretched out on his back and scuttled beneath the apron of chicken wire, only his feet protruding.

Leaning down, Sam asked if Lester needed anything.

In a muffled voice Lester said he had his pliers and screwdriver set with him. "Looks like a loose wire," he mumbled a few minutes later.

"The parade marshal's ready to start," the 4-H leader groaned, her voice taking on a note of panic.

"Don't give up," Sam said. "You can always fall in toward the rear of the procession."

The woman faced him. "You really think somebody like Lester is going to do us any good?"

Sam resisted the urge to dress down the woman only because he knew this opinion of Lester was widely held in the town and she was no more guilty of intolerance than the next citizen. "Yes, I do," he said, hoping his confidence was not misplaced.

From beneath the float, he heard Lester say, "Who's driving this thing?"

"I am," said a pimply faced teen.

Lester slid out from under the float. "Git in and try 'er then."

The young man raised his eyebrows, clearly signalling that he did not believe in miracles, especially ones produced by the town character.

Then to the amazement of everyone but Sam and Lester, the float purred to life, accompanied by the cheers of the now exultant 4-H group. The leader turned a mystified smile on Lester. "I guess I owe you my thanks," she said before hurrying after the float, which was slowly moving toward its assigned position.

"Good job," Sam said.

Lester merely shrugged. "She didn't think I could do it. None of 'em did."

Clapping Lester on the shoulder, Sam chuckled. "You sure fooled them, didn't you?"

Lester didn't seem pleased. "Now if somethin' goes wrong, they'll just blame stupid ole Lester." He shrugged Sam's hand off and started down the alley.

"Aren't you going to watch the parade?" Sam called after him.

"I got a special place to watch where they can't find me."

Sam sighed. Based on what he'd witnessed, Lester's habitual fears seemed justified. Despite his natural caution, Sam couldn't help but be buoyed in his conviction that Lester's problems arose more from external stimuli than from a psychosis of some sort.

"Don't forget about tonight," Sam called after him.

Lester waved his hand in acknowledgment before disappearing behind a Dumpster.

Just then Sam was jostled aside as a red-faced, doughy teenager, burdened by the tuba he carried, ran toward his assigned slot in the last row of the high-school marching band. No sooner had the boy shouldered his instrument than a lanky kid in a top-heavy white bearskin hat bleated on his whistle, extended his baton and cavorted down the street. Behind him the band struggled manfully in their hot uniforms to march and simultaneously play "Stars and Stripes Forever."

Smiling, Sam reclaimed his spot against the planter to enjoy the parade. A hook-and-ladder truck startling the bystanders with blasts from the siren, a vintage car transporting Mayor and Mrs. Jackson, an aging troop of American Legionnaires keeping step behind their standard bearer, bicycle riders trailing red, white and blue crepe-paper streamers, and even a mounted group from the regional quarter-horse club. And this didn't include the floats sponsored by the Boy Scouts, the Cougar Booster Club and the Methodist Youth Fellowship or the shiny convertibles from which fresh-faced queen candidates waved at the crowd.

The down-home patriotism of the event moved Sam. The only thing that would make it any better was if Blake and Bart could be experiencing this with him. And Kate.

Amazing Kate. After a busy day at the clinic yesterday, he'd called her last night wanting to reassure her that he'd meant every word he'd said to her. However, she'd seemed restive, remote. But when he'd asked if she had any regrets, she'd sighed, then said, "I keep telling myself I should have."

"That's no answer," he'd reminded her.

After a pause, she'd quietly answered the question. "No, Sam. No regrets."

He glanced toward the lemonade stand, then strolled in that direction, weaving among the onlookers clustered on the sidewalk. Several acknowledged him with fingers to their caps or a mumbled "Hi, Doc." Standing in line for the lemonade, he felt a hand on his shoulder. Turning, he acknowledged Keith Appleby, the bank president. "Good to see you. This is quite a celebration."

"I'm pleased you're enjoying it. It's not exactly big city stuff, but we do our best." Appleby turned to the older man beside him. "Have you met our new doctor?"

"Don't believe so," the thin-lipped stranger said, scrutinizing Sam.

"Sam Gray, meet Paul Manley, retired farmer and one of the bank's most astute board members." The man had to be Kate's father-in-law. His facial expression was neutral, and Sam wondered if his astuteness extended to sizing up people, especially one intent on pursuing his daughter-in-law.

Sam shook Manley's hand. "Pleased to meet you."

The men made small talk as they purchased their drinks. Before they parted company, Keith said, "Too bad you didn't have a chance to know Paul's son Ed. You'd have liked him."

"Pret' near everybody did." Paul held his lemonade awkwardly.

Keith went on. "You've probably met Kate, Ed's widow."

Sam hoped his face didn't give him away even as he regretted the need for duplicity. "I've had the pleasure."

"Ed loved that girl something fierce." The older man focused his eyes on the horizon as if checking the weather.

"He sure did," Keith agreed. "Everybody in town thought they were just about the perfect couple."

What did you say to that, Sam wondered, aware that he was feeling intensely uncomfortable. "A good marriage is enviable," he finally offered.

"And rare," Paul said.

"And rare," Sam echoed.

To Sam's everlasting relief, Keith changed the subject at that point and soon the two men drifted away, leaving him to sort out the intricacies of small-town relationships. And to reflect that perhaps he needed to be more sensitive to Kate's concerns about how folks in Salt Flats would view their interest in one another.

With an earsplitting "Go, Cougars," the Pep Club float rolled past. Then he saw Kate standing across the street—her blond hair pulled up into a chignon, her V-necked red T-shirt revealing her lovely curves, her blue denim skirt flaring gracefully over her hips. Despite the lemonade, his mouth went dry. She was everything he wanted in a woman. As if drawn by his gaze, she spotted him, and her mouth curved in a spontaneous smile. But then, as if she'd been caught in a lapse of judgment, she turned away and began talking animatedly with the white-haired woman beside her.

Sam's stomach muscles contracted. Why should something so right feel so awkward?

"DAMN IT, QUIT NAGGING, Jenny!" Todd stood in the kitchen, his golf bag slung over one shoulder. "So what if it's Fourth of July? It's not every day I get a chance to play Cherry Creek Country Club."

"I'm not nagging, but is it too much to expect you to spend a holiday with your wife and son?" The tomato in Jenny's hand slipped from her trembling fingers and dropped to the floor, splattering seeds and tomato pulp on the woodwork and tile.

Todd's face froze in disgust. "Now look what you've done."

From his high chair, Parker clanged his spoon on the tray and set up a chant, "Mama bad, mama bad, mama bad."

Jenny clenched her teeth. "I'll clean it up, okay?"

"Damn right." He shook his head. "Can't you do anything without screwing up?"

She advanced a step, heedless of the mess at her feet.
"What's that supposed to mean?"

He rolled his eyes. "Jeez, Jenny, get a life. You're
so wrapped up in that baby you're no fun anymore."

"Is that your major priority?" She spat out the word.
"Fun?"

"Well, ex–cuse me for living." He checked his
watch. "I've gotta go."

Her voice felt squeezed, as if she had a balloon
lodged in her windpipe. "Will you be back in time for
the neighborhood parade?" She'd worked all week dec-
orating Parker's stroller and making him an Uncle Sam
suit.

He flipped his golf hat on his head. "I'll be back
when I get back." Then he marched out to the garage.

She started to follow him, to unload a string of in-
vectives, but then stopped. What was there to say? He
wouldn't be back for the parade or for anything else
that was important to her. It would be like all the other
times. She might as well face it. He didn't care.

A moment later she heard the roar of the sports car
engine, followed by the squeal of tires. "Mama bad,
mama bad." Parker grinned toothily at her, then threw
his spoon across the room.

She couldn't help herself. She sank to the floor, oblivious to the wet tomato seeds sticking to her knees. She
was beyond mad, beyond sad.

She pounded her fists against her thighs, wishing she
could cry. But she was empty. Just empty.

She'd done everything to avoid having to admit to
herself she'd failed. But now it was clear. She couldn't
change Todd. And she didn't like what trying to change
herself had meant. There was only one conclusion.

The marriage was over.

LESTER HUDDLED in the corner of the clinic waiting room, riffling through the pages of a dog-eared *Popular Mechanics* and jerking his head each time firecrackers sounded in the distance.

Sam checked on him periodically, when he wasn't treating the few patients who had drifted in throughout the early evening—a woman with multiple wasp stings, a rash-covered toddler and a teenager with a burned arm. During a lull, Sam grabbed sodas for him and Lester, then sat down beside the man. "You doing okay?"

"Okay, okay. But is it almost over, Doc?"

"The fireworks?" Lester's head bobbed up and down. "No. What you're hearing is just local folks in their yards. The main display hasn't started yet."

"You won't leave me then, Doc? Please say you won't leave Lester."

Sam was puzzled. Lester's panic was real, seemingly unjustified by the event. "Only if I have an emergency. Otherwise, I'll be right here with you."

Lester gulped, his baleful eyes full of concern. "Don't want no 'mergencies, then. No, sir. No 'mergencies."

Sam drained his soda, then rose to his feet. "I have a few reports to finish. Then I'll come sit with you."

"Lester'll be waiting right here, Doc."

After completing his paperwork, Sam rejoined Lester. When the first window-rattling boom sounded, Lester flinched, then leaned over covering his eyes with his grease-stained hands. At the second burst, he rocked back and forth, keening.

Alarmed, Sam put an arm around the man's shoulders. "I'm here, Lester, I'm here."

Another explosion and Sam thought he heard Lester

say, "Where's Daddy?" And again, "Where's Mama?"

Sam leaned closer. "What is it? What about your daddy?"

But Lester was in another world. "I didn't do it, I didn't!"

Sam knelt in front of Lester and shook him slightly. "It's okay. You're safe."

"No!" Lester looked up, his eyes glazed, his stare unfocused. "I promise. I won't tell." He cringed as if responding to scenes in his head. "Don't hit me again, please." In the distance a bottle-rocket wail punctuated the silence. Lester's voice rose in desperation. "Please! I won't tell."

Sam pulled the man to his feet and enfolded him in his arms. Shudders racked Lester's body. "Listen to me. You're okay. I'm here. Nobody's going to hurt you."

Suddenly, Lester went limp, resting his head on Sam's shoulder. "Aunt Julia will."

Sam's mind raced with possibilities, the least of which was that Julia Jakes had been physically abusive. But there was more going on here. "Come on, Lester. Let's go into my office. I'll turn on some music so you can't hear the fireworks so clearly. Then we'll talk."

Lester permitted himself to be led into the office where Sam helped him into a chair and wrapped him in a blanket. Deliberately taking his time, Sam selected a mellow Wynton Marsalis CD, then pulled his office chair around the desk so he could sit close to Lester. He sat without speaking, allowing Lester time to calm down. When he heard Lester's breathing return to normal, he spoke softly. "Why don't you tell me about your daddy and mama? About why you're so frightened?"

Lester shook his head emphatically. "Can't. That Aunt Julia, she'll get me."

Grabbing Lester's hands, Sam looked intently into his eyes. "You don't have to be afraid of your aunt. I'll help you."

Lester's eyes darted around the room, before settling back on Sam's. "You promise?"

"I promise." Sam dropped Lester's hands and sat back in his chair. "It's time you unloaded that bag of worries you've been carrying." On a sudden hunch, Sam continued. "Tell me about the tornado, Lester. Tell me what happened."

Again, Lester seemed to go to a faraway place. "Can't. Aunt Julia, she'll hit me."

"No!" Sam's voice was forceful. "She won't hit you. I won't let her." Sam waited, letting the soothing music do its work. "Now, then. Where were you when the tornado came?"

Haltingly, in bits and pieces the story came out. "Daddy hollered, 'Lester! Julia! You run to the storm cellar. After Mama and I tend to the animals, we'll be there. Run, now. Run!'" Lester's eyes rounded. "Lester was so scared. There was this awful wind and green sky and roaring noises."

"Did you get to the storm shelter?" Sam prompted.

"Storm shelter?" Lester focused again. "I hate that place! Dark, cobwebs. And noise on top of me, loud, terrible noise."

"And Aunt Julia? Was she with you?"

"She's the one did it! Not Lester, not me!" His body arched, as if flinching from the truth.

Sam proceeded quietly, cautiously. "Did what, Lester?"

For a moment Lester looked flustered, and Sam

feared he would fall back to his standard defense of his aunt. But in that next fraction of a second, when he again fixed his eyes on Sam, he must've realized it was time to speak the truth that had poisoned him for so long. "Aunt Julia, she was all crying and scared. She kept screaming, 'We'll be killed.' Then she did it. That awful thing."

"What, Lester?" Sam prodded.

"She locked the door." Lester began sobbing.

But Sam needed the whole story. "She locked the storm cellar door?"

He nodded, then added through his tears, "And Daddy and Mama, I heard 'em knocking, knocking, knocking." He covered his ears with his hands. "She wouldn't let me unlock the door. She held me so tight I couldn't move."

The full horror of the scene registered itself on Sam's mind. The terrified little boy powerless to avert the tragedy. The child living for years with the fear of retribution if he ever revealed Julia's role.

With effort, Sam reined in his rage. "Thank you, Lester. Now I can help you."

Lester looked mournfully at Sam. "She'll kill me."

Sam gripped him by the shoulders. "No, Lester, she won't. And until we figure out what to do, you're coming to my house tonight."

"You won't tell on me?"

"You've done nothing wrong, Lester. Not then, not now." He stood. "I'll bring you a cup of coffee." He glanced at the desk clock. "The fireworks are nearly over. Then we'll go home. In the morning we'll figure out what to do."

"But Aunt Julia—"

"She's not your worry anymore. Leave her to me."

The man wiped his face with a corner of the blanket. "Okay."

Sam raised his eyes in solemn appeal. *Lord, help me find a way.*

THE DAY AFTER THE HOLIDAY, Kate hid in her studio, fully aware that that was exactly what she was doing—hiding. From the townspeople, from the Manleys, from Sam, from herself. And worrying. Jenny had answered none of the phone calls she'd made yesterday throughout the day and evening. Not surprisingly, looking at the painting she'd attempted, her art had suffered. Dull. Lifeless. Trite. She threw down her brush in disgust and wiped her palms over her jeans. Everything was out of kilter.

She'd lived her entire life being the "good girl," considering symbolic pats on the head the ultimate prize. Now the "good girl" warred with the woman who yearned to cast aside the shackles of conventionality.

Although Charlene might come close to understanding, Kate couldn't imagine anyone else would. On the phone she'd told Sam she had no regrets. And she didn't. But the obstacles were formidable. Insurmountable.

She left her stool and wandered to the window. Outside Charger ran up and down the fence line as if attempting to herd the cattle watching him with stolid expressions. She'd have to end it with Sam. Somehow. She hugged herself against the chill sent up and down her spine merely by thinking about telling him. Leaning her forehead against the glass, she admitted goodbyes hurt. Badly.

Movement in her peripheral vision pulled her attention back to the scene before her. The postman. She straightened up, chastising herself for morbid self-indulgence. What had to be done would be done. Soon.

To walk off some of her frustration, she left the studio, whistled for Charger and started down the lane to the mailbox. To the west, angry, dark clouds were massing. A sudden stiff breeze, forerunner of the storm, bent the crepe myrtle bushes lining the lane and the spring-damp smell of rain caused her to hurry. She pulled the packet of mail, bound by a rubber band, from the box and with Charger urging her on, just made it to the house before the skies unloaded.

Thunder rattled the windows as she removed the rubber band and sorted through the magazines, catalogues, flyers and letters. Then she saw it. Her heart stopped. It was a big envelope. And the return address was Lupe Santiago's.

She sank into a chair at the kitchen table, holding the fateful envelope, her mouth tasting like talcum powder. She found herself missing Ed. If he were only here. He would calm her down, pick up the pieces when she was rejected. Slowly and deliberately she slit the envelope, then withdrew a letter and several attached pages.

Her eyes swam as she read the first word. "Congratulations!" She scanned the page in disbelief. She'd been accepted for the session starting the last week in July. She shook her head. Lupe Santiago wanted *her?*

She stood up and paced around the kitchen. She wanted to celebrate, call someone, share the news. But who would care? Jean, of course. Charlene, maybe. And Sam? Her elation turned to panic.

Oh, God, Sam. She crumpled into her chair.

But she had her out now, didn't she?

CHAPTER EIGHT

THE NEXT DAY, Sam, his mouth set in a grim line, drove steadily west in a driving rain toward Julia Jakes's place.

"I shouldn't a told." Lester, huddled next to him in the passenger seat, shook his head violently. "No sir."

"You did exactly the right thing. The trouble started a long time ago and it needs to be settled."

When thunder reverberated across the prairie sky, Lester winced. Sam reached out a hand to calm him. "Remember, Lester, I'll be with you. The social worker will be there. We want to help you and your aunt."

"But Aunt Julia—"

"Let me deal with her, okay?"

Lester sent him a sideways glance, then nodded. "Okay."

Sam gripped the wheel and hoped to hell they could somehow gain Julia's cooperation. Last night at Sam's, Lester had immediately dropped into the sleep of the dead. Sam, however, had lain awake fighting mad. First thing this morning he'd reached the county social services office and after he'd outlined the situation, one of their people had agreed to meet them at Julia's farm.

When he pulled off the highway and parked near a ramshackle dwelling, Lester began to rock back and forth, moaning softly. Sam placed a hand on his knee.

"Let's go, Lester. It's almost over." Like a whipped pup, Lester trailed him into the house.

Julia Jakes sat stoically in a wooden rocker, her arms folded across her chest, her chin thrust forward. She glared at Sam. "You again!" Then she turned on Lester. "Couldn't leave well enough alone, could you, boy?"

Lester ducked his head, shuffled toward the worn, sagging couch, then sat, his knuckled hands clamped on his jutting knees.

A round-faced woman with hair arranged in a coronet of braids looked up from the paperwork spread on her lap. She acknowledged Sam with a nod, then turned to Lester. "Hello, Lester," she said with an encouraging smile. "I'm Lola Fletcher from social services. The doctor tells me you may need some help."

"We don't need nothin'!" Julia's querulous protest caused Lester to shift uncomfortably. "Lester 'n me get along fine. Government's got no call to barge in here."

Sam, trying to keep his voice under control, faced her. "Miss Jakes, Lester told me something very troubling last night. With Mrs. Fletcher's assistance, we need to get to the bottom of it and, if necessary, secure you and Lester help."

"Mind your own damn business," Julia shot back. "There ain't no trouble."

Lola Fletcher leaned forward. "From what I understand, Miss Jakes, this *is* our business. Now let's all settle down and discuss the problem." She arched her eyebrows at Sam, who picked up on the cue, recapping Lester's account of the events of his parents' deaths.

When he came to the part about Julia's locking the storm cellar door, she leaped to her feet and screeched,

"Goddamn liar!" Then she wheeled on Lester. "Bad boy! You know nothing happened."

Lola Fletcher stood, advanced to Julia, put an arm around her shoulder and firmly led her back to her seat. "Don't make this any harder than it is. I need to hear what Lester has to say." She remained standing at Julia's side as if to reinforce her authority. "Lester, why don't you tell us what happened?"

Ashen, Lester looked at Sam for reassurance. "Go on, it's okay."

Lester hesitated, stole a frightened glance at Julia, then looked back at Sam, who nodded his encouragement. "Um, what Doc said, it's true."

"Your aunt locked the cellar door?" Lola Fletcher prompted, clamping a hand on the back of Julia's rocker.

"Yes'm."

Julia strained in her chair, but Lola continued. "Did your aunt insist it was your fault the door was locked?"

Lester studied a wrinkle in his jeans.

"Just tell her the truth," Sam said quietly.

"Yes'm."

Julia tensed. "You ain't going to believe anything that worthless boy says, are you? Why, everybody knows he's crazy."

It was all Sam could do to keep himself under control.

"On the contrary, Miss Jakes," Lola said. "Since your nephew has requested assistance through Dr. Gray, I'm offering Lester lodging in a group home, subject to his consent, until you and he both can be evaluated and get some counseling."

Julia's face was crimson. "See what you done, boy?"

Lester cringed.

Ignoring Julia, Sam stood up, then extended his hand to Lester. "C'mon, Lester, let me help you pack up a few things."

Lester eyed Julia, who fixed him with a menacing glare. Finally, gripping Sam's hand, he rose to his feet. "You mean you're not gonna leave me with Aunt Julia?"

Sam held Lester by the shoulders, steadying him. "No. You'll be spending a few days in a nice, safe place."

"Like at your house last night?" Lester's expression brightened hopefully.

"Like at my house." As Sam led Lester toward the upstairs bedrooms, he whispered, "You don't have to be afraid anymore."

Lester gave Sam a gap-toothed smile, then spoke words Sam knew he would never forget. "Doc, you know somethin'? You're Lester's best friend."

BY LATE AFTERNOON the storm had passed, leaving rain-freshened flowers, greener pastures and cooler temperatures. On her way home from the grocery, Kate decided to stop by the Manleys' to share her good news. Paul was sitting on the front porch reading *USA Today*. As she approached, he set the newspaper aside and peered at her over the rims of his wire-framed glasses. "This is a surprise," he said.

"A happy one, I hope." Smiling, she perched on the top step.

"Always."

Ed's father was a man of few words, but the "always" held a world of warmth. "I have some good news I'd like to share with you and Jean."

For a moment, Kate thought she detected a flicker of

worry in his eyes, but then decided she'd been mistaken when he said, "Good news is always welcome." He stood up. "I'll fetch Jean." He hesitated with his hand on the latch of the screen door. "Before I do, though, I wanted to tell you I met your Dr. Gray at the parade yesterday."

Such was the neutrality in his voice that Kate had no idea how to respond, although the "your" raised a definite red flag. Should she react or let it pass? Distinctly uneasy, she merely said, "I saw him there, too. Great parade, wasn't it?"

He shrugged noncommittally. "A little warm for my liking." He opened the door. "Back in a minute."

It was a "little warm" for her liking at the moment. Paul had never been an easy man to read, but she sensed he had intended to send her a message. But what kind? Well, she wouldn't worry too much about it since she planned to take care of "her" Dr. Gray as soon as possible. In fact, she'd left a message on his answering machine suggesting a meeting at his earliest convenience.

She stood up and wandered the width of the porch, studying the hanging baskets full of lush begonias. It should all be cut and dried, this business with Sam. But he had given her a precious gift, her sense of self, and for that she would always be grateful.

"Kate, what a pleasant surprise!" Her mother-in-law, a beaming smile lighting her face, swept out the door, her arms extended for a hug. Behind her, her husband carefully closed the door. "Paul tells me you have news." She gestured to a wicker rocker. "Sit down, honey, and tell us about it."

Kate took the proffered chair while the Manleys, eyeing her expectantly, settled on the glider. "Paul, Jean may have told you that I decided last spring to get more serious about my painting.'' She licked her dry lips. ''It's something Ed had encouraged me to do.'' In response, Paul merely nodded. ''So in early June I applied for a four-week workshop in Santa Fe.''

Jean, her eyes sparkling, put a hand to her chest. ''And?''

''I've been accepted.''

''That's wonderful!'' Jean exclaimed, then turned to her husband. ''Did you hear that? Our Kate's on her way.''

''Santa Fe?'' Paul appeared to be meditating on the subject. ''When is this?''

''Soon. I need to be there by the end of July.''

''In three weeks, you say?'' Something about her news seemed to be important to Paul.

She nodded. ''Is there a problem?''

Jean punched her husband playfully with her elbow. ''Paul, for heaven's sake, can't you tell her how pleased we are?''

Her father-in-law leaned forward. ''I'm sorry, Kate. Of course, I'm happy for you. I was just getting the facts straight, that's all.'' He pulled out a handkerchief and made a show of cleaning his glasses. ''Ed—'' his voice faltered ''—he'd have been so proud of you.''

Paul still had difficulty talking openly about his son, and Kate knew his approval was heartfelt. ''Yes, I think he would have.''

''Do the girls know?'' Jean was practically bobbing with excitement.

''No. I plan to tell them as soon as I get my schedule pinned down.''

''They'll be so excited,'' Jean said.

"I hope so." Although given the puzzling way Jenny had been acting lately, she wasn't so sure.

Paul replaced his glasses and said in a firmer voice, "Don't you ever doubt it."

"I'm not sure what folks around here will think of my traipsing off to paint."

"Pooh." Jean patted her hand. "What do they know, anyway?"

"Thank you both for your encouragement. It's a big step for me." Kate rose to her feet. "I need to get my groceries home. Frozen food isn't very forgiving."

Jean pushed up from the glider. "Let me walk you to the car."

Before picking up his newspaper, Paul gave a thin smile. "It was nice of you to drop by."

Jean tucked her arm through Kate's. "This is such exciting news, Kate. You let me know if there's anything I can help with while you're gone—watering houseplants, gathering mail, whatever. We'd keep Charger, but with Paul's allergies…"

Kate squeezed Jean's arm. "Thanks, but Charger can go to the kennel. I imagine I'll have quite a list for you, though. And thanks, too, for your support."

When they reached the truck, Jean detained her. With a sinking sensation, Kate noticed her mother-in-law's expression sober. Jean spoke in a low voice. "This will be for the best, you'll see." She glanced around as if checking to be sure she was out of earshot of the porch. "I don't know quite how to say this, but I've been concerned that maybe you were getting too friendly with Dr. Gray." Before Kate could formulate a reply, the older woman went on. "I just don't know how that would sit with Paul. He always thought you and Ed were such a perfect couple. But we know you'd never do anything to dishonor Ed's memory. You're far too sensible. Santa Fe will be just the ticket.''

Out of the blue came an overwhelming sadness— loss—that choked Kate, making it difficult to reply. Finally, as she climbed behind the wheel, she found her voice. ''Yes, Jean. Just the ticket.''

Driving home, through her tears, she consoled herself by repeating the phrase again and again. ''Just the ticket.''

KATE HAD TRIED to eat dinner, but her stomach was in knots, the food tasteless. According to the message left on her machine, Sam, barring an emergency, would be here at eight. She paced the back porch. Fifteen more minutes, and still she didn't know what she'd say to him. Where would she find the courage to cast herself adrift when all she could think about was how wonderful it felt to be in his arms? Yet, like it or not, this was about a whole lot more than her needs. The accusation thundered in her ears. *We know you'd never do anything to dishonor Ed's memory.* But she already had.

Or had she? Did she have an obligation to remain faithful to a dead man?

She gripped a post and clung to it for dear life. What had seemed crystal-clear this morning was obscure in the twilight. And her rebellious heart didn't seem to have the remotest interest in listening to her head. She leaned her forehead against the smooth wood of the post. What was the matter with her anyway?

Abruptly Charger raced around the corner of the house, headed toward the lane. Then Kate heard. The purr of an engine, the crunch of tires. Her mouth turned to dust.

She pushed away from the post and started across the

lawn, hugging herself against the inevitable. And then Sam was there. Pulling her into his warm embrace, soothing her fluttering heart with words of endearment.

With a supreme effort, she pulled away. In his eyes, happiness faded, replaced by bafflement. Beside them Charger lunged, thwarted in his efforts to get Sam's attention. Still he didn't look away. Then came the words that blocked escape. "Kate, what is it?"

DEALING WITH LESTER had meant Sam had been unable to see Kate last night. And when he'd gotten her message today, he'd assumed she was as eager as he to be together. But looking down at her now, he knew something was very wrong. His foreboding increased when she didn't immediately answer his question. Instead she ducked her head and remained motionless. With a small sigh, she finally looked up. "We need to talk."

He laid his hands on her shoulders. "Is this about Sunday night?"

"Not exactly," she murmured. "Please," she nodded toward the house, "come sit down."

He trailed her to the porch where she stopped short. "Let's stay out here."

He felt like a leaf swept up in a whirlpool, helpless to reverse the flow of events. "Okay." She perched on a metal patio chair, carefully arranging the pleats of her skirt. He chose to lean against the railing where he could study her face. He didn't speak, fearing that whatever he said would be wrong.

She brushed back a tendril of hair that had escaped the band low on her neck. "Sam, I'm going away."

Whatever he'd expected she might say, it certainly wasn't that. He was stunned. Leaving Salt Flats? "Going away?" he finally managed.

"Not permanently," she added. "For four weeks. To Santa Fe."

"Santa Fe?" he echoed stupidly, wondering if he'd somehow slipped down a rabbit hole.

"Early in June I applied for a workshop with Lupe Santiago, the famous artist. Today I learned I've been accepted."

He pushed off the railing and knelt in front of her, clasping her hands. "That's wonderful, Kate. I'm so pleased for you. That's quite a validation of your talent." He tipped up her chin. "You had me scared there for a minute."

Inexplicably, she pulled her hands away and averted her face. Perplexed, he stood up, pulled a chair close and sat down. "Four weeks? That's not long. You don't need to apologize. I'm happy for you. And I'll be right here when you get—"

"Sam, don't!"

Her ominous words caught him up short and he sank back in his chair, lacing his fingers over his chest. He'd forgotten an important rule—that a doctor's most effective diagnostic tool was listening. He didn't know what the hell was going on with Kate, but the cavern in his stomach told him it wasn't good. "Talk to me, Kate."

She gripped the arms of her chair, then began. From the start, he knew better than to interrupt. "This opportunity is an answer to a prayer. Not just because it's a great chance for me to learn and to see if my art has any merit, but because it's the best thing for you and me. This gives us a clear conclusion to whatever's been going on between us."

It was only because he cared so desperately that he didn't stop her right there. *Whatever's been going on? Try love, Kate.*

"You're new in town. You're lonely. I'm lonely." Her voice wavered. "And we're both vulnerable. Sunday night was a beautiful one-time thing."

He couldn't help himself. "You said, 'no regrets.'"

She stood and, locking her hands in front of her, paced to the railing where she stopped and then faced him. "I meant it, Sam. I mean it still. You—" her voice caught "—you made me feel like a woman again. For that, I could never be sorry."

Like a boulder poised to set an avalanche in motion, the anticipated objection loomed in his awareness.

"But it was a quicksilver kind of thing. Lovely, exciting and...foolish."

"It was many things, Kate. But 'foolish' wasn't one of them. Not for me." She turned away, fingering a trailing ivy leaf. He waited.

"I mean 'foolish' in the sense that we didn't take into consideration the fact that there can be no future in our relationship. We're adults and while we don't necessarily regret our actions, they were irresponsible." She hurried on, seemingly carried away with her arguments. "You have the boys to think about. They've had enough changes without worrying about Daddy and some woman. Then there's your practice. You'll get more patients if you're not the subject of gossip. Then, of course, I can only imagine what the Manleys would think. Or my daughters."

During the last part of her list, he'd slowly gotten to his feet and, wrapping his arms beneath her breasts, had pulled her back tight against his chest, capturing her hands in his. "Listen to you. Trying so hard to discourage me. To be logical." He planted a kiss against her neck, feeling her shiver in his arms. "It won't work. And there *is* a future. There has to be."

She didn't move. From the corner of the porch, he could hear Charger yawning, then licking his muzzle. Sam continued. "Believe me, I understand all about trying to please everyone else. I've spent much of my life doing what I thought other people wanted or expected. My parents, my brother, my ex-wife, my partners in the practice. I've been there, done that. And you know what?" He paused, letting his words sink in. "It doesn't work. Because in the long run, no matter how hard you try, you can't please other people. At least not until you've done what you need to do for yourself."

He turned her in his arms, breathing in the lilies-of-the-valley freshness of her skin. "So go to Santa Fe. Learn all you can. But when you come back, I'll be here waiting for you."

Her eyes widened in dismay. "Sam, I—"

He shushed her with a finger. "Because I love you and I can wait."

She sagged against him, burying her face in his chest. He could feel her shoulders shaking under his palms, sense the tears dampening his shirt front. Then he heard her muffled voice. "Please don't make this so difficult."

He bent his mouth to her ear. "Is it so wrong to want to prove to you that what we have is for keeps? To hope that while you're away, you'll remember how much we need each other?"

Her eyes swimming, she looked up at him. "Oh, Sam" was all she could say before he caught her lips and she answered with a tenderness that made him ache with longing.

Then, trembling in his arms, she murmured his name again and again. "You make it so hard to resist."

He kissed her throat, just at the tender place where her pulse throbbed. "Then don't."

She wound her arms around his neck, her breasts abrading his chest, causing sharp pangs to race to his groin. Her voice was thick with need. "Once more?"

He picked her up in his arms. "For now, Kate, for now."

Yet even as he made love to her, he knew he would have to set her free. That only then could she truly come home. To him.

SAM LEFT SHORTLY AFTER MIDNIGHT. Kate lay in bed, aware that every part of her body was tingling, flushed with Sam's incredible lovemaking. Once more she'd felt her body come alive under a man's hands and mouth. Once more pure sensation had lifted her out of herself.

She should've been stronger in her resolve. Earlier, she'd been up-front with Sam. He'd known where she stood.

She rolled over on her side and stared out the window. But all her reasoned comments hadn't stopped him from saying it again before he left. *I love you. I can wait.* It was too much to take in. Santa Fe would help. While she was gone, surely they'd both come to their senses. She would return home, immerse herself in her work. He'd be busier with his practice and his sons. They'd be friends. But as for the other? As she'd said, "a quicksilver kind of thing."

Sated, she drifted off to sleep, only to be awakened a little before one by the phone. Her immediate reaction was dread, but then she reassured herself that it was probably Sam calling to say a final good-night. She got out of bed, pulled a robe around her nakedness and stumbled to the phone. "Hello?"

"Mom?"

Her chest heaved. Her daughter's voice sounded tinny, strained. "Jenny, are you all right?"

"I-I'm sorry to call so late, but—"

"That's all right, honey. You sound upset."

"Mom, I—" There was no doubt then. Jenny was crying.

"What is it? You'll feel better when you get it out." Kate clasped one hand around her waist, as if to clamp down the fear.

"It's Todd, he—"

"What, darling?"

"I-I can't go on." Jenny hiccuped, then continued, her voice stronger. "I'm leaving him."

A thousand questions rushed through Kate's mind, but she sensed the last thing her daughter needed at this moment was a maternal third degree. "Oh, Jenny. I'm so sorry."

"It's been awful. I didn't know how to tell you." Jenny dissolved again, sniffling into the phone. "He-he doesn't love me. I know that now."

"What can I do to help?"

There was a long silence. Finally Kate heard her daughter gulp. Then in a hesitant voice, heavy with pain, Jenny answered. "Mom, I have to get out of here. Could Parker and I come home? I could leave tomorrow."

Kate doubled over, sinking to the floor. The enormity of Jenny's situation and of the new role she herself would be asked to fulfill hit her with the force of a cannonball. Clearing her throat, she summoned her voice. "Of course you can. Of course you can."

"I think maybe, well, that this move could be permanent."

Kate closed her eyes, praying she'd say the right thing. "You get yourself and the baby here. Then we'll face it together. One day at a time."

CHAPTER NINE

KATE SPENT the better part of the next day setting up the crib, grocery shopping, attending to myriad details and trying to keep her mind from rioting out of control. The full story would have to wait until Jenny arrived. Nevertheless, she'd spent wakeful hours in the middle of the night whipping herself for not questioning Jenny more thoroughly.

It was midafternoon as she was preparing a roast for the oven before she finally accepted the full implications of the situation. Poor Jenny, her self-esteem had to be at rock-bottom. And if this was a permanent split, she would be in Salt Flats indefinitely. She would need a job. Child care would be an issue. Unless Kate volunteered. Unworthy though the thought was, she couldn't help wondering when, now, she would ever complete Ed's portrait.

And that brought her to the workshop. There was no choice. She had to turn it down, and Jenny must never know of the missed opportunity. Kate cradled the roasting pan in her arms, overwhelmed with disappointment. She'd had even more riding on Santa Fe than she'd thought. Opening the oven door, she shoved in the roast, then balled her fists willing the self-indulgent tears away. Tears would change nothing.

Without further thought, she stepped to the phone and

within five minutes had withdrawn from the workshop. And from a dream.

As she cut up vegetables for a salad, she finally turned her thoughts to the topic she'd been avoiding— Sam. There wouldn't be any Santa Fe to defuse their situation, but having her daughter and grandson under her roof would definitely preclude a repeat of tempestuous evenings like last night. There was huge irony in the fact that Jenny and Parker would write *finis* to her relationship with Sam far more effectively than a New Mexico retreat.

Once preparations for dinner had been made, Kate could no longer put off the call to Jean. Reluctantly she dialed the familiar number. After exchanging greetings with her mother-in-law, Kate launched in. "Jenny and Parker will be arriving late this afternoon. She's left Todd."

"Oh, Kate, I'm so sorry. I wish I could say I'm surprised."

"For the moment, I don't think we should tell anyone. It's Jenny's place to decide how and when she wants to spread this news."

"You're absolutely right, although I don't imagine she'll be able to keep it under wraps for long." Jean sighed heavily. "The poor thing. What can Paul and I do?"

"All any of us can do at the moment is offer our support. Later I suppose we'll need to help her make some plans."

"I hate what this means for her and Parker."

"Me, too. Me, too." Kate felt the weight of the world sinking ever more heavily on her shoulders.

"But wait." Jean's voice became more urgent. "What about your trip to Santa Fe?"

"I've cancelled. Jenny and Parker come first."

"Of course they do, but I'm sorry you have to miss this wonderful opportunity."

"I'll be fine, really. It's just one of those things."

"When she arrives, give Jenny our love and let us know when she feels like company."

"I will. She loves you very much, you know."

"And we love her." Jean paused, then added tearily, "And we love you."

"Thanks, Jean. You and Paul mean a lot to me."

When she broke the connection, Kate stood holding the receiver in her hand, readjusting her thinking. She was many things—a library volunteer, an artist, a friend, a daughter-in-law. But first and foremost, she was a mother and a grandmother.

All the rest had become incidental.

AFTER FIFTY MILES of what seemed like nonstop irritability, Parker had finally given up and fallen asleep in his car seat. Jenny gripped the wheel more tightly as she shifted in her seat to alleviate an ache low in her back. She'd worked from dawn to dusk yesterday crating up what needed to be shipped and packing the essentials in the car. The only good news was that the knockdown-dragout fight she'd expected when Todd had returned from his oh-so-important golf outing had never materialized. When she'd told him she was taking Parker and leaving, his first comment had been, "I guess this is it, then." In fact, he'd acted more relieved than upset. Duh. Why had it taken her so long to admit the truth?

But Salt Flats? Where were all her fancy ideas now? When she'd left Oklahoma, never in her wildest dreams had she imagined returning except for brief visits. Although she'd never confess it to another living soul, Denver had been a disappointment. She hadn't made the kind of friends she'd had in high school. All the shopping excursions, parties, theater outings and meals at fancy restaurants she'd pictured had never materialized. At least not after she got pregnant. It was as if, then, Todd totally lost interest in her. That sure as hell wasn't how it was supposed to be.

And she'd been helpless to know how to fix it.

So here she was driving through her hometown, with its familiar, never-changing landmarks—the Kreme Kup drive-in, the Rexall drugstore, the buff-brick high school—on her way to the ranch. And to her mother, who'd want to know all the gory details she was too tired even to think about.

As she drove past the cemetery where her father was buried, she had a sudden, powerful sense of his presence. Soothing. Welcoming. That's when she finally lost it. Careful not to wake Parker, she pulled off the road, pausing until she could control the sobbing pent-up for all these hours. When she could breathe again, she spoke softly. "Oh, Daddy, what am I going to do?"

No answer came. With a sinking heart, Jenny recognized another important truth. It was grow-up time.

ENCOURAGED, Sam carefully locked the door of the clinic. Today had been the busiest day so far for his practice. Even Nellie had acted moderately upbeat, although when his back was turned, she'd switched *Big Bands of the 50s* for his Rolling Stones CD. In his good mood, he'd gone so far as to tell her "Slow Boat to China" was almost palatable.

His high spirits were tempered, however, by Kate's behavior last night. Her words had said one thing, her

incredible body quite another. He understood the valid-
ity of what she was telling him. Her relationships were
entrenched. And inevitably they *would* change if the
two of them made a public commitment. For Kate, who
had lived all her life in Salt Flats, that had to feel risky.

But surely, in time, they could work through that.
What was between them was special, too special to give
up on. So he would be as patient, as circumspect and
as sensitive as she needed him to be.

He paused, brushing his hand over the brass name-
plate tacked up beside the door. Sam V. Gray, M.D.
Despite naysayers, especially his father, he'd achieved
his goal of a small-town family practice. Now he had
another even more important goal—the "family" part.
And if Kate needed time, he had plenty to give.

He'd left just early enough to pick up some flowers
at the florist's before they closed. All day he'd planned
to surprise Kate by dropping them off on his way home.
The flowers were a nice gesture, but he had to admit
they were only an excuse. He wanted like hell to see
her again. To encourage her to go to Santa Fe. To tell
her she'd wait a very long time before he would lose
interest. And to be sure she understood he'd meant what
he said last night. He loved her. With everything he had.

AFTER DINNER while Jenny was upstairs unpacking the
baby's things, Kate sat on the porch cuddling her towheaded grandson, breathing in the Ivory-soap baby
smell of him. Charger sat at her knee, occasionally sniff-
ing at the strange object in her arms. She scratched his
head reassuringly.

Parker stirred and pointed to Charger, who, satisfied
with his mistress's attention, was settling in his accus-

tomed place in the corner. "Arf, arf," her grandson
said.

"That's right, sweetheart. Doggie." Kate wrapped
both arms around him and sighed with contentment
when he lay back against her shoulder, his eyes drooping. Poor baby. His life had been turned topsy-turvy,
and from what little Jenny had told her, chances didn't
look good that Todd would be much of a factor in his
life.

Recognizing Jenny's fragility, Kate had worked hard
to control her anger at Todd. Her daughter could be
difficult, but she was also very loveable. Todd's im-
maturity and selfishness were evident. How had Jenny
put it? "It was always about him—what he wanted,
what he needed, what made him happy." Kate found it
hard to muster much sympathy for a young man who
craved instant gratification at the expense of his family.

Jenny had barely touched her dinner. A bite of meat,
a spoonful of potatoes, a nibble of salad. Even her favorite chocolate cake had failed to tempt her. Her
makeup had worn off, her hair hung lankly at her shoulders and red-rimmed eyes signaled both physical and
emotional exhaustion. Kate felt a swift, intense longing
for Ed, for his steadiness and guidance. Together they
could have faced this. But alone?

Looking down, she saw that Parker had fallen asleep,
one chubby hand clutching a button on her blouse. She
began humming softly, but stopped abruptly when she
heard a vehicle turn down her lane. Jenny hadn't mentioned telling any of her friends she was home, but
maybe she—

Momentarily, Kate's breathing stopped. There was no
mistaking the white Suburban. What was Sam doing
here?

She didn't know how to handle his arrival, held captive as she was by the sleeping toddler. She waited for what seemed a long time as Sam climbed out of the truck and walked in slow motion toward her, carrying in his hands a bouquet of daisies and baby's breath.

Grinning, he mounted the steps, nodding toward Parker. "Friend of yours?"

She tried for a smile that never made it to her lips. "My grandson."

Sam cocked his head inquiringly. "From Denver?"

"From Denver." She struggled to go on. "This is Parker."

"Jenny's boy?" He waited on the next-to-top step of the porch.

She nodded, swallowing the cotton in her mouth. "They arrived just a little while ago."

"Is this an unexpected visit?"

"It's more than a visit." There. She'd said it.

He stepped up on the porch, set the flowers on the railing and moved toward her. "Kate, you look so worried. What is it?"

"Jenny has left her husband. She's moved home with the baby."

Expecting Sam to be concerned about the invasion of their privacy, she wasn't prepared for what he did next. He kneeled beside her and put an arm around her, pulling her and the baby close. "She couldn't have come to a better place."

Kate rested her head momentarily against him. If only he knew how helpless she felt.

"What about Santa Fe?"

She couldn't make a sound. She simply shook her head. Then when Parker stirred, she straightened up and shifted him so he lay against her chest, his head nestled on her shoulder.

"I'm sorry," he whispered. "I hope sometime you'll have another chance." He got to his feet and retrieved the flowers. "These are for you," he said, laying them gently in her lap. Then he stepped back and leaned against the railing, his arms folded across his chest, his eyes full of compassion. "Because I love you."

"Sam, don't—"

"Kate, I couldn't turn it off even if I wanted to. Which I don't."

"But can't you see? Everything's changed."

"Do you really believe that?"

Her breath caught, and for a confused moment she didn't know whether she believed it or not. "I have other obligations now." She looked down at Parker. "I'm somebody's grandmother, for heaven's sakes."

"What's that got to do with you and me?"

The man was dense as a post. She lowered her voice. "What happened last night...before..."

"Was just the beginning."

"Didn't you understand anything I said last night?"

He grinned an infuriatingly mischievous grin. "Yes. But I like to believe actions speak louder than words."

Cradling the baby, she abruptly stood. "Sam—"

The screen door creaked and their heads swiveled to Jenny, who stood as if rooted, looking from Kate to Sam. "Um, am I interrupting something?"

Kate steadied her voice. "Certainly not. Come on out. I'd like you to meet Sam Gray."

Jenny stood her ground. "The doctor?"

Sam stepped forward, his hand extended. "You must be Jenny."

Very deliberately Jenny closed the door behind her, ignoring Sam's hand. "How do you do."

For the life of her, Kate couldn't think of a thing to say. Sam came to the rescue. "Your mother tells me you're home for a while."

"For good," Jenny said bluntly. She swiped back her shoulder-length blond hair, then relieved Kate of Parker.

"Salt Flats is a nice place," Sam said, deliberately overlooking Jenny's sneer. "Since you just arrived, I'll shove off so you two can visit. See you around, Jenny." He nodded at the daisies clutched in Kate's hand. "Enjoy the flowers, Kate. Good night."

In silence the two women stood watching until long after the Suburban had cleared their vision. Then Jenny spoke, her disapproval evident. "Mind telling me what that was all about?"

"Sam's become a good friend."

"And a close stargazing buddy?" She chuckled sardonically. "A regular free spirit, what with that ponytail and all."

"Aren't you being a bit judgmental?"

"Don't lecture *me,* Mother. I saw how he looked at you. How uncomfortable you were when I caught you—"

"*Caught* me? Now see here—"

"No, you see here." Jenny's chin quivered. "Are you telling me these daisies are some sort of—" she sputtered "—friendly prescription?"

"Jenny, please." Kate strained for the right tone. "You've got this all wrong."

"I don't think so. Haven't you any pride at all?" Then as she wheeled to go back in the house, she shot a parting sally over her shoulder. "And what about

Daddy, huh? What about him?'' The door slammed behind her.

In the back of her head, Kate felt the miserable throbbing of a headache. Jenny's rudeness could be chalked
up to her exhaustion. But her insinuations? Uncomfortably close to the truth.

Massaging the nape of her neck, Kate wondered what
in the world she was going to do. Less than twenty-four
hours ago she'd only *thought* she had troubles.

"HOO, BOY," Sam muttered as he drove away from
Kate's. He'd stumbled into it big-time. Jenny, a petite
blonde, attractive in a high-school cheerleaderish kind
of way, had cut him dead. And the tension between her
and Kate was obvious. Maybe it would have been better
for Kate if he hadn't shown up this evening, but from
the looks of things, Jenny wouldn't have been happy
under any circumstances to learn of his interest in her
mother. The flowers, of course, had been a dead giveaway.

Kate clearly believed Jenny's arrival changed things
with him. He could tell how nervous she was with
Jenny, worried no doubt about what her daughter might
think. Then there was that business about being a grandmother, as if that made any difference in his feelings.
He couldn't help grinning. He loved it. He'd slept with
a grandmother. Some grandmother! She was only the
sexiest, most responsive woman he'd ever known.

But there she was—doing it again. Dwelling on the
obstacles. He'd grant they were real enough to her, but
they could be overcome. Well, now he had two women
to win over—Kate *and* Jenny. Kate would have to understand. He couldn't give up. He loved her too much.

That settled, he turned his thoughts to Lester whom

he'd visited briefly over the noon hour. The poor guy was understandably confused by events, still harboring the fear that his aunt would punish him for exposing her secret. Lola Fletcher had assured both him and Lester that counseling would be expedited so the matter could be resolved as soon as possible. Sam hoped to hell the intervention would turn Julia Jakes around. Despite her negative influence, Lester needed her. There were no other relatives, and Lester was incapable of living on his own.

When he arrived home, Sam pulled a TV dinner from the freezer, stuck it in the oven, then began sorting through the mail. When the phone rang, he couldn't help hoping it wasn't a patient.

It wasn't. It was Marcia. Frowning, he rubbed his thumb and forefinger over his brow. "Hi. What's up?"

She told him briefly about the boys' recent Little League game and their dental checkup. Then she got to the point. "But that isn't the main reason I called. I don't quite know how to tell you this, but Blake says he doesn't want to come for your scheduled weekend."

Sam's heart sank. His worst fear was materializing. "Did he say why?"

"No. He won't talk about it." He could hear the puzzlement in her voice. "Did something happen last time?"

Yeah, something happened, but how was he supposed to tell Marcia? He sidestepped the question. "I was afraid Salt Flats would be too tame for them."

"I don't think it's that. Besides, however much you and I disagree about things, we've worked hard to keep the boys out of it." She hesitated. "But I've never seen Blake this upset."

"Would it help if I talked with him?"

"It couldn't hurt."

Sam felt a flash of panic. What if that didn't work? What if Blake wouldn't come again? Maybe he should offer to let them skip a week. He roamed the living room, clutching the phone.

"Okay. I'll call him tomorrow. And I'll plan something really fun for his next visit."

"I hated to bother you with this."

"No, that's quite all right. We need to talk about these things."

"The only clue I have is something Bart said. But you know him. You can never tell when he's putting you on."

He didn't want to ask the question, but he had to. "What was that?"

"Something about some woman named Kate. Does that mean anything to you?"

Okay, so he'd blown it at the Great Salt Plains Park. And his feeble explanation hadn't made a dent. One kiss and he was toast with his son. "Yeah, that sheds some light. Thanks."

"Sam?" Her question was laden with curiosity.

"I've had a long day, Marcia. I appreciate your concern. I'll get in touch with the boys tomorrow. Good night, now." Before she could prolong the conversation, he hung up, aware of a sour taste in his mouth. God help him. Had he let his feelings for Kate obscure his obligations as a father? Or was Blake just that vulnerable? In either case, he had some thinking to do.

THE NEXT MORNING Kate sat in the kitchen watching Parker squish bananas and arrange then rearrange Cheerios on his high chair tray. Every now and then, with a triumphant flourish, he'd actually put a few in his mouth. Sun streamed through the window, birds chirped and Charger sat, paws extended, happily studying his new buddy. It should be a joyful new day. But all Kate could think about was last night and Jenny's stony face.

When they'd gone in the house after Sam left, her daughter had made it clear that further discussion was out of the question. It was just as well. Kate doubted there would have been any positive outcomes.

From Parker's cheek, she plucked a Cheerio held in place by banana goop. "Had enough, fella?"

By way of response, he ran his sticky fingers through his curly hair and shouted, "Done!" After she washed him off, she set him on the floor. He took a few tottering steps before turning, bewildered, back to her. "Mama?" He looked around, his huge blue eyes wide with concern. "Mama!" he said more urgently.

Kate knelt beside him, placing a finger to her lips. "Shh. Mama's sleeping." From his expression, Kate couldn't tell if he was ready to howl in protest or go on with his baby life. With a flash of inspiration, she opened the cabinet behind her and pulled out a set of colorful plastic bowls and several spoons. Easily diverted, he plopped down on his diaper-padded bottom and began playing with them.

She was glad Jenny was catching up on her sleep and it was certainly no hardship to spend time with her darling grandson. Inevitably, though, she and Jenny would have to talk. The sooner the better. It was not, however, a conversation she was looking forward to. If only Sam hadn't arrived when he did...

She thought guiltily of the daisies she'd hidden away in her bathroom, knowing intuitively that displaying them openly would be an affront to Jenny. Like it or not, Kate could see Jenny's viewpoint. Home to her meant Dad and Mom. Not Mom and some stranger. Rachel had encouraged her, but Jenny wouldn't. Though an adult, she was still daddy's girl.

Hearing a car outside, she looked out the window. Charlene and Amanda. Kate scooped up Parker and stepped out on the porch. Charlene left Amanda in the 4Runner and hurried up the walk bearing a frozen casserole. "Oh, isn't he a cherub?" She patted the baby's shoulder, then went on. "I heard Jenny and Parker were visiting and thought this lasagna might come in handy."

"But how—"

"Brandi Moody was standing outside the drugstore yesterday and saw them drive by. Why didn't you tell me they were coming?"

Kate took hold of Parker's fingers, now gripping hunks of her hair, and attempted to extricate them. "I didn't know until late Wednesday night."

"A quick surprise trip?" Charlene was studying her with concern.

"You could say that."

"Kate, something's the matter. You look like hell. Are you sleeping all right?"

"Gee, you sure know how to make a girl feel good."

"You're evading the issue."

Just then Parker lunged, arms outstretched, for Charlene, who barely managed to catch him and hold on to the casserole at the same time. Kate wiped her hands down the sides of her jeans, hoping she could avoid answering her friend. No such luck.

"Kate?" Charlene urged. "Are you and Jenny still having difficulties?"

"It's more complicated than that."

Parker played happily with the open collar of Charlene's blouse. "Well?"

Kate glanced nervously toward the house. "Not now, Charlene. I'll call you later." She waved toward the 4Runner. "How's our girl?"

"Ecstatic to be out of the house. She's actually begun to think life will get better. We're on our way to Enid to check in with the orthopedist."

"Want to take Parker along?" Kate grinned. "He seems pretty attached."

"Somehow, I don't think Jenny would like that. Where is she, by the way?"

"Still sleeping." To move off the subject of her daughter, Kate walked to the SUV and exchanged greetings with Amanda.

"Guess we'd better get a move on," Charlene said, handing Parker back to Kate. "Let me know when you feel like talking."

"I will."

Charlene started the motor, but just before pulling away, she grinned teasingly at Kate. "Hope you liked the second batch of flowers as well as the first!" Then she roared off down the lane.

Kate stood there sputtering. How had Charlene known? A lightbulb went on. Of course. Mavis Hortell, Salt Flats's one and only florist.

It was after eleven when Jenny finally rolled out of bed, refreshed by the marathon sleep, but worried about Parker. She pulled on her ratty terry-cloth robe, a remnant from college days, and hurried downstairs. The house was ominously quiet. The kitchen had been cleaned up and the diaper bag was missing from the corner where she'd left it last night. Glancing around, she noticed a note on the kitchen table. Mom had taken the baby to the park and grocery store.

She fixed herself a glass of orange juice and sat at the table munching on a banana and sipping the juice. At least she had a little peace and quiet to consider what she needed to say to her mother. Things like how weird it was to be here, waiting for Daddy to walk into the house or bound down the stairs. Like how betrayed she felt by the fleeting blush that had passed over her mother's face when that doctor had mentioned the daisies. Like how scary it was to think about being a single mother. If she'd hoped to come home and find comforting normalcy, Dr. Gray's little visit had squelched that notion.

What in hell was her mother thinking? Judging from the looks of him, the man had to be considerably younger. Jenny set down the banana, only half-eaten. The other weird thing was that it was as if her mother was a different person, somebody she didn't know. She slumped, then laid her head in her arms. She was so tired. It would feel heavenly just to crawl back between the covers and sleep the whole day away, oblivious to the pain and confusion.

She must've dozed off because at first she couldn't tell if the phone was ringing or she was dreaming. Rousing herself, she cleared her throat, then picked up. "Hello?"

A deep, warm, female voice with the hint of a Spanish accent responded. "Good morning. Am I speaking with Kate Manley?"

"No, this is her daughter. Mother isn't here right now."

"Would you be so kind as to take a message, then?"

"Just a minute." Jenny scrounged in a drawer for a notepad and pencil. "Okay, I'm ready."

"This is Lupe Santiago in Santa Fe." Then she spelled her name. "Your mother left word with my secretary that for personal reasons she wouldn't be able to come to my workshop." She laughed. "But you're her daughter, so you already know this, no?" The woman rattled on in her lilting manner while Jenny tried to make sense of what she was saying. Workshop? What workshop? Santa Fe? "Do you think you could have your mother call me as soon as she can? She is most talented, don't you agree?"

Jenny mustered a faint "Yes."

"It would be my very great privilege to work with her. She has already paid her tuition. If she can come later, I will make room for her in my September workshop. Please have her call so we can make arrangements." Ms. Santiago then gave Jenny the number, rechecking to be sure it had been copied correctly.

"I'll tell her."

"Bueno. Goodbye, Kate's daughter."

Bewildered, Jenny replaced the receiver. Maybe Sam Gray was merely the start of her mother's secret life. Santa Fe was a big-time art colony. Daddy had always praised Mom's work, but... Jenny guessed she and Parker had thrown a monkey wrench into her mother's plans. Yet another reason to feel crummy.

She had no time to ponder these developments since Kate and Parker arrived home just then. Jenny wiped the sleep out of her eyes, raked a hand through her uncombed hair and watched them come up the walk. Parker was lucky to have a youthful grandmother. That made her think of her own grandmother. She'd go see her this afternoon. Try to explain about Todd and the mess of her marriage. She desperately needed Grandma's understanding.

"Mama, Barney." Parker toddled toward her holding a small purple stuffed dinosaur. "Pahkah's," he announced proudly, mangling his name.

She knelt to examine his prize. "Morning, Mom."

Kate paused in the act of taking the groceries out of the sack. "Hi, honey. Sleep well?"

"Well and long. I'm sorry I wasn't up to get Parker's breakfast."

"That's what grandmothers are for."

Jenny stood. "Do you mind if I shower real quick and get dressed before lunch? You can turn on cartoons for Parker."

"Run along. We'll be fine."

Jenny dashed upstairs. She should have told her mother about the message from Lupe Santiago, but she wanted time to think about things first. If her mother went to Santa Fe, could she handle things here by herself? What if she found a job? Who would take care of Parker?

But... She paused in the act of taking off her robe. It might be best for her mother to get away from Sam Gray. Then the good doctor would just have to take his flowers to somebody else. And maybe when her mother came home, she'd have reverted to the Kate Manley who'd been Ed's wife and her mother. It was something to think about.

As she stepped into the shower, another thought—a frightening one—hit her. Maybe her mother didn't want to be that Kate Manley anymore. Jenny gulped, reminded of her long-harbored fear. Maybe her mother had never wanted to be that Kate Manley.

CHAPTER TEN

AFTER A TENSE LUNCH, Kate knocked on Jenny's bedroom door. Since Parker was down for his nap, this would be as good a time as any to clear the air. At the mumbled, "Come in," Kate entered the room. Jenny sat on the floor in front of an opened bureau drawer sorting clothes into piles.

"Don't you think it's time we talked?" Kate asked, perching gingerly on the edge of the bed, strewn with belts, scarves and lingerie.

Keeping her attention on her task, Jenny merely shrugged.

"I know you have quite a few things on your mind. I want very much to help."

"You are. You're letting me live here."

"This is your home, Jenny," Kate said quietly.

"Maybe."

Maybe? "I know it's not Denver, but what I meant was—"

"I know what you meant." Jenny dropped a pile of T-shirts into the open drawer. "But it doesn't feel like home."

Kate realized her fingers were gripping the ridges of the chenille bedspread. "Why not?"

Jenny slammed the drawer shut, then spun around to face Kate. "For one thing, Daddy's not here."

Kate searched for soothing words. "I know it's hard.

For months, I struggled. Expecting to hear his feet stomping off mud on the back porch, smelling his aftershave every time I opened his closet, turning on football, which I don't even like, because it was Sunday afternoon. I still have moments like that. But I have to live with the reality, and, honey, so do you. He's gone.''

"So I'm just supposed to accept it and forget him?"

"No," Kate said gently. "We'll never forget him. Nor should we. But he'd want us to move on."

"Obviously that hasn't been a problem for you." Jenny's face was a mask of hostility.

Kate slid to the floor, staring into her daughter's teary eyes with disbelief. "Spit it out, Jenny. What's bugging you?"

"Mother, I have enough problems of my own without coming home to find a man on your doorstep. For Pete's sake, you're forty-two!"

Kate stifled the urge to laugh hysterically. Instead, she succumbed to her own sarcastic impulse. "Just a dried-up old prune of a woman, right?"

Jenny rolled her eyes. "That's not what I meant. It's just that—"

"Just that you can't admit your mother might have some interest in another man. Isn't that right?"

Jenny's expression turned to stone. "Do you?"

"Would that be so terrible?"

"What do you think? My marriage is on the rocks, I have no home, no job, I come here to find you—" she stammered "—acting like one of my single friends."

"That's what I am, Jenny. Single." She plunged on. "And that's what you'll soon be. Are you prepared to spend the rest of your life without a man? Never to fall in love again?"

Jenny fiddled with the buttons on a cardigan, avoiding Kate's eyes.

Kate continued. "I'll take your silence for a 'no.' So is it fair to deny me those same possibilities?"

No answer.

"That having been said, you'll be pleased to know I've come to the same conclusion you have. I've told Sam there's no future. I like him a great deal. I want him as a friend. But it's not the time for me to begin a new relationship. With him or anybody." Wearily, she rose to her feet. "I hope that news comforts you."

Without raising her head, Jenny slowly buttoned the sweater. "I wouldn't want you to give up anything on my account." The set of her daughter's jaw belied her words.

"I'm not. You and Parker come first. You're my priority." She walked toward the door, then paused. "Please let me help you through this rough patch."

"I'll figure it out myself."

Kate nodded at the predictability of her daughter's response. "Whatever. But remember, I'm here and I love you."

Jenny finally glanced up, her expression neutral. "I'm planning to take Parker to see Grandma and Grandpa when he wakes up."

"That's a good idea," Kate said noncommittally.

"Okay, then." Jenny tossed her head, flipping her hair back. "For your information, Monday I have an appointment with a lawyer. About the divorce." Apparently sensing her mother needed answers to unasked questions, she went on. "Don't suggest counseling. It's too late for that." Suddenly, Jenny seemed to shrink. "From now on, it's Parker and me. I'll be getting a job and a place to live, so you won't have to put up with us forever."

Kate's heart turned over at further evidence of her daughter's stubborn streak. "You two aren't a hardship, Jenny."

"I just don't want to be a burden."

There was something weighted in her comment as if it had even greater significance than the words suggested, but Kate couldn't imagine what. "That will never happen," she said before leaving the room.

In the hallway, Kate shook her head, trying to sort out the conversation. Jenny's resentment over her relationship with Sam was natural, but whether Kate's reassurances had made a dent, she hadn't a clue. She was troubled by Jenny's remark about being a burden. She hoped she'd never done anything to make either of her daughters feel that way.

She started down the stairs and was nearly to the bottom before another puzzling aspect of the conversation hit her. She herself had been downright defensive about Sam. Justifying her actions, including the ones Jenny knew nothing about. *Especially* the ones that had made her feel young and sexy.

Giving up Sam wasn't as easy as she was letting on.

PARKER'S PLAYFUL PRATTLING couldn't lessen Jenny's guilt as she drove to her grandparents' house. She'd treated her mother like crap. Even during the conversation, she'd known she sounded sullen, selfish, insensitive. All those worst traits Todd, too, had provoked in her. But at the same time, the thought of her mother having feelings for another man, no matter who, caused her to ice up.

She should have known better than to have a serious

conversation with her mother when she was on the verge of falling apart herself. Communication had never been easy between them. Not like it had been between her mother and Rachel.

And despite reassurances regarding Sam Gray, Jenny wasn't convinced. The fire in her mother's eyes when she'd talked about the man didn't get there overnight. Santa Fe was seeming like a better idea all the time. She'd find out what Grandma knew about Dr. Gray. Maybe, between them, they could work something out.

AFTER WAVING Jenny and Parker goodbye, Kate returned to the kitchen and finished cleaning up the lunch dishes. At the end of the counter, she stopped, staring at a note sticking out of the phone book. In Jenny's handwriting was Lupe Santiago's name followed by an out-of-town number. Odd that Jenny hadn't mentioned it before she left.

Still holding the note, Kate wandered from the kitchen across the yard to her studio. She'd already cancelled her registration. What could Lupe Santiago want? Inside the studio, the mingled odors of paints, solvents and a eucalyptus-scented candle she often burned for inspiration stopped her in her tracks—the familiarity of her special place and an overpowering sense of lost promise filling her with melancholy.

She turned on one lamp and settled at her drawing board, idly studying her sketches of Ed. Workmanlike. Spiritless. She had been nuts to think she had any business going to Santa Fe to study. When she'd felt the stirring of ambition following the grim months after Ed's death, she must have deluded herself into euphoric overconfidence. Nothing in front of her confirmed talent.

She tapped her drawing pencil on the edge of the table. Well, no need to second-guess herself. Circumstances had swiftly put an end to any pretensions. Yet something she'd captured in a full-frontal drawing of Ed's face mocked her, and she could again hear him saying, "Don't let yourself down."

Idly she began sketching, not Ed, but a toddler, one with curly hair, big eyes and chubby fingers. Before she knew it, she was covering page after page with drawings of Parker. After a couple of hours, she stopped briefly. She stood and stretched, elated that whether or not she ever studied with Lupe Santiago or anyone else, her art was great therapy. She enjoyed it. That was value in itself.

She picked up a small canvas and set it on her easel and with a lightness of heart she hadn't experienced in the past few days, began daubing on the first splashes of color that would become her grandson.

"Mom?"

Kate jumped, pivoting to see Jenny, with Parker in her arms, standing just inside the door. "Goodness, you startled me."

"We couldn't find you in the house." Jenny strolled around the room. "What are you doing?"

Kate nodded toward the sketches of Parker. "Trying my darnedest to capture our little munchkin's likeness."

Jenny picked up one of the renderings, holding it near Parker's face. "Wow. This is really good."

Kate recognized the surprise in her daughter's comment. "He's an inspiring model."

"Grandma sends her love."

"How was your visit?"

"Fine. She was very understanding." With her free hand, Jenny shuffled through the sketches, but stopped when she came to the first one of Ed. "Is this supposed to be Dad?"

Sharing her work on Ed's portrait at this stage made Kate self-conscious. "Yes."

Jenny held it to the light, frowning. "It looks sort of like him."

"But not exactly?"

"No, he was more…"

"What?"

Jenny set the sheet down. "I don't know. More relaxed or something. He looks stiff here."

Kate sighed. "I know. I can't seem to get what I'm after."

"Maybe you're trying too hard."

Sometimes Jenny was amazingly perceptive. "That, plus maybe a lack of talent."

"There you go again!"

Puzzled, Kate said, "What do you mean?"

"Selling yourself short. Daddy used to hate it when you did that."

Kate smiled ruefully. "I can't help it."

"Well, start trying. And start in Santa Fe."

"What are you talking about?"

"The workshop. Were you ever going to tell me about it?"

"Tell you what?"

"That you canceled out on a once-in-a-lifetime chance because Parker and I came home?"

"Any mother would have done that."

"Well, you don't have to. Ms. Santiago called today. She's saving a place in her September workshop and wants you to call her back. She thinks you're very talented."

Kate could hardly absorb what Jenny was saying.

"That's nice of her, but it's not important now. And I already saw the note. Why didn't you tell me earlier before you went to Grandma's?"

Jenny fussed with Parker's bib overall fastener. "It slipped my mind."

A tick of irritation nudged Kate. "I guess it wasn't that important to you."

Jenny's face flamed. "Believe me, Mother, it was very important to me."

Parker began squirming just then, his hands scrabbling at Jenny's shoulder. "Down! Pahkah down!" Jenny set him on his feet, secured his hand in hers and started toward the door. Grasping the knob, she turned back toward Kate. "The last thing I want to do is cause you any more trouble than I already have. Call Ms. Santiago. Tell her you'll come."

"But—"

"I don't need you. I can handle my life by myself."

If Kate hadn't been so dumbfounded and concerned, she'd have been tempted to grin at hearing her daughter's familiar mantra. "I know you're capable of—"

"Go to Santa Fe. Please." Parker began tugging on Jenny's hand and whining. "I don't want to feel that you missed a golden opportunity because of me. Not again."

Jenny and Parker were halfway to the house before Kate registered the last two words Jenny had flung at her. *Not again.* She sank, defeated, onto a stool. What in the world was Jenny talking about? She had never missed anything because of her daughter.

THAT EVENING SAM WANDERED out of the house, his cell phone tucked in his hand, and sat on the weathered glider staring at the distant line where the fields met the evening sky. In odd moments during the day he'd racked his brain to find a way to help Blake. To explain. With no success. He couldn't blame the kid, really. Blake was right. His father's attention *had* been diverted. How could he help his son see that love wasn't exclusive?

Sighing, Sam punched in the number and waited, his stomach in a knot, until Marcia answered. After a perfunctory greeting, she put Blake on.

"'Lo." His son's voice held little warmth.

"Blake? How's it goin', buddy?"

"Mom said I had to talk to you. Whaddaya want?"

Sam stood and began prowling the yard. "Something's bothering you. Does it have anything to do with Kate?"

Blake was silent.

"Son?"

Finally the boy spoke. "You kissed her."

"Yes, I did."

Blake's voice seemed to catch in his throat. "You like her better'n me."

"Why would you say that?"

"She's a grown-up. And you're all the time making us see her."

Sam clutched the phone, praying for guidance. "Think about that. Did you enjoy fishing?"

"Uh-huh."

"How about watching the stars?"

"I guess."

"And digging the salt crystals?"

"I hated that!"

"Did you hate it at the time, or only after Bart told you I kissed Kate there?"

"Who cares? I don't wanna come to that dumb old town ever again!"

Trying to ignore the hurt and do the right thing, Sam responded, "That's not a choice. This is where I live. I love you, fella, and in the long run I don't think you'd want to do without a dad, would you?"

"No," Blake conceded. "But *she'll* be there."

"You may be right. But is it Kate you don't like or the idea of Kate and me being together?"

Blake hesitated before answering, apparently mulling over the question. "Kate's okay, I guess. But how come you kissed her?"

"Because I like her." Sam swallowed. "Quite a lot."

"You gonna marry her?"

"That would depend on her, wouldn't it?"

That stopped him. Finally, he said in a baffled voice, "Why wouldn't she want a neat guy like you?"

For the first time in the conversation, Sam felt himself relax. "She has other people to think about. Things she wants to do." He paused, then went on. "Just like I do. I have you and Bart to think about, work to do. But there's room in my life for all of that."

Silence.

"You don't stop loving your mother or your brother because you love me, do you?"

"I guess not."

Sam sucked in his breath and continued. "And I will never stop loving you just because I love someone else."

Blake was silent, as if working it out in his mind. "Do you love Kate?"

Blake's question hovered between them, and Sam knew his son deserved and needed an honest answer.

"Yes, I do."

"That's weird."

Sam grimaced. "Okay 'weird'?"

"I dunno."

"Maybe we can talk more about this when you come for your next visit."

"Maybe."

"Feel better, son?"

"A little." Blake's tone brightened. "Wanna talk to Bart?"

"Sure."

While Blake went to get his brother, Sam expelled a relieved sigh. He felt renewed confidence that eventually he could work things out with Blake.

With Kate he wasn't so sure.

AFTER HIS BATH and bedtime story, Parker dropped off immediately. Jenny knew she had no choice but to go downstairs where her mother would be waiting for her. To talk, Kate had said. But for a few more minutes, she'd sit here rocking in the dark, listening to her son's steady breathing. Dinner had been strained, especially after Kate refused to call Lupe Santiago to tell her she'd reconsidered.

Jenny hated herself. She was always messing up someone's life—her mother's, Todd's, Parker's. The last thing she needed at this moment was a mother-daughter chat. Now, added to the usual dynamics, was her mother's ridiculous infatuation with Sam Gray. And it wasn't merely her own suspicion anymore. Grandma had hinted that there might be something going on between them.

Although Grandma had understood about Todd and made her feel better about what had gone wrong in the marriage and her decision to file for divorce, she'd cau-

tioned Jenny not to work herself up over her mother
and Dr. Gray. Easy for her to say! Had Grandma ever
seen the two of them together?

At least Grandma had agreed that it was too bad Kate
wasn't going to Santa Fe. In a sudden flash of inspiration, her grandmother's eyes had twinkled and she'd
laid a finger on her cheek. "I may have an idea. Let
me talk to Grandpa." Although Jenny had pressed, her
grandmother had refused further comment.

Sighing, she heaved herself out of the rocker and
placed one reluctant foot in front of the other. She didn't
want it to be like this with her mother. But she doubted
their upcoming talk would change anything.

WHEN JENNY CAME into the living room, Kate set down
the magazine she'd been pretending to read. "Parker
asleep?"

"Out like a light," Jenny said, curling up in Ed's
recliner, as if its arms could comfort her as her father's
had.

Jenny's impassive expression signaled the ball was
in her mother's court. Kate took a deep breath and
launched in. "Would you like to call Rachel?"

"I talked with her Wednesday. She's working a
three-day trip now. I said I'd get back to her next
week."

"Like the rest of us, I'm sure she's concerned about
you."

"Nobody needs to get in an uproar. I'll be *fine*."
Jenny's nostrils flared. "I'll see the attorney, get my
finances squared away and look for a job."

"About your finances—"

"Until the lawyers can work out an interim arrangement, I may have to mooch off you."

"It isn't mooching. You're my daughter, for heaven's sake."

Jenny nestled deeper into the recliner. "I hate it, though. I feel like some damn albatross tied around your neck."

Kate tried a faint chuckle. "Now there's a picture."

"Well, it's true. Lupe Santiago is offering you an exciting opportunity and then I come dragging home with a child, no husband and no job. Great timing, huh?"

Kate frowned, wishing she knew what to say. "Jenny, you sound like you're trying to convince yourself you're a burden."

"Haven't I always been?"

"Nonsense. You've sometimes presented some interesting challenges," Kate smiled at the recollections, "but that's all part of being a parent."

Jenny merely shrugged.

As before, Kate had the distinct sense that something important wasn't being said. "What's going on here?"

Still nothing.

"Jenny?" Kate leaned forward, tense with expectation.

Jenny, staring into her lap, mumbled something Kate couldn't quite hear. Something that sounded like, "It's all my fault."

"Honey, what did you say?"

Her daughter looked up, eyes filled with angry tears. "I said," she carefully enunciated each syllable, "It's all my fault."

"What on earth are you talking about?"

"Everything. Daddy having to leave school, you missing out on the study-abroad program, the financial struggles you two had being saddled with a baby, and—''

Kate's heart plummeted. ''Wait a minute.'' She waved her hand as if clearing confusion from her brain. ''Are you suggesting we didn't want you?''

Jenny sprang to her feet and walked to the window, where she stood fingering the drapes, staring out into the night.

Kate was right behind her. ''Jenny, darling, that's utter foolishness. Your dad and I were young, but we loved you right from the day we learned I was pregnant.'' She laid a hand on her daughter's shoulder, but Jenny flinched and Kate reluctantly moved away.

''How could you love me? In those days, wasn't pregnancy out of wedlock kind of shocking?''

''Oh, honey, how could we not?'' She couldn't stand to know that Jenny had ever harbored such thoughts, but it explained a lot. ''Some people were surprised, maybe even disapproving, but that wasn't the important thing. Your dad and I were very much in love. You were the special, God-given proof of that.''

''What about Grandma and Grandpa? Your parents?''

Kate made a quick decision. Since her parents were both dead, there was little purpose in bringing up their disapproval. ''Jean and Paul were supportive of us from the beginning. And all four parents attended the wedding.'' Kate remembered with a pang how her rigid father nearly hadn't come to the ceremony.

''But if it hadn't been for me, Daddy could've earned his degree, and you could've been a famous artist. You wouldn't have had to come back here to Salt Flats—''

''That's all might-have-beens, Jenny, and never really mattered.'' Kate edged closer again, placing her hand on Jenny's shoulder. This time Jenny suffered it to remain. "Your father and I never looked back. We had each other." Her voice softened. "And we had you. We were young and strong with a lot of faith in the future. Think about it. Together we built a successful ranching business, we had two healthy, bright children, we lived in a solid community of caring friends and neighbors. Whatever made you think we weren't happy?"

Jenny let her fingers slip down the pleat of the drape. Tears clung to her eyelashes. "Daddy so desperately wanted Rachel and me to go to college. I always figured that was because if we did, he wouldn't mind so much that he never got his degree." A lone tear escaped and ran down her cheek. "And the way he was always encouraging you about your painting. He told me once how bad he felt that he couldn't send you abroad to study. To make up for, you know, when you couldn't go. Because of me."

"Oh, honey." Kate gripped her daughter by the shoulders and turned her into an embrace. "I can't bear that you've been blaming yourself all these years." She held Jenny's tear-stained face between her hands. "Listen to me. There is nothing your dad or I would've changed about our lives. Least of all you!"

With the back of her wrist Jenny dabbed at her tears, then turned away. "If you and Daddy were so happy, how can you even think about another man?"

A leaden weight descended on Kate. Her arms fell to her sides. How on earth could she explain? "This may sound odd to you, but it's the truth. The reason I can have feelings for Sam is precisely because of the love I shared with your father." Kate folded her arms and leaned against the wall. "Listen to me, Jenny. Someday you'll love a man with your whole heart. Forgive me, but I doubt you ever felt that way about Todd." She waited until Jenny shrugged. "It's a wonderful feeling. But when the man you love dies, there is always the memory of that kind of love, the longing for it."

Jenny turned around, her face pale, her eyes hollow. "So Sam is important to you?"

Kate swallowed the lump in her throat. "He's made me believe in the possibilities."

"That's not answering the question."

How could she still be equivocating about Sam? Jenny was right. She didn't want to answer. "I know."

Kate had done all she could do. Said all she could say. Yet Jenny's expression remained skeptical.

"Well, at the very least, you've given me plenty to think about," Jenny said. "If you don't mind, I think I'll turn in now."

"A hug first?" Kate ventured.

Jenny hesitated, then walked into her arms.

They stood entwined for several seconds, the warmth of her daughter's body and Jenny's whispered "thank you" reassuring Kate that they'd made another kind of connection as well.

When the phone rang, they broke apart and Jenny picked up. "Hi, Grandma... He's sound asleep. Mom and I have been chatting... Grandpa said that? Wow!"

Kate watched, as a smile formed on Jenny's face. What could Paul have done to create such a metamorphosis?

Jenny continued her end of the conversation. "When?... That soon?... It's a great idea." She paused, eyeing Kate. "It might take some convincing, though. Mom's a hard sell, but I think I can persuade her."

Kate suddenly felt as if she were being swept along on some mysterious tide of events.

"She wouldn't dare defy both of us... Good night, Grandma. Oh, and thank Grandpa." A triumphant look on her face, Jenny hung up the phone.

Kate advanced toward her. "What?"

"You're going to Santa Fe. When you were originally scheduled to go."

"I think not!"

"You don't have to worry about Parker and me. It's all settled."

"What are you talking about?"

"Grandpa is going to remodel the upstairs so Parker and I will have an apartment there."

"But—"

"Let me finish. They're offering me free lodging in exchange for helping them with the heavier chores around the house. I'd be in town, close to the day care. That'll be important as soon as I find a job." Jenny sounded upbeat for the first time since she'd been home. "It'll be a perfect arrangement for everybody. I can help take care of Grandma and Grandpa, Parker will have built-in attention, and you—"

"—will be lonely."

Jenny grinned the same mischievous grin she'd given her mother as a child when she'd pulled a fast one. "Not hardly. You'll be in Santa Fe." She started for the stairs. "Good night, Mom."

Her head swimming, Kate managed a "'Night."

Jenny turned at the bottom of the stairs. "I expect you to call Lupe Santiago first thing in the morning."

Kate had never intended to chase Jenny away. But the sparkle in her daughter's eyes was genuine. And there would be advantages for Jean and Paul in having Jenny and the baby with them. Kate threw Jenny a kiss. "Yes, ma'am."

CHAPTER ELEVEN

JENNY STEPPED from the cool interior of the offices of Hellmann and Bates, attorneys-at-law, into the blazing midafternoon sun. Pausing to put on her sunglasses, she blinked away tears she thought had dried up days ago. The divorce was underway. Not once had Todd bothered to call, even to check on Parker. When she'd left Denver, he'd told her his attorney would be in touch. She hadn't imagined that would be their only communication.

Now, to make matters worse, Berta Jackson was bearing down on her, practically salivating with anticipation. "Yoo-hoo, Jenny," she hollered, breaking into a trot.

Jenny awaited the inevitable polite conversation peppered with outwardly solicitous questions no doubt aimed at mining dirt. The news of her move home would get out soon enough. She might as well get it over with. "Hello, Berta. How are you?"

The older woman, flushed and breathless, managed a brief answer. "Hot."

"July in Oklahoma was never my favorite season."

Berta fanned herself with her checkbook. "July's nice in Colorado, though."

Jenny nodded, deciding to let Berta work for her nuggets.

"Why would you trade those cool mountains for the scorching plains?"

"Sometimes there's not much choice."

Berta's eyebrows shot up. "Oh?"

"Family matters, you know."

"No, I didn't. Is everything all right with Kate?"

Jenny started walking in the direction of her car, parked in front of the clinic. Berta followed. "Yes, she's fine."

"What a relief. I thought maybe you'd heard about her and Sam Gray."

Damn. Berta had her. Her remark had no suitable answer, like the old do-you-still-beat-your-wife question. "Heard what?"

Berta smiled smugly. "Some folks believe they might be, er, making whoopee."

Making whoopee! God help her, if it hadn't been her own mother they were discussing, Jenny would've burst out laughing. "I don't think so," she replied coolly.

Berta shrugged. "Well, you know Salt Flats. A rumor a minute."

Oh, yeah, she knew Salt Flats, all right. For that reason, she decided to lay it on the line. At least she'd have the satisfaction of knowing that Berta, as instigator of the gossip chain, had the facts. "There is one item that is not rumor, Berta. Todd and I are getting a divorce."

Berta had the grace to feign surprise. "I had no idea. You poor thing."

"On the contrary, I'll be fine. This does mean, however, that my baby and I are back in Salt Flats for good. In fact, in a week or ten days, we'll be moving in with my grandparents."

"Jean and Paul?"

Who else? "Yes. It should work out well for all of us."

"But what will you do, how will you—"

Jenny didn't need the mayor's wife raising the frightening specter of her economic future. "It's been nice talking to you, Berta. There's my car and I need to get home to Parker. 'Bye now." Without a backward glance, she hurried toward her car, leaving Berta gaping.

Just then the front door of the clinic exploded outward and a red-faced Julia Jakes emerged, followed by an angry-looking Sam Gray. "You can't just kick me out," Julia said stridently.

"I can, and I have." Sam stood his ground beside the door.

Several pedestrians stopped to watch, and Julia took this as her cue to play to the crowd. "You've already done enough damage, mister." Her voice grew louder. "Lester and me don't need no counseling." Addressing the growing group of bystanders, she flapped her arms at Sam. "You're not much of a doctor, comin' here and messing everything up. I told you to leave Lester alone, and I meant it."

Sam waited, as if indulging a child's tantrum.

"You folks, if you know what's good for you, you'll find another doctor." Her voice rose on a wave of indignation. "One that won't meddle in your family business. One that ain't a damn hippie!" With that, she shot Sam a menacing look, then turned and marched toward the parking lot, muttering under her breath.

Unwittingly Jenny found herself siding with the doctor, whose eyes scanned the onlookers. "Sorry about that," he said with a shake of his head before reentering the clinic.

"I declare," a voice behind her said. Berta. Inadvertently, the woman had stumbled on a bonanza.

Jenny climbed in her car, grateful to escape, yet curious about the scene she'd just witnessed. Dr. Sam's patients apparently weren't *all* satisfied. Yet with somebody like Julia Jakes, you had to consider the source.

On the way home, Jenny made a decision. She couldn't hole up forever. Especially after having run into Berta. It was time to get in touch with her friends still living in the area. She wondered if her mother had felt this same need to escape prying eyes and wagging tongues after her dad had died. Withdrawing wasn't healthy. But it was natural.

Her mother had been having no trouble socializing lately, Jenny thought, remembering Sam Gray facing down Julia Jakes outside the clinic a few moments ago. Over the weekend, he'd telephoned Kate several times. Each time the snatches of conversation Jenny had overheard sounded awkward, as if her mother were straining for a neutral topic. At one point Kate had politely explained she was going to Santa Fe and there would be no need for Sam to concern himself about her.

Instead of being reassured, Jenny had felt an icy premonition. Her mother's tone had sounded phony as hell.

"ARE YOU AVOIDING ME?"

Startled by the abrupt question, Kate looked up from the library journal she'd been studying. Sam had materialized out of nowhere and loomed, unsmiling, over the circulation desk Wednesday night.

Kate glanced sideways at the only other occupant of the library, a farm wife looking up recipes for green tomato pickles. "If I said yes?" she whispered.

"I'd say there was a reason." He checked his watch. "Fifteen minutes till closing. Then we'll talk." He nodded toward the periodical section. "I'll wait for you over there." He wheeled around, picked up a magazine without seeming to look at the title and settled in an armchair at the far end of the library.

Kate rested her chin on her hand. What was there to say? That it had been fun while it lasted? That she'd been derailed by her own shaky emotions? That no matter how wild and wonderful her time with him had been, she had inescapable obligations?

She closed her eyes, willing away the memory of Sam's hands caressing her, his mouth at her breast, his smile of satisfaction... Stop it! She was not some hormonal teenager. Despite her reservations about Jenny's decision to move in with the Manleys, Santa Fe couldn't come soon enough to suit her.

SAM OBSERVED KATE over the top of his gardening magazine, his anxiety mounting. He figured she was once again lining up all the reasons their relationship wouldn't work. The irony was that her devotion to her family and friends was one of the very reasons he loved her. And she was right. They *did* have to consider others. But in the end, he and Kate had to decide what was best for them. Maybe going to Santa Fe was just what she needed to get perspective. To realize how much he cared for her and that, together, they could overcome the obstacles she seemed determined to set in their path.

At nine o'clock the other library patron, a pleasant-faced woman, gathered the notecards on which she'd been scribbling and bid a prolonged goodbye to Kate. Sam waited. As the woman left, she looked directly at him, arching an eyebrow in disapproval.

After the door shut, Sam strolled toward Kate, who was busily straightening up the desk. He put his elbows on the counter, grinning broadly and nodding toward the exit. "Am I compromising you?"

She looked up, her fair skin flushed. "At the very least, you're fueling rumors."

"You know what?" He fixed his eyes on her. "Right this minute I don't care what other people think. But I care a lot about what you think."

"And I think we better get out of here."

"And go where?"

"Home."

"Not before we talk."

"Please, Sam." Her eyes were pleading.

"Was it your plan to leave for Santa Fe without so much as a goodbye?"

She reached under the desk, picked up her purse and edged around the counter. "There's nothing more to say."

"Kate, we can talk here, we can go to your car, whatever. But we need to talk. *I* need to talk."

In the sag of her shoulders, he read concession. "If I agree, will you let this be it until I leave for New Mexico?"

"If that's the way you want it."

She turned off the main lights and stood in the semi-darkness. "All right. But we can't stay here. We'll sit in my car."

He put a hand under her elbow and escorted her outside. "Why do you make it seem as if we're doing something wrong? We're not, you know."

"It's complicated, Sam."

"It doesn't have to be."

They had reached her car. She stopped and confronted him. "That's not fair. Are you going to stand there and tell me our relationship isn't causing problems for you, too?''

She had him there. ''No.'' He opened the car door for her. She slid behind the wheel. He skirted the car, then settled in the passenger seat.

Kate gripped the steering wheel as if proving to passing motorists she was in full control. Finally she turned to him. ''So?''

''Gossip isn't the issue. It will run its course and human nature being what it is, most folks will be happy for us once we're an established couple.''

''Sam, that's not going to happen.''

''I hope it will. I'll wait.''

''You're insufferable, you know. Arrogant to a fault.''

''Guilty as charged.'' He put a hand along the seat back and massaged her shoulder. ''I guess I'll just have to keep telling you until you believe me.'' His voice rasped. ''I love you.''

Shaking his hand off, she said, ''But earlier you acknowledged problems.''

He shrugged in admission. ''Blake isn't sure he wants to share me with a woman.''

''See? That's what I mean. He's been through a lot. You can't blame him.''

''He's a kid, Kate. I'm being as sensitive to him as I know how, but I'm not going to let him dictate the next forty or fifty years of my life.'' He paused, letting that idea sink in. ''Your daughters may not understand, either. I sense Jenny is less than thrilled, but she's dealing with a lot of personal stuff. In time, she'll come around.'' He reached for her right hand and pulled it slowly into his grasp, turning her, as he did so, to plumb the depths of her uncertain eyes. "Kate, don't be too quick to give up on us."

"Oh, Sam, you're making this so hard."

"If it's hard, that ought to prove what you're feeling is genuine."

She looked down, as if facing him were too painful. "Please, can you let it be for now?" she asked in a reedy voice.

He squeezed her hand. "Sure. If that's what you need. I won't bring this up again before you leave." He cupped her chin so she had to look at him. "But when you come back from Santa Fe, we'll talk again. In the meantime, remember that I love you and we have the rest of our lives to be together." He released her hand, leaned over and pecked her on the cheek and with one last lingering gaze drank her in. "Thanks for listening. Good night."

Hoping he'd done a sufficient sell-job, he waited on the sidewalk till she started her car and pulled away from the curb. He plunged his hands in his pockets, then walked toward his truck. It had been a long time, if ever, since he'd loved someone so completely.

WHILE KATE WAS at the library, Jenny worked on her resumé, woefully aware her credentials included only two years of college and a few months of child-rearing. Fortunately before she could get too discouraged, Rachel phoned. "Should I come? I can rearrange my schedule." Rachel's voice held warmth and concern, and Jenny was sorely tempted to accept her sister's generous offer.

"Maybe later," Jenny conceded. "The hard part's over. Making the decision to come home, hiring an attorney, facing the relentless gossips of Salt Flats."

"I'm proud of you, sis. I never thought you were very happy with Todd, but it's hard to admit a mistake."

"It's Parker I'm most concerned about." Jenny's voice quavered. "He'll always wonder why his father doesn't take more interest in him."

"Don't project. Todd may not have been a good husband, but he might come around where the baby is concerned."

A surge of bitterness swept over Jenny. "You're more optimistic than I am."

Ever intuitive, Rachel must have sensed the need for a change of subject. "How's it going with Mom?"

"We're getting along, if that's what you mean. I move to Grandpa and Grandma's next week. That'll help. Mom's pulling this self-sacrificing routine, but Grandma and I convinced her to go to her workshop in Santa Fe. She needs to get away."

"I agree that Santa Fe will be good for her, but what do you mean she *needs* to get away?"

"I'm talking about Dr. Gray."

"So there's more to this than she's been letting on?"

"If you ask me, more than she's even admitting to herself. It's weird, Rach!"

"I'm not there, of course, but it doesn't sound weird to me. I told her to go for it."

"You what?" Jenny couldn't believe her ears. Wasn't that just like her naive sister?

"She's young, for heaven's sake."

"But Daddy—"

"He's gone, Jenny. Mother isn't. Do you want her to live alone the rest of her life?"

Jenny started to respond, then paused. *Did she?* Lonely was a cold place to be, as she was finding out.

With a sigh, she gave the only answer she could. "I don't know."

"You're dealing with some tough stuff. Lots of stressful changes. But life goes on."

"Not always the way I'd like it to, either," Jenny admitted.

Rachel's voice softened. "Are you sure you don't want me to come?"

Moved by her sister's offer, Jenny blinked away the mist covering her eyes. "I'm sure. This is something I have to face myself." Even if it was almost unbearable.

"Don't be too hard on yourself." Rachel paused. "Or on Mom."

They said their goodbyes, then Jenny hung up the receiver, aware that her sister had raised some serious questions. Questions that didn't have easy answers.

LATE THURSDAY AFTERNOON Sam worked at his desk. He'd seen his last patient and was catching up on some paperwork before Lola Fletcher arrived with her update on Lester and Julia Jakes. He was bushed. After leaving Kate last night, he hadn't had much time for reflection. A semi and a compact car had collided west of town just before midnight. He and the paramedics had worked on the victims for hours.

When Nellie appeared at the door, he straightened. "Do you need me to wait?"

"Thanks, Nellie, but you go on home. Lola and I just have a few things to figure out about Lester."

"Well, I hope one of them is the way to keep that Jakes woman out of our clinic. She made quite a scene the other day. Why, she called you every name in the book."

Sam was enjoying Nellie's indignation on his behalf. "Not so great for business, huh?"

"Her outburst certainly explains some of Lester's behavior."

"She has her troubles, too." Sam could afford to be generous knowing what he did about Julia. "But they need to be dealt with privately, not in front of our patients."

"Hmmph." As if by second nature, Nellie crossed the room and began fluffing the pillows on the sofa and then aligned the medical journals piled on a corner of Sam's desk. "Do you have a big weekend on tap with your sons?"

"We're going to attempt water-skiing. What about you?"

Her face reddening, Nellie wiped imaginary flecks of dust off the desk. "Mel, er, Dr. Floyd, and I will be covering for you, of course."

Sam sensed there was more. "What else?"

"Oh," she replied casually, "the church picnic."

"You'll be going together?" Hell, he was as shameless as the other Salt Flats gossips.

"Dr. Floyd has been kind enough to offer to escort me." She finished her contrived cleaning duties and looked up. "Will that be all for today?"

"Yes, Nellie. Have a good evening." *Kind enough to escort me?* The Emily-Post phrase gave her away. He'd be very surprised if Mel hadn't picked up on Sam's diagnosis of Nellie's actions and prescribed a surefire treatment—himself.

After Nellie left, Sam wandered into the reception area to await Lola Fletcher, who arrived shortly. He escorted her to his office where she sat, extracting some papers from her briefcase.

"How's Lester?" Sam asked.

"Disoriented a bit. Still fearful of his aunt. But he's calmed down in the past few days." She smiled. "And he's already fixed the toaster and the clothes dryer at the group home. It's as if he has a sixth sense."

The germ of an idea grew in Sam's mind. "I wonder if there's a way to turn that talent into a permanent job. It might help restore some of Lester's confidence."

Lola cocked her head, as if considering the idea. "You could be right. By the way, your visits mean a lot to Lester. You're the one person he counts on. You'll be interested to know that one of our counselors was successful in getting Julia into the office yesterday for a session. And while I can't say great strides were made, at least she agreed to come back. With any luck, maybe Lester can go home soon—as long as his aunt understands that our office will be making periodic home visitations."

"For what it's worth, I appreciate all you're doing for Lester."

After they concluded their business and Lola left, Sam made a notation in the clinic appointment book that he'd be visiting Lester between twelve-thirty and one tomorrow. Then he returned to his office and started going through his mail, surprised when he came across an envelope with Charlene's return address. And even more surprised when he opened it. The Klingers were throwing a party for Kate a week from Saturday night, the day before she was due to leave for Santa Fe. And he was invited.

A slow grin spread across his face. He'd told Kate he wouldn't bother her about their relationship before she left. But he hadn't promised he wouldn't see her.

Besides, he reasoned, it would be downright unneighborly to turn down Roy and Charlene.

SUNDAY KATE FOUND herself oddly touched by the fact that two more family members occupied places at the Manleys' dinner table. Parker's high chair was drawn up beside Jenny in the place where Rachel had customarily sat. Still, though, there was the void made by Ed's empty chair.

Paul, generally taciturn, was ebullient, running on and on about the improvements he was making to the upstairs. "I'm gonna have a toy chest under the dormer window and a built-in bookshelf on the opposite wall. Then I thought…"

As Paul spoke, Kate watched Jenny, her face alive with possibility. Jean, too, hung on her husband's every word. Kate tried to convince herself this move was the best solution. Jenny and Parker clearly gave the Manleys a renewed purpose. And Jean's angina attack just this past week pointed to the value of having Jenny there to keep an eye on things. Jenny would be living in town where her friends were. It all made sense. Except for that place in Kate's heart where the easy mother-daughter bond she'd always hoped for was missing.

"…and this will help you, too, Kate."

The way her father-in-law spoke her name brought her attention back to the dinner table. "I'm sorry. What did you say?"

"That having the kids under our roof will permit you to go worry-free to New Mexico. You can paint your heart out."

Worry-free? She wished. Besides Jenny's situation, she had two other major concerns. One, her painting had not been going well. Lupe Santiago might well regret her decision to include Kate. Second, there was Sam. Sam, who had refused to give up. True, he hadn't tried to change her mind. In fact, she hadn't seen him since that night at the library, nor had he called. Somehow, though, she didn't think anything was over. Not for him.

Nor for her, if she was honest. Already she missed him desperately.

"Mom, aren't you excited about Santa Fe?"

"Excited...and scared."

"Don't you ever be scared, Kate. You'll show them." Jean's eyes were full of encouragement and love.

Kate was touched by her mother-in-law's vote of confidence. "I'll do my best to make you proud."

Paul took off his glasses, carefully cleaned them on his white handkerchief, then wiped his eyes. "You already do," he said.

But would that continue, Kate wondered, if she let her heart lead?

For Kate the next week passed in a whirl—helping settle Jenny and Parker at the Manleys', prepaying her bills, arranging care for Charger and, worst of all, selecting which of her painting projects to take with her to Santa Fe, Ed's unfinished portrait chief among them.

As she pulled up to the Klingers' house Saturday night, she was dumbfounded. Strings of Chinese lanterns crisscrossed the yard, Roy's gigantic smoker was set up near picnic tables covered with red-and-white checkered tablecloths and a huge banner—LOCAL ARTIST MAKES GOOD! GO, KATE!—hung above the patio door. At least a dozen people already milled around, drinks in hand.

Leave it to Charlene. The promised "intimate gathering" had obviously mushroomed. Kate had never been comfortable in the limelight. Before she could give in to embarrassment, Minnie Odom waved and came to greet her. "The artist arrives!" she trumpeted to the others. Soon Kate was surrounded by well-wishers. Arnold Johnson placed a beer in her hand while Ethel Portman prattled on about a trip she and Toad had taken to Santa Fe years ago to attend the horse races.

Toad joined them for the tail end of Ethel's story. "Hot and dusty, that's how I remember it. Full of all these art galleries with high-priced junk. Nothin' there a real man'd want to spend any money on."

"Hush, now," Ethel said, putting an arm around Kate. "You don't wanna go hurting her feelings."

Toad took a minute to process his social gaffe. "Well, uh, I guess, *your* painting's okay," he mumbled. "Just hard to figure how selling art puts food on anybody's table."

Kate laughed. "It doesn't, unless you're extremely successful. I paint because I like to."

Toad shook his head in bewilderment. "Guess we're all different. Me? For fun, I'd rather hook a big catfish."

Just then Paul, Jean, Jenny and Parker arrived, and Kate's attention was diverted. "Don't you look pretty!" Jean said, taking in Kate's black slacks topped by a black-and-orange batik tunic top. Parker held out his arms, and Kate scooped him up, excusing herself to find her hostess. Nodding to friends, stopping occasionally to allow folks to admire Parker, Kate finally made it to the kitchen where Charlene was taking huge bowls of potato salad and coleslaw from the refrigerator.

"I'd offer to help, but, as you can see, my hands are full," Kate said, then planted a kiss on Parker's curly head.

"Nonsense, you're the guest of honor. Besides, if I want it, Berta will lend a hand." She grinned. "And an earful."

Kate groaned. "What now?"

"The latest? Lester will go home to live with Julia only under a social worker's supervision, and other than blaming her troubles on Sam Gray, she won't say a word to anybody."

"Strange."

"That about sums it up. But Sam doesn't need that kind of aggravation."

Parker put a hand to Kate's nose. "Nose," he crowed.

Grateful for the change of subject, Kate gave Parker an Eskimo kiss.

Charlene gathered up the potato salad, but before heading toward the patio, she paused. "Kate, what about you and Sam?"

"Please. There *is* no Sam and me."

"Uh-huh," Charlene said with a don't-try-to-fool-me look. "We'll see about that."

Kate held the door for her, then sought out Amanda who was holding court from the chaise longue, reveling in her invalid role. While Kate chatted with her, more and more people arrived until Kate was hard-pressed to name any respectable Salt Flats resident who wasn't in attendance. Amanda, however, had no trouble coming up with the missing. "Mom," she called to her mother. "Why isn't Dr. Gray here yet? I gotta tell him how cool my therapist is."

Kate blanched. Sam had been invited? What was

Charlene up to now? She had been on edge about being the center of attention, but now her insides turned to aspic. All she wanted was to get out of town, to put miles and weeks between Sam and herself.

Jenny, who'd been standing nearby, sidled up to her. "Was this your idea?" she said acerbically.

"What?"

"Inviting the good doctor?"

"No, it wasn't."

"Maybe, then, you've come to your senses." And with that, Jenny took Parker and turned to join a group of her friends.

Kate stood, an island in the sea of partiers. The men clustered around the smoker, discussing methods of cooking ribs. The older women sat in the chairs rimming the yard while the younger ones helped Charlene set the food out. The happy voices of children playing hide-and-seek echoed from the front of the house.

Could any of these people guess that her main motivation for going to Santa Fe was not her burning desire to create, not her expressed need for independence, nor even her deathbed promise to Ed. No. The force driving her now? Simply put, she was running away.

SAM, DETAINED by a call from a specialist in Oklahoma City regarding a puzzling case, arrived belatedly at the Klingers' party. It was near dusk, and the brightly colored lights danced in the gentle southerly breeze. Folks were already settled at the picnic tables, and judging by the volume of some of the voices, Roy had not been stingy with the beer. He paused on the fringe of the yard, looking for Kate.

And there she was, slim and elegant in a silky-looking outfit, her hair drawn up on the back of her head exposing that soft place at the nape of her neck where she tasted of flowers. With her long, graceful fingers, she was gesturing as if describing how a painting is born. Then she laughed, her head thrown back, her body arched in delight. Lord, she was beautiful. He swallowed the lump in his throat.

When he started across the lawn, Jenny left the chair in which she'd been sitting and approached him. "What are you doing here?" she asked, her eyes unforgiving.

"I was invited."

"You didn't have to come."

His good feelings evaporated. "You don't like me much, do you?"

"I don't know you well enough to make a judgment. All I know is you seem a little too interested in my mother."

"And that would be so terrible?"

"She's not available."

The message was clear. "At the risk of offending you further, I'd like to point out she doesn't need a keeper. She's perfectly capable of making her own decisions."

Jenny studied him impassively, then shrugged. "Time will tell," she said, then abruptly returned to her seat.

It was going to be harder to win Jenny over than he'd imagined. He reminded himself she was hurting—so many things were changing in her life. He couldn't blame her for lashing out. For needing Kate as her anchor. For resenting him.

"Dr. Sam, Dr. Sam!" He looked up. Hobbling toward him on her crutches was Amanda, looking like a particularly impish Orphan Annie. "See? I can do wheelies!" She pivoted on the crutches.

"Whoa, squirt. Not a great idea. You don't want to take another tumble, do you?"

"Nah, but if I have to be a cripple, I might as well learn some tricks."

He pointed his finger at her. "I imagine you know quite a few tricks."

"Yeah," she grinned, "like how to get my doctor to cut off his ponytail."

"Think you're gonna win that bet, do you?"

"My therapist says it's in the bag."

"I dunno. I'm not making an appointment at the barbershop just yet."

"You will. And don't forget, if I complete my therapy without complaining, I get to watch."

"It's a deal."

"Did Bart and Blake come last weekend?"

"Yes, but once we started water-skiing, they didn't want to do anything else."

"Wish I could go," she said wistfully.

"Want to trade a water-skiing trip for letting me keep the ponytail?"

"No way!"

He gave her a mock punch on the arm. "You're too smart for me. You knew all along I'd take you water-skiing anyway."

"Yeah. You're a pushover." And off she went, toward a girl with long dark hair who was playing with a kitten.

Great kid, he mused. Like his own. They'd had a good weekend together on the lake. Blake, however, had remained cautious, reserving his affection, as if he didn't want Sam to get any big ideas that he'd forgotten about Kate and the kiss. He sighed. Between Jenny and Blake, approval was hard to come by.

When he joined the group by the smoker, Charlene handed him a plate. "Get some food, and make yourself at home."

After he served himself, he looked around for a place to sit. "Over here, Sam," a deep voice bellowed.

Lucky for Sam he didn't drop his plate. Beckoning to him with a big smile was Mel Floyd. Beside him sat Nellie, her adoring expression focused directly on the retired doctor. And over their heads, seated with a group under a huge cottonwood tree was Kate, staring at him with surprise and...misgiving?

AROUND ELEVEN the party-goers began gathering up their folding chairs, collecting their tired children and heading for home. Most paused to wish Kate well, although she could read in their eyes that they hadn't a clue why she would leave Salt Flats for the dubious attractions of Santa Fe. It had been a great party, especially once she'd gotten over her self-consciousness. There'd been an abrupt moment of panic when she'd spotted Sam. Panic and something else. Fierce longing. But he'd been circumspect. Even though some, like Ethel and Berta, had sent searching looks at both of them throughout the evening, they would carry home not so much as a shred of confirmation of their suspicions, for which Kate was immensely grateful.

"Don't you go all bohemian on us, now," Charlene said when Kate thanked her for the party.

"Fat chance!" Kate laughed and hugged her good friend. "I'll be lucky if Lupe Santiago doesn't send me packing after the first day."

Charlene drew back, holding her at arm's length. "Will you quit that! For once, believe in yourself. I do!"

Charlene was a generous friend, and Kate appreciated her encouragement. ''I know,'' she whispered, hugging Charlene again. ''You're the best!''

Charlene shooed her toward her car. ''Go now. And don't forget to bring me those turquoise earrings you promised.''

Kate turned away, walking slowly beneath the Chinese lanterns toward her car, parked beside an ancient lilac bush. She was reaching for the door, when she heard a low voice from the direction of the fence bordering the bush. ''Kate?''

She stopped, the blood pounding in her head. ''Sam?''

He stepped forward, his dark pants and black golf shirt camouflaging him in the darkness. ''It's my turn.'' He came even closer. ''To wish you well.''

''But—''

His lips lowered to hers and he seared her mouth with all the fire she'd been trying so hard to forget. She jerked away. ''Sam, don't. What are you doing here anyway?''

In the moonlight she could see the pain in his eyes. But then he shifted gears, grinning cockily. ''I couldn't very well turn down my first Salt Flats social invitation, could I?''

''I don't mean what you're doing at the party. I mean,'' she gestured at the car, the bush, the ground, *''here.''*

''Giving you one last thing to think about while you're gone.''

One hand ran up and down her bare arm. Her flesh burned under his touch. She shuddered. ''I have to go,'' she whispered urgently.

''I know, love. But, remember. I'll be waiting. As

long as it takes.'' With that, he gathered her in his arms and kissed her again—expertly. Her hands just naturally seemed to find his shoulders, his back, his waist. She wanted to take his strength, his warmth, the feel of him with her on her journey. To remember his eyes fastened on her, his fingers arousing her, his breath mingled with hers. This wasn't sensible. This wasn't Kate.

His lips had just left hers, his eyes compelling her to look at him, when she heard words that froze the blood pulsing through her body.

"*Mo-ther,* how could you!"

CHAPTER TWELVE

JENNY STOOD stock-still, her heart racing, far-off voices indistinguishable in the haze of her anger. Her senses narrowed on her mother's startled eyes, on Sam Gray's arm encircling her mother's shoulders, on the awful image still crowding her brain. For a long moment, she thought she was going to be sick. That was no friendly farewell kiss she had just witnessed.

Recoiling, she covered her mouth, wheeled and ran down the Klingers' long driveway. Even though she didn't turn around to look, she knew her mother was following when she heard Kate call, "Jenny, please, wait!"

Please what? Wait to hear a plea for understanding? Wait to be told her mother was in love with another man, one young enough to have kids still in grade school? Jenny kept running, finally cutting through a field and flopping, exhausted, onto a weathered wooden hay trailer. Her sides aching, she drew in deep, ragged breaths, fatalistically anticipating her mother's arrival.

"Jenny." Kate, winded, her arms wrapped around her waist, walked the last few steps toward her. "It's not what you think."

"Oh?" This was going to be rich. "And what do I think?"

"I—I suppose that..." Her mother seemed at a loss

for words. "I don't know, I suppose you think I lied when I told you it was over with Sam."

Jenny's lips thinned. "Uh, yeah."

"Sam was just saying goodbye."

"Right."

"I didn't intend for it to happen."

"It looked pretty meaningful to me." Jenny's stomach lurched again. "I know the difference between friendship and lust."

"Lust?" Kate looked shocked.

"Do you like 'passion' better?" Jenny pulled her knees to her chest. "Mom, that was disgusting."

With a sigh of resignation, Kate leaned on the trailer. "Okay. I can understand how it must have looked to you. How painful it was to see me in another man's arms." She hesitated, then looked directly at Jenny. "But he's a fine man, Jenny. I can't just turn off what I'm feeling for him. But I'm trying."

"Not very hard, it appears." Jenny wanted desperately to clap her hands over her ears and shut out her mother's voice. All she could think of was how her father had always called the three of them "his girls," how he'd enlisted his daughters' help to find Kate just the perfect Christmas gift, how he'd smelled of grain and grass and spring wind. She blinked back tears.

"I don't want to leave when you're feeling this way."

"I'll get over it," Jenny said, even though she doubted it. "Besides, maybe you'll meet someone else in Santa Fe." It was a cheap shot, but she was beyond caring.

"I'm not looking for anyone. And I haven't been. Sometimes life just happens."

"Tell me about it." Jenny couldn't keep the edge out of her voice.

"Is there anything I can say to make things better between us?"

Jenny balled her fists, determined not to cry. "Yes. Goodbye." She swallowed the lump in her throat. "Maybe you'll come to your senses in Santa Fe."

"Oh, Jenny. Please, let's not leave things like this." Her mother reached out her hand, but Jenny couldn't break through the steel bands of her hurt to accept it.

"You were the one in the big clinch. Not me."

Kate straightened and looked long and hard at her. "I love you, and I'm sorry I've disappointed you. But this is my life we're talking about, and I'm the one who has to decide how to live it. I hope someday you'll understand." She hesitated as if hoping Jenny would respond.

After a few moments during which Jenny said nothing, her mother spoke quietly, "That's it, then. I'll be in touch." She laid a hand tentatively on Jenny's knee. "Take care of yourself, honey." Then she walked away.

Moonlight silvered the fields and a canopy of stars twinkled overhead, but Jenny saw only the vast empty space growing between her and her retreating mother.

SAM HAD WATCHED helplessly as Kate ran after Jenny, knowing full well there was nothing he could do. He didn't imagine either of the women needed his interference, nor did he think anything he might say would make a difference. It was unfortunate Jenny had appeared when she did. Damn. He'd only made things more complicated for Kate. But despite his concern, he couldn't regret the kiss, nor Kate's ardent response.

Leaning against her car, he ground his heels into the dirt and waited.

Then he saw Kate, walking slowly up the driveway. Her hands were thrust inside the pockets of her slacks, her shoulders drooped and her head was downcast. Forlorn. That was the word that came to him. His heart sank. He wanted to go to her, but he sensed she needed time and, in fact, was pacing her return.

She stopped a few feet from him and raised her eyes, raw with hurt. He shoved off the car and approached her. Before he could speak, she held up her palm. "Sam, please. Don't say anything. It would be more than I can bear."

"It didn't go well, then?"

She shook her head. "I don't know if she'll ever forgive me."

He took another step toward her. "It isn't a matter of forgiveness. What you—*we*—did was the most natural thing in the world."

"Not to her."

Venturing the last step, he tilted her chin. "I'm sure our kiss *was* upsetting to Jenny. She's emotionally devastated right now. Her whole life has turned upside down. But has it occurred to you she needs to lash out at someone? Someone who's safe?"

"Me?" Kate said in a small voice.

"Who safer? She wants to control what's left of her world." He grinned wryly. "Unfortunately, she's not allowing for changes in others. Our relationship has to be hurtful and confusing to her. But give her time."

"Are you always this insightful, Doctor?"

"I try to be. Especially where you're concerned."

"Oh, Sam. It's all too much. Please don't press me."

"I won't. You have all the time in the world."

"That doesn't seem fair."

He fingered a strand of her hair. "It's not a matter of 'fair.' I know what I want, Kate. You. And I'm willing to be patient."

She ducked her head. "I need to go home."

"It's all right. I'm not going to try to kiss you again."

She peeked through her lashes. "You're not?"

"No. I've done enough damage for one night."

She looked up at him, her face a plea for understanding. "Thank you. I-I'll see you when I get back."

"I'm counting on it." He assisted her into her car, then before succumbing to the temptation to kiss her after all, he swung around and headed for his own vehicle.

THE STRAIGHT TWO-LANE HIGHWAY through the desolate country of western Oklahoma and the Panhandle of Texas gave Kate plenty of time the next day to think. About Sam. About her own lack of willpower. And especially about Jenny, whose frosty, wounded eyes had haunted her all the way from Salt Flats. She acknowledged that Sam had a point—Jenny needed to lash out. But she didn't need her mother to hand her the whip.

Kate tossed and turned that night in her Amarillo motel bed and awakened with a bad case of jitters, which two cups of coffee did nothing to alleviate. In addition to her other concerns, she was only hours away from Santa Fe and the judgment of Lupe Santiago and the other workshop participants, who undoubtedly were years younger and infinitely more gifted. When she crossed the New Mexico state line, butterflies took up residence in her stomach and multiplied with each passing mile. She couldn't remember when she'd ever felt

more unsure of herself. In the trunk was the painting of
Ed, mute testimony to the fact she lacked talent. Icy
with trepidation, she managed to navigate through Santa
Fe and northeast into the mountains where the studio
was located.

A small cedar sign at the side of the highway directed
her up a winding gravel road that rose steadily between
scrubby trees, yucca and rocky outcroppings. Finally,
the road widened and before her she saw a two-story
log building with a veranda running the entire length of
the house. With panic, she also noted cars bearing several different out-of-state plates, parked off to the right.
A welcome flag fluttered from the porch overhang. Several people stood on the veranda, as if awaiting her
arrival. Kate gulped. There was no turning back.

She parked and had just started unloading her lug-
gage, when a beaming man with lovely silver hair
headed toward her. ''Welcome to Casa Santiago.'' He
extended his hand. ''I'm Eugenio Santiago, Lupe's husband.'' After Kate introduced herself, he took her bags
and escorted her toward the house. ''We are most happy
to have you here.''

''And I to be here.''

As they neared the veranda, a tiny, vibrant-looking
woman wearing jeans, a concho belt and a faded denim
shirt approached them. Her salt-and-pepper hair, which
reached nearly to her waist, was drawn back and held
in place by a leather thong. But it was her remarkable
dark eyes that arrested Kate. In their depths were enthusiasm, warmth, life. ''I am Lupe. You must be our
Kate Manley, no?''

''How did you—?''

''Easy. You are the last to arrive.'' She laughed,
looking at Kate with approval. ''But by no means the

least.'' With that she hooked her arm through Kate's.
''Do not be afraid, little one. I am not a tigress. You
are exactly where you are supposed to be.''

Kate couldn't find her voice. She'd never met the
woman, yet Lupe read her easily. Amazingly, Kate
found herself relaxing. Lupe was right. She *was* supposed to be here.

NELLIE LOOKED DIFFERENT. Studying her as she stood
framed by his office door, Sam couldn't for the life of
him figure out what had changed. She waited, the hint
of a grin causing her lips to twitch. Finally she spoke.
''What do you think?''

A loaded question if he ever heard one. He opted for
''Nice.''

''Mel, er, Dr. Floyd, hasn't seen me yet.'' She looked
somewhat more anxious. ''Do you think he'll like it?''

''I'm sure he will,'' Sam ventured, still at sea.

''You know what they say. 'Blondes have more
fun.'''

He looked again. The tight curls were more relaxed
and the color was definitely more…youthful. Even her
skin looked…peachier. Was that a word? He was
speechless, but finally managed another ''Nice.''

''Thank you.'' She came into the room and laid the
charts for the day's patients on his desk. ''I know we're
not officially open yet, but Lester's waiting outside.''
In a return to the old Nellie, she said, ''He doesn't have
an appointment you know.''

''It won't take long. Send him in.'' When she turned
to leave, he added, ''And, Nellie, would you mind
changing that Burt Bacharach CD you've had in the
system for days now?''

She shot him a chiding look, but said nothing, and

before Lester arrived, the equally saccharine strains of the Mystic Moods Orchestra floated down from the overhead speakers.

A knock on the door was followed by Lester's voice. "It's me, Lester. Gotta see you, Doc."

Sam rose, opened the door and greeted Lester. "Have a seat. What can I do for you today?"

"Don't need to sit." Lester stood pigeon-toed, rotating his greasy ball cap between his fingers. "Just wanna warn you 'bout Aunt Julia." He looked at Sam, his eyes wide. "She's mad at you."

"I know."

"She told me I'm not s'posed to see you again. You cause trouble she says." Lester clapped the hat on his head. "But I told her Lester's a man. She can't tell him what to do."

"That's true. You are a man. But you need your aunt. She gives you a home. And you need a home, right?"

Lester nodded, his hangdog expression indicating a lack of enthusiasm.

"Your aunt is upset with me because I wanted both of you to get some help. You don't need to go on thinking you had anything to do with your parents' deaths."

"That's what that man said I talked to at the group home."

"And your aunt doesn't need to be afraid anymore."

Lester looked startled. "Aunt Julia? She's never afraid of anything."

Sam put a hand on Lester's shoulder. "Don't be too sure, Lester. We're all afraid of something."

"Not you!"

"Yes, me."

"What?" Lester stuck his chin out.

"Making mistakes, same as everybody."

"You don't make no mistakes, Doc."

"We all do, my friend. We all do."

"But you're not afraid of Aunt Julia?"

"No. Don't worry about that."

Lester smiled, revealing his scraggly yellow teeth. "Okay." He looked around as if suddenly uncomfortable in the professional setting. "Gotta go, now."

"Okay. I'll see you soon, Lester."

After Lester left, Sam shook his head in bewilderment. Such a good, simple soul to have suffered such injustices at the hands of his aunt and the intolerant of the town.

After he'd seen all his patients, Sam sat in his office trying to read a medical journal. The day had passed quickly, for which he was grateful, but it was the nights that were interminable since Kate left. Then he had too much time to miss her. Too much time to question whether she would come around as he had convinced himself she must. Too much time to think about Jenny. Without her acceptance, he had concluded his battle would be all uphill. The boys were coming this weekend and that, at least, was something to look forward to.

But then there was Blake. Another challenge. Sam tapped the magazine impatiently against the desk. That last evening with Kate, he'd felt confident. Now questions assaulted him from every side.

When the phone rang at his elbow, he was startled out of his reverie. The caller identified herself as Mary Davis, the 4-H leader whom Lester had helped with the Fourth of July parade float. She surprised him by saying the youngsters had spent their last meeting discussing their erroneous judgment of Lester. Now they were looking for a way to make amends. Hesitantly, Mrs.

Davis offered their suggestion. Sam couldn't stop the grin that split his face. "Help you? I'd be delighted. And you know what? I think your plan just might work."

PARKER SPLASHED HAPPILY in the plastic wading pool set up in the Manleys' backyard. Jean and Jenny sat in webbed lawn chairs alongside the pool shelling peas. Every now and then Jenny reached down to retrieve one of the toy boats Parker had thrown over the side. It was late afternoon, but the temperature still sat at 95 degrees.

Jean set her pan on a chairside metal table and rubbed her knuckles. "Have you talked with your mother yet?"

Jenny continued shelling peas without looking up. "No," she said, hoping Grandma would let the subject die, but knowing she wouldn't.

"Is there a reason for that? She's been gone five days."

"I haven't been here when she's called."

"And you can't pick up a telephone?" Grandma's voice was neutral, but Jenny felt trapped.

"You may as well know. We didn't part on the best of terms."

Jean picked up her bowl of peas and started shelling again. "I guessed as much. Care to say why?"

Jenny longed to escape, but she also knew she desperately needed to confide in someone. "It's about Sam Gray."

"You told me you thought the trip to Santa Fe would take care of that."

"That was before."

Her grandmother's eyebrows rose. "Before what?"

"The Klingers' party."

"Why don't you tell me what happened?"

Jenny considered her words. She didn't want to hurt Grandma or Grandpa nor did she want to be disloyal to her mother, but, damn it, somebody had to do something about Sam Gray. "I caught them kissing."

"She's an attractive woman," Grandma said evenly.

"Yes, but she loved Daddy. And he was crazy about her. It doesn't make any sense for her to make goo-goo eyes at another man."

"'Goo-goo eyes'? Is that what you think your mother's doing?"

"At the very least."

"So who is it you're upset with? Dr. Gray or Kate?"

"Both of them," she said. "I mean she's a respectable widow, not some restless woman on the make. And he's almost young enough for me to date, for Pete's sake."

Grandma laid a hand on her arm. "When you live as long as I have, you learn some things are beyond anyone's control."

"Like what?"

"Attraction." Her grandmother closed her eyes, then opened them before going on. "I don't like to think about Kate with another man. After all, my son adored her. I know she loved him, too. But…"

Jenny's heart sank at the word. She didn't want to hear what was coming.

"But your mother is a young woman, Jenny. Even though forty-two may sound ancient to you, she's in her prime. I've been thinking a lot about this in the past several days. Ask yourself whether your father would want your mother to be alone for the rest of her life. Ed was a generous man. I don't think that's what he'd wish for her." She paused, watching while Parker put his head in the water and blew noisy bubbles. "I don't know about Dr. Gray, whether he's right for her or not. But I've come to the conclusion that's up to the two of them. Not to you and me."

"But, Grandma—"

"Stop it, honey. You're working yourself up about something that may never happen. In the meantime, why don't you try putting yourself in your mother's shoes? When I did that, it helped me see things in a totally different light. It's only fair."

It was useless to argue. Jenny felt even more miserable than she had before talking with her grandmother. It was as if her whole thought process was distorted. Surely she wasn't the only one out of step. But it sure felt like it. "Thanks." Jenny stood and scooped a dripping Parker from the pool. "I need to get him into his pajamas. I'll finish the peas later."

With that, she fled the backyard and the sad, knowing look on her grandmother's face.

"I WAS HOPIN'" we could go water-skiing again today," Bart said Sunday after lunch as he stood at the living room window watching the trees sway in the wind.

"Too gusty, son," Sam said, silently wondering what new entertainment he could dream up.

"Maybe we could go fishing," Blake suggested from the sofa where he sat channel surfing.

"Too windy for that, too. But we might go to the park and shoot some hoops."

Bart shrugged, and Blake brightened. "I guess that'd be okay."

Fortunately the wind had calmed some by the time they reached the park. Two tennis courts with weeds sprouting between the cracks in the concrete boasted basketball goals. Between the courts and the playground area at the far end were picnic tables, a goldfish pond and a band shell. Several families picnicked, their tablecloths weighted down by mustard and pickle jars.

Sam had his work cut out for him in the two-on-one game. The boys seemed to communicate by special telepathy and kept him on the run. He was amazed how they'd improved since last winter.

Flushed and happy, Bart and Blake had finally had enough. Sam glanced at his watch. They'd have to leave for Enid within the hour. "Ready, guys?"

"Can't we climb on the monkey bars first?" Bart asked.

Sam smiled. "Sure."

The boys dashed on ahead. Walking among the picnic tables toward the playground, Sam was hailed by Ethel Portman. "Those your boys?"

"Yes."

"Cute," she said, then turned to introduce him to her husband Toad and her niece and family visiting from Tulsa. By the time Sam tore himself away, Bart and Blake were waving triumphantly from the top of the jungle gym. Several parents and small children clustered at the swings, merry-go-round and seesaws. He was just passing the slide when he became aware that at the top sat Jenny with Parker wedged between her legs. When she spotted him, she looked away and shoved down the slide, Parker laughing delightedly.

He waited. When she stood at the bottom, clutching Parker's hand, he moved closer. "Hello, Jenny."

"Dr. Gray," she acknowledged with a chill in her voice.

"I don't suppose you're pleased to see me."

"It's a public place."

"I'd like the opportunity sometime to talk with you about Kate."

"That won't be necessary."

He bit his lip. She wasn't making this easy. "I care about her. I wouldn't hurt her for anything."

"I would certainly hope not." She looked down at Parker, who was tugging at her hand.

Just then Bart and Blake ran up. "Hi, kid," Blake said hunkering down and addressing Parker, who smiled adoringly at the "big boy."

"Blake and Bart, this is Mrs. Manley's daughter Jenny and her son Parker."

Bart mumbled a "hello," then Blake stood up and echoed the greeting.

"Nice to meet you," Jenny said, then abruptly added, "Parker wants to swing, so we'll be off now."

Bart screwed up his face, then blurted out, "Wait! I gotta figure this out. If you're Mrs. Manley's daughter, then—" He frowned in concentration.

Groaning inwardly, Sam completed his deduction. "—this little guy is her grandson."

Blake stared at Sam with disgust.

"Yeah," Bart concluded, "Mrs. Manley's old then, isn't she, Dad?"

Over the boys' head, Sam caught Jenny's I-told-you-so look. "You don't have to be old to be a grandmother, son. Kate isn't."

"I guess," Blake mumbled, studying the toe of his sneakers. "But still." Finally he looked up at Sam. "Dad, I don't get it. Why would you wanna kiss a grandma?"

Jenny gasped, turned on her heel and started toward the swings. Suddenly the sole of her sandal caught on an exposed tree root and she fell flat. Sam ran toward her and picked her up by the elbows. The boys knelt beside a wailing Parker, soothing him. Red-faced, Jenny hobbled toward a nearby bench, supported by Sam. "Are you okay?"

She wiggled her foot. "Yeah, my ankle's fine. And the skinned knee isn't too bad."

Kneeling in front of her, Sam cradled her foot and rotated it in his hand. "Seems all right. A little alcohol will take care of the knee." He stood. "I'm sorry, Jenny. About the fall. And about what the boys said."

She looked up, unsmiling. "Apparently I'm not the only one who's seen something no one was intended to see."

"There's much more to it, Jenny."

"I'll just bet there is."

"Don't make it sound like something ugly. Please."

"Isn't it?"

He didn't know when he'd felt so helpless. "No. It's special. And you may as well know, I'd like to make it permanent." Her expression should have stopped him, but he hurtled on, "Your mother loved your father very much. I've never doubted that. But I'm hoping her heart is big enough for two men in her life. And that yours is, too." He held his breath, waiting for her reply.

"We'll see," was all she said.

"Dr. Gray, Dr. Gray!" Ethel Portman was bearing down on them. "I wanted to meet your boys." She arrived, breathless, and presented a huge sugar cookie to Parker and each of the twins. "Why, I declare, aren't they precious?"

Bart puckered his mouth as if he'd sucked a lemon. Sam gave the boys a warning look. Politely, they responded to the introductions and thanked her for the cookie. Then Ethel stood back and beamed approvingly at Sam and Jenny. "I'm so pleased to see the two of you together. I was just telling my niece what a handsome couple you make." She batted her eyes, then waggled her fingers. "I need to get back to my group now. But I'm so thrilled I saw you. Why, you look like a regular little family."

Jenny's look could have fried ice cream and Sam felt a tectonic shift in the area of his stomach. He didn't even want to think about what else could go wrong.

CHAPTER THIRTEEN

THE WARM MORNING SUN streaming through the high clerestory windows in the studio and the dry mountain air, aromatic with sage, filled Kate with contentment. Around her, working at individual easels, were eleven other students, now friends, ranging from nineteen to seventy-seven with talents as diverse as their ages and backgrounds. From that very first evening over a week ago when they'd shared their stories around the huge refectory table in the dining room, Kate had felt at home, thriving on the talk of fellow artists, grateful for a respite from her artistic isolation.

Lupe, as colorful as a tropical bird in a hand-dyed jade skirt and a gold peasant blouse, moved among them, her body language as expressive as her snapping eyes. Pausing at the easel of the workshop's youngest participant, she said, "Ellen, the space—it is all yours. Don't be afraid to use it."

Kate experienced a momentary sense of panic when Lupe moved, then, to examine her rendering of one of the Navajo women selling jewelry in the open-air market. Palette suspended in her hand, Kate waited apprehensively, as Lupe stood back, her fist under her chin. "The shadows are good—alive but subtle. Where, though, is going to be the color, the vibrancy?"

Using her palette knife, Kate pointed to the seated figure. "The woman."

"Ah, yes. The woman. But what is it about the woman? Think. Who is she? Who are you creating her to be?" Lupe started forward, patting Kate on the shoulder. "When you decide, splash your color, your light."

Looking at the painting, Kate recognized the focal point—the woman's hands. Feverishly, she bent to her work. Almost unconsciously, she mulled over Lupe's question. "Who are you creating her to be?" With a start, Kate realized she could ask the same of herself. Who was she in the process of becoming? Did she dare splash her life with color?

Her thoughts turned to Jenny and the recent phone call she'd had from her. Nothing had been mentioned about that last awful scene between them. Her daughter had confined her remarks to Parker's antics, local gossip and her job search. The conversation was pleasant enough although, under the guise of freeing Kate to focus on the workshop, Jenny had suggested they talk further only in case of emergency. Sometimes, absorbed as she was in the workshop, Kate could almost forget about Salt Flats and the decisions she would soon be forced to make. Almost, but not quite.

The first day of class here, Lupe had asked another important question. "Where," she had said, "is the source of your light?" Of course, she was talking about painting. But when Kate contemplated the source of her own light, of the "color" in her life, she was left with one inescapable answer. Sam.

SAM STARED at his coffee mug, oblivious to the sounds of conversation echoing around him in the Main Street Café. Kate had been gone nearly two weeks and he had no idea how he would endure two more. It took every ounce of will to keep from writing her or picking up the phone. His gallant gesture of giving her time apart may have been the most foolish decision he'd ever made. Certainly it was one of the loneliest.

Millie set down his bowl of oatmeal with a clatter. "You look glum, Doc. Your girl stand you up?"

He roused himself. "Girl? You know I don't have a girl."

She crossed one foot over the other and leaned both hands on the table. "That's not what I heard?"

He went on alert. "Oh?"

"Yeah, folks're sayin' what a swell-looking couple you two make."

"What the heck are you talking about?"

She straightened, a triumphant look on her face. "Why, you and Jenny Lanagan, of course." Before he could offer a protest, she sashayed toward the serving counter.

But what was there to protest? The truth had never stood in the way of a good story in this burg. He nursed his coffee until Mary Davis, the 4-H leader, and her husband arrived for the meeting they'd arranged earlier in the week.

Mary introduced her husband Joe, the business teacher at the high school. After the men shook hands, Mary got right to the point. "If you can work it out with social services and we can find a vacant building, I think, with Joe's help, the kids can set Lester up in business."

"Each year," Joe explained, "we have a school project aimed at giving the students a hands-on experience with private enterprise. Many of Mary's 4-H members are in my classes. If Lester can repair the engines and appliances, the youngsters could handle the bookkeeping, advertising and that kind of thing. He'd have a regular business, and we'd follow through each year."

"It sounds great," Sam said. "Lester needs people to believe in him and support him. I'll talk to Lola Fletcher and get back to you." He swigged the last of his coffee, then politely excused himself.

When he arrived at the clinic, he cornered Nellie. "Give me the straight scoop. Have you heard any rumors about me lately?"

"Would those be the ones about your, uh, interesting hairstyle, the ones about you and Kate Manley, or the ones about you and Jenny Lanagan?"

Sam groaned. "So Millie didn't make it up, then?"

"Doubtful. She was just passing on the latest." She eyed him speculatively. "Any truth in that last one?"

"None." He leaned back against the wall. "Where do people get these ideas, anyway?"

"Beats me," Nellie said, moving around him to pick up an armful of charts, which she thrust at him.

He took the charts and, shaking his head, moved toward his office. No sooner had he arrived than Nellie put a call through to him from Amanda Klinger. "Are you ready to pay up?" she asked in an excited voice.

"Is it time already?" He grinned, anticipating her answer.

"Bailey discharged me yesterday. No more physiotherapy, except the exercises I have to do at home."

"You're sure you didn't whine or complain?"

She snorted. "Not once. Ask Bailey."

"Okay, okay, I believe you. When do you want to meet?"

"Noon today at the barbershop." She giggled. "This is gonna be *so* fun!"

"For you, maybe."

"Don't you dare chicken out, Dr. Sam."

He dangled the phone from his ear. "Twelve o'clock. I'll be there."

At least one topic of gossip would be put to rest. About the others? He hoped to God Kate didn't get wind of the ridiculous notion that he was seeing Jenny socially, but he had no doubt, if given the occasion, Jenny would nip that one in the bud, big time.

SAM'S STEPS SLOWED as he approached the barbershop. What the heck was going on? The place was as crowded as he'd ever seen it. Amanda stood outside next to the barber pole, a huge grin lighting up her face. "Ready?"

He nodded toward the interior where Toad, Ethel, Berta, Charlene, Roy, Lester, Mel and several others waited. "Looks like there are a few customers ahead of me."

Amanda took him by the elbow. "Them? They're the audience," she said triumphantly.

Audience? Why, that little rascal. She'd set him up. "Whoa, we didn't talk about this."

She started forward. "C'mon, Dr. Sam. You promised."

He was greeted with hoots, catcalls and scattered applause. Lou Carney, the barber, with scissors in one hand and comb in the other, stood poised like an athlete ready for the starting whistle.

"What do you s'pose he really looks like?"

"Scalp him, Lou."

"'Bout time he got rid of that hippie do."

Amanda shoved him down into the chair. Just before Floyd administered the first ceremonial snip, Lester shuffled forward and whispered in Sam's ear. "Don't worry, Doc. It don't hurt none."

As Lou bent to his work, Sam looked around at the friendly, smiling faces, and for the first time since moving to Salt Flats had the distinct impression that he was starting to belong.

AFTER A FUSSY SPELL, Parker had finally fallen asleep. Jenny hoped he wasn't coming down with something. They'd been to the city pool that afternoon, and he was probably just tired and maybe had had too much sun. At the pool a group of her girlfriends had invited her to go to Enid with them and their husbands for dinner and a movie, but she wasn't ready yet to be with couples. Besides they all seemed inordinately curious about her reaction to the news of Sam Gray's haircut. Jeez, didn't these people have anything else to think about?

She sure did. Several days ago Todd had finally called, but only to give her the name of his attorney and to discuss a possible interim financial arrangement. He'd politely inquired about Parker, but had mentioned nothing about visitation.

And, besides all that, she had something else weighing on her mind. Grandma's words, which wouldn't stay buried. About putting herself in her mother's shoes. If Mom wanted a new life, did that necessarily mean she was betraying Dad? Was it selfish of Jenny to stand between Sam Gray and her mother? Worse yet, was she letting her own unhappiness color her perceptions of her mother? Bottom line, was she acting like a child instead of an adult?

If Grandma believed her dad wouldn't have wished a lifetime of loneliness on her mother, why couldn't she? It was up to her mother and Sam to figure it out, Grandma had concluded. Jenny sighed. But she wasn't making it easy, was she? And, somehow, the way she'd been acting toward her mother didn't feel good. It didn't feel good at all.

She wandered into the kitchen, fixed herself a glass of iced tea and decided to join Grandpa and Grandma on the front porch, where they sat every evening after dinner, temperature permitting. Passing through the darkened living room, Jenny paused, picking up an unaccustomed scolding tone in her grandmother's voice. She knew she shouldn't be eavesdropping, but she couldn't help herself when she heard Grandma say, "I know you don't like it, Paul. I'm not sure I do. But Ed's dead. Kate was a good wife. She's a fine mother and we couldn't ask for a better daughter-in-law. She deserves a chance for happiness."

The creaking of her grandfather's rocking chair ceased abruptly. "You women with your heads full of romance."

Patiently Jean continued, "It's about much more than romance. It's about companionship, security, belonging to someone."

"But she loved Ed," Paul insisted stubbornly.

"Of course she did. But she can love again. She needs to love again. We can't stand in the way of her happiness. Not you, not me, not Jenny, not Rachel. Kate's too precious to us."

Jenny set the iced tea down on a table and clasped her cold hands together.

Her grandmother's voice rose. "Paul, you need to move on. We all do." Jenny heard her grandmother stand. "Anything else is pure selfishness."

The word pierced Jenny. *Selfishness.* Sudden tears started in her eyes. She loved her mother, but she certainly hadn't been demonstrating that lately. In fact, she'd been downright self-absorbed. Damn. She swiped at her eyes before Grandma came into the room.

Now she had even more to think about. Because, in her heart, she knew her grandmother was right. Her mother deserved a chance for happiness.

THE NEXT EVENING, a balmy Saturday, Jean and Paul Manley went to Enid for their monthly ballroom dance club outing, leaving the house to Jenny and Parker. The baby fussed just as he had the previous night, and Jenny tried everything she knew to do—rocking, bathing, walking. But still he fretted. Finally she carried him to his bed, praying he would soon drop off. She'd taken his temperature earlier in the evening. Somewhat elevated, but not dangerously so. If he wasn't better in the morning, she'd be forced to call Dr. Gray.

One ear cocked for Parker, she undressed and slipped on a shorty gown and robe. She'd just finished brushing her teeth, when hair rose on the back of her neck. Something was wrong. Dropping the toothbrush in the sink, she dashed into Parker's room. He was lying on his back jerking and writhing. His eyes were rolled back in his head, and his skin was a terrifying shade of blue. Panic ballooned in Jenny's brain, and for a moment she couldn't think. When she picked him up, his skin was on fire and his seizures continued. Desperate, she ran to the phone and, with shaking fingers, located Dr. Gray's after-hours number in the directory. Fortunately, he answered on the second ring.

Cold, paralyzing fear made it hard for her to speak. "This is Jenny Lanagan. It's Parker. He's burning up and shaking. Oh, God, I can't get him to stop!"

"Are you at your grandparents'?"

"Yes. Help me. What should I do?" She could hardly think for Parker quaking in her arms.

"I'll be right there."

"Oh, thank you. But hurry! Please!" Numb, she listened as he succinctly told her that Parker was probably having a febrile convulsion and advised her what to do.

After she hung up, she tried desperately to follow his suggestions, grateful beyond belief that he would be here soon. She laid Parker on her bed, unbuttoning his pajamas and then gently turning him on his side. Minutes that seemed like hours dragged by, and still he twitched spasmodically, seemingly unconscious. How long had it been? Five minutes? Ten? What if she was losing her baby?

Finally, just as she heard a car turn in the driveway, the spasms stopped. Jenny sagged with relief. Parker's crying was a welcome sound, and he appeared to be breathing normally again.

As Sam had instructed her, she removed the child's pajamas, dampened a towel, and wrapped him in it, cradling him as she carried him downstairs and answered the door. She'd never been so glad to see anyone in her life, and when Sam stepped into the living room, she couldn't help it. She burst into tears.

"It's okay, Jenny." He laid a palm on Parker's forehead, then patted her shoulder. "Relax. The worst is over." He led her to a chair and helped her sit down. When she looked up at him through misty eyes, she could find no hint of impatience or resentment. "What you just witnessed looks very scary, but febrile convulsions are quite common. Parker spiked a fever. Now we need to discover what caused it. Why don't you cuddle the little guy for a few minutes? He's had a rough time. Then I'll look him over."

When Parker's cries reduced to whimpers, Sam took the toddler from her and laid him on the sofa. From his bag, he extracted his instruments and proceeded to examine him.

Jenny couldn't sit still. She rose and peered over Sam's shoulder. "What do you think?"

Sam looked up from the thermometer he'd just pulled from Parker's ear. "He's going to be fine." His calm words eased the tightness in Jenny's chest. "I'll write a prescription, but for now, you need to keep him cool and bring this fever down. I don't think it's his throat or ears. My best guess is a urinary infection. Bring him into the office Monday morning and we'll take another look." He took out a pad and pen. "Meanwhile, here are some instructions." When he finished writing, he said, "Parker should drop off to sleep pretty soon. That was quite a jolt to his system."

"I was so scared." She clasped her still-trembling hands.

"Of course you were." Sam wrapped Parker in the towel and handed him back to Jenny, who sank gratefully into the rocking chair. Sam moved across the room and flicked a switch. "This ceiling fan should help keep him cool." Then he perched against the edge of the library table, his arms folded across his chest, looking down at Jenny and Parker. "Now, Jenny, how about you? Are *you* okay?"

She saw the concern in his deep blue eyes and felt her body flood with warmth. He cared about Parker. He cared about her. "My heart rate's about to return to normal, I think. I didn't know it was possible to feel such panic."

"But you kept your head and handled the situation very well."

In a small voice, she made a painful admission. "I don't know what I'd have done without you."

"You'd have managed." He smiled reassuringly. "The main thing is, your son is going to be all right."

Jenny studied Parker, whose long blond lashes fluttered against his now-rosy cheeks. "I love him so much," she said quietly.

"That's obvious. He's lucky to have you for a mother."

Jenny ran her hand tenderly over her son's curls. "He's what keeps me going."

"You've had some rough times lately, haven't you?" Sam's expression was somber.

She bit her lip, fighting tears. "Yes."

"And I haven't helped."

She looked up. "What do you mean?"

"The way I feel about Kate." He cleared his throat as if unsure how to proceed. "You loved your father. It must hurt, you know, thinking about Kate and me. Together."

She managed a nod, knowing that if she spoke she would break down again.

"All I can tell you, Jenny, is that I love your mother. With all my heart. I didn't set out to make things difficult for you or your sister or the Manleys. I owe you the truth." He leaned forward, his expression earnest. "From the first night I saw Kate in the library, something special happened. It's as if, with her, I've come home. I've told her how I feel." He paused again. "Now, it's up to her."

Parker's even breathing, the distant meowing of the neighbor's cat, the ticking of the grandfather clock seemed amplified in Jenny's ears. It was no longer conjecture—Sam Gray loved her mother. And in her heart,

Jenny knew something else. Her mother loved him. "And to the rest of us, I suppose." Jenny shifted Parker to her shoulder. "I guess I've been pretty selfish."

"Don't be too hard on yourself. The idea of your mother and me must've been a shock. But I can tell you this. I would never do anything to hurt Kate."

Jenny thought about what he'd said. He'd made no attempt to win her over. Instead, he'd spoken from the heart. "I believe you."

"I'm glad." He hesitated. "And relieved." He stooped to pick up his bag. "I'll see you and Parker at the clinic Monday morning. Between now and then, if you get worried, call me immediately."

Jenny stood carefully so as not to disturb her sleeping son. "Thank you, Doctor."

"How about 'Sam?'"

Smiling tentatively, she echoed the word. "Sam." At the door, she turned to him. "Thank you for coming tonight. I'll never forget what a help you were."

With two fingers to his forehead, he acknowledged her thanks. "It's what I do."

"That's why you're special." The words just popped out. Hearing them voiced, she came to an important realization. He was no longer the enemy.

"Good night," he said, turning to walk toward his car.

A bubble of relief made her feel twenty pounds lighter, and just as he reached his vehicle, she went out onto the front porch and called after him, "Hey, Sam, I forgot to tell you. That's a cool haircut!"

He paused, his hand on the door handle, then laughed, a warm hearty sound in the stillness. "Makes me almost presentable, huh?"

She waved in acknowledgment, then as he drove off,

stood barefoot on the porch, feeling better than she'd felt in a long, long time, totally unaware of the car slowing almost to a stop in front of the house.

MONDAY MORNING HAD BEEN HECTIC for Sam—two emergencies and a waiting room full of patients. He'd already seen Parker Lanagan and his suspicion had been confirmed—an easily treatable urinary infection. Best of all, Jenny had been genuinely open and friendly.

Nellie had a noon appointment at the beauty shop, and he'd promised Mary Davis that during his lunch break he'd check out a vacant building Arnold Johnson was willing to make available for Lester's repair service.

The Davises and Lester were waiting when he arrived at the site of what had obviously once been a service station. Lester walked toward him, waving his hands. "Look at this, Doc. Whooee. Ain't it somethin'?"

"All it needs is a big sign," Sam spread his arms, "reading 'Lester's Repair Shop.'"

"Uh, no, it needs a counter, my tools, a storage bin, and—"

"You've got this all figured out, huh?"

"Yessiree. Lester can do it." He grinned at the other three.

Joe Davis motioned to Sam. "Arnold's willing to let us have it for a song. Needs some work, but I've talked to the shop teacher at school. He thinks he can pull together a group of fellas to make the necessary repairs."

Mary piped up, "And the 4-H kids want to have a grand opening celebration."

Sam looked at Lester, who was grinning from ear to ear, then back at the kind faces of the Davises. "Sounds good to me. I'd like to kick in a thousand bucks for the supplies. How soon do you think Lester can be up and running?''

"Coupla weeks, outside," Joe said.

Mary nodded enthusiastically "Why don't we plan on Sunday, August twentieth, for the party?''

Sam knew that date. Kate would return from Santa Fe then. He willed away the thought of what that might mean and turned back to Lester. "Looks like you're in business, pal.''

"I can fix those engines. I know I can.''

"We know it, too, Lester," Mary said, her eyes shining with approval.

Sam whistled all the way back to the clinic. In Oklahoma City, he would never have had a chance to be involved with a project like Lester's shop. This was exactly what he'd been looking for—a place to make a difference. And to belong.

He remained upbeat right up until Nellie returned from the beauty shop and stood over his desk, quivering with outrage, her newly coiffed hair regrettably reminding him of a Valkyrie. "I can't believe what they're saying about you," she finally sputtered.

Sam stared at her blankly. "Who?''

"The women at the beauty shop.''

Sam clasped his hands and summoned patience. "Nellie, what exactly are you talking about?''

"You and Jenny Lanagan.''

"What about Jenny and me?''

"I tried to tell them you'd never do anything improper. By now, though, it's probably all over town.''

"What, for God's sake?''

"Everyone knows Jean and Paul Manley go dancing in Enid the first Saturday of every month. So Jenny was alone at their house. That's what.'' She gathered herself for the juiciest tidbit. ''Eula Phinster just happened to be driving past and spotted your car parked at the Manleys' late Saturday night. She went around the block several times to be sure—''

''I'll just bet she did.'' Sam couldn't believe what he was hearing.

Nellie leaned forward, her hands on the desk. ''But that's not the worst. She saw Jenny standing on the porch practically naked.''

''I assure you she was fully clothed in her nightwear. You knew I'd made an emergency call there when Parker had his febrile convulsion. Didn't you tell them that?''

''Sure, and a lot more—like how lucky they are to have a doctor who makes house calls, but a fat lot of good it did. All my talking didn't make much of a dent, since you apparently stayed at the Manleys' for almost an hour. What could you have been thinking?''

''Nellie, Nellie,'' Sam said wearily, ''just when I was beginning to enjoy this town.''

KATE SAT ON A LOG BENCH on the Santiago property. To the southwest the city of Santa Fe spread across the desert floor, lights coming on gradually as darkness approached. The sunset was an artist's dream—magentas, pinks, blue-violets, misty grays. Kate inhaled deeply, drawing in the pungent fragrance of piñon and sagebrush. Off to her left a lizard scuttled beneath a rock.

A little over seven days from now she'd be going home. Home. The word sounded almost alien.

For the past three weeks her world had been centered here at Casa Santiago. She'd learned so much. It seemed at times as if she'd burst with ideas. She couldn't cover canvas fast enough. Ed had been right all along. She'd needed an experience like this. Now nothing could stop her.

Except herself. And the painting of Ed, looming as an obstacle between her soul and genuine creativity. Lupe had advised her to put it away. To work on other subjects. But her failure still lay over her like a coat of armor.

Lost in her thoughts, she was unaware that Lupe stood behind her until the woman gently touched her shoulder. "A beautiful evening, no?"

Kate smiled up at her mentor, then moved to make room for Lupe beside her. "Perfect."

Lupe joined her, but neither woman spoke for several minutes. "It's been good for you, this time here?" Lupe finally asked.

"Oh, yes. I've learned so much. And there is so much more I want to try. I can't thank you enough."

"Ah, thank-yous. The best thank-you, my Kate, is the work itself. And yours is very good. I hope you are pleased."

"I am, but—"

"But the husband? He worries you. Am I right?"

Kate nodded, trying to find the words to express how deeply she felt the failure. "It isn't coming, Lupe. In my head I can see the painting. But my hands won't cooperate. I've tried and tried. I can't capture him."

Lupe gazed out at the vista before them, her eyes focused on something in the distance. Finally she spoke. "You cannot 'capture' him, little one. No." She turned and faced Kate, her eyes intense with meaning. "You must free him."

"What do you mean?"

"You are, perhaps, trying to control this husband?"

She nodded knowingly. "This cannot be. The art, it is not something you *do*. It is something that comes through you. If you struggle to make the picture, to control its shape and meaning, you do not let go. You must let go. Become the vessel for your art, not the manipulator. When the time is right, the husband will come. You will see."

Kate's eyes filled. "Thank you," she whispered.

Lupe put an arm around Kate. "One last thing, if you will forgive an old lady. I sense you are struggling with some important question. It is not just the art that must be set free. Set yourself free, too. Then—" she laid her head against Kate's "—all will be well. Yes, all will be well."

Kate trembled with emotion, her heart overflowing with gratitude for this wise and generous woman. If only someday all could, indeed, be well.

CHAPTER FOURTEEN

SAM SAT AT THE CONTROLS of the boat chuckling at the interaction between Amanda, who had anointed herself water-skiing instructor, and his boys, who were determined to prove their athletic prowess even though both were still struggling to master the sport and tended to fall at least as often as they stayed up.

Amanda leaned over the stern, her voice shrill. "Keep your knees together."

Twenty yards behind the boat, Bart bobbed in the water, grappling for the ski that had come off during his latest attempt. Sam circled, slowing as the rope approached Bart's shoulder.

When Sam idled the motor, Blake added his two cents' worth. "You're standing up too soon, dork."

Bart blew a mouthful of water toward his mentors. "You're not so hot, either, Blake!"

Sam propped an elbow on the gunwale and called to his son. "One more time. You've almost got it, kiddo."

"No thanks to *them*." Bart nodded at the other two youngsters, then awkwardly managed to get the ski on. "Okay, Dad."

Sam straightened the boat and eased forward, slowly pulling the rope taut.

"I wish I could try it," Amanda said.

"Not yet," Sam advised, craning his neck to see if Bart was ready. "You still need to baby that leg."

"Go!" Bart frowned with concentration as Sam gunned the boat forward. Then like a champagne cork exploding from a bottle, the boy was up, mixed delight and terror on his face.

Amanda clapped her hands excitedly. "Yea, Bart!"

"You did it!" Blake's cheer was filled with pride.

Sam steered closer to the mirrorlike water near the shoreline. This weekend with his sons had been one of the best so far. Blake seemed to have forgotten he was supposed to be angry with his father, and both twins had readily accepted Amanda as "one of the boys." Out here on the lake, Sam could almost forget the ridiculous rumors swirling about him and Jenny, which no amount of damage control had curtailed.

He glanced over his shoulder, watching in amazement as Bart negotiated the wake, emerging triumphantly on the port side. Behind him, Blake and Amanda applauded again.

One more week until Kate returned. Then facts, not innuendoes, would prevail. He felt a flicker of fear. That was supposing things went the way he hoped with Kate. The way it had to be. A life without her was unimaginable.

Just then Bart hit the wake of another boat and fell spectacularly. "Down!" Amanda and Blake yelled simultaneously. Sam maneuvered close to Bart, who handed up the skis and climbed into the boat, dripping water over the seat cushions and laughing gleefully. "That was a blast!"

Sam handed him a dry towel. "Good job, Bart." He checked his watch. "That's it for today, kids."

"Thanks, Dr. Sam," Amanda said.

"Yeah, thanks," the boys said as one.

As they headed toward the boat ramp, Amanda took

charge of the conversation. "Mother and I are baby-sitting tonight. With Parker. She says I'm not old enough to do it by myself."

Bart twitched his nose in disgust. "Ugh. Babies. All they do is poop!"

"Parker's not so bad," Blake said.

Amanda, too, came to the toddler's defense. "'Not so bad?' He's adorable."

"Did you know our dad kissed his grandmother?" Bart asked, a mischievous gleam in his eye.

Sam cringed, checking to see how Blake was reacting. Miraculously, instead of sulking, he was studying Amanda with interest, as if awaiting her judgment.

"Cool!" Amanda said, excitedly. "Kate's one of my favorite people. Maybe she and your dad'll get married."

"Married!" As if rejecting a mouthful of brussels sprouts, Blake spit out the word.

"What's the problem?" Out of the corner of his eye Sam caught Amanda flipping the corner of her towel at Blake.

"They're *old!*" Blake folded his hands across his chest.

"Who's old?" Sam challenged as he slowed the boat and took his place among the craft circling the ramp. "Surely not me!" Shifting in his seat, he watched, curious, as the youngsters continued their exchange.

Amanda rolled her eyes. "Boys are *so* dumb!"

"Are not!" Bart retorted.

"Look, morons, what's the big deal? You want your dad to live all by himself forever? Huh? So what if he likes Kate? If ya gotta have a stepmother, you might as well have a good one." The longer she talked, the more she sounded like a patronizing schoolmarm. "You think people can't be in love just because they're somebody's parents? Just because they've got a few gray hairs?'' She gestured toward Sam. ''Look at him, you guys. He's a stud.''

Although Sam hardly thought of himself in that way, he was grateful for Amanda's advocacy. Bart giggled. ''Dad? A stud?''

''That's what I said, dork. And Kate is the nicest grown-up I know. So what's the big deal?''

Blake studied his father, a frown of concentration wrinkling his forehead, then darted a furtive look at Amanda. ''I dunno. Maybe it wouldn't be so bad....''

Bart, huddling beneath a beach towel, watched his brother. ''What wouldn't?''

Amanda's eyes widened in anticipation.

Blake kicked his bare foot against the engine casing. ''If, you know...if Dad liked Kate.''

''That's lame, Blake.'' Amanda poked his arm. ''It'd be super!''

Sam bit his lip to keep from grinning. ''Super'' wasn't half of what it would be.

''Girls!'' Bart and Blake chorused.

MONDAY MORNING Sam dialed Mel Floyd, hopeful he could accommodate him on short notice. After making his irregular request, he explained further. ''So, Mel, do you think you can hold down the fort by yourself? We'll only be gone Saturday, back home before noon Sunday... Great. I think it'll be good for her, too, but mum's the word.''

Sam hung up the phone, fanned the tickets on his desk and grinned, anticipating the results of his little surprise. This caper gave him something to look forward to, helped to keep his mind occupied. Otherwise, he'd go nuts. Kate was due home Sunday, the same day as Lester's grand opening. He couldn't wait to see her. But he'd have to take his cue from her. Up to a point.

Lester. He dialed the phone again and was put right through to Lola Fletcher. "How're things coming for Sunday?"

"Mary and Joe are doing a phenomenal job and Lester's beside himself. Have you seen the renovations yet?"

"No, but I hope to get by there this afternoon."

"There's more good news," Lola went on. "Julia's therapy is producing some positive results. There's a reason she was so afraid of telling the truth about the deaths of Lester's parents."

"What's that?"

"She confessed that because she was the oldest, she'd always believed the Jakes farm should have been hers, not her brother's. Furthermore, she'd always been terrified of storms and was genuinely frightened out of her wits by the tornado. After her sister and brother-in-law were killed in the storm, she thought people would assume she'd murdered them to claim her rightful inheritance."

Sam shook his head wearily. "So she made poor Lester the scapegoat?"

"Looks like it."

"God, the things people do to each other." He slumped back in his chair. "Will Lester be going home to live, then?"

"On a trial basis, starting Wednesday. I hope it works out."

"Me, too. Thanks for all you've done, Lola."

"And you, Sam."

He hung up, wondering whether Julia Jakes could change much, but hoping she would at least try.

When he rose in anticipation of seeing his four o'clock patient, he noticed the tickets still lying on his desk. No time like the present, he decided. He cornered Nellie in the supply room. "You busy Saturday night?"

She looked up, as if the question had come from the ionosphere. "First Kate, then Jenny, and now you're—how do the young people put it?—hitting on *me?*"

Sam chuckled. "We may as well keep those tongues wagging, Nellie. Good exercise for the epiglottis."

She threw him a long-suffering look.

"Well, are you?"

She fluffed her hair in mock coquetry. "What did you have in mind?"

"There's an, uh, event in Oklahoma City and I think it's important for us to attend."

"A professional meeting?"

Sam hedged. "Not exactly. But something I think would give a new, productive dimension to our working relationship."

"Really, Doctor. You know I help Mel," she corrected herself "*Dr. Floyd,* on the weekends you're off."

"Won't work, Nellie. I've already talked with Mel. He approves our going off to the city. We'd be gone less than twenty-four hours."

"What about Lester's grand opening?"

"We'll return in plenty of time." He leaned against the door, folding his arms across his chest and smiling engagingly. "So you're out of objections."

Nellie eyed him skeptically. "You're sure this is something that will result in professional improvement?"

"Absolutely," Sam said, his face a mask of innocence.

She studied him for the crack in his veracity. Finally she shrugged. "You're the doctor. Okay."

Sam chuckled all the way to the examining room.

SAYING GOODBYE to Lupe Santiago had left Kate feeling as if she'd lost her mooring. Now retracing her route, drawing closer and closer to Oklahoma, she found her stomach knotting. Casa Santiago—and all it represented—had embraced her, protected her and given her confidence in her talent. Reentry. That was the word her workshop friend Ellen had used to describe the inevitable letdown facing them back home. It wouldn't be just the accumulated mail, the catching up on local events or the rude awakening of mundane chores. Worse. No one would understand where she'd been, what had happened, how she'd changed.

Not to mention the complex web of relationships to be negotiated. She gripped the steering wheel more tightly. And a decision to be communicated. To Sam. Soon.

She'd thought a lot about Lupe's admonitions and had reached two inescapable conclusions. She hadn't freed Ed. And she hadn't freed herself.

She didn't know if she ever could. That being the case, it was unfair to delude herself or mislead Sam. She had her art. She had her family. That had to be enough.

Naturally in Sam's first few weeks in Salt Flats, he had gravitated toward someone welcoming. Undoubtedly as an attractive, available man, he'd craved affection. Intimacy. True, she'd enjoyed feeling desirable.

Alive. But that alone wasn't justification for making what could be an awful mistake.

She sighed, then slowed slightly as she crossed the Canadian River in the far northwest corner of the Texas Panhandle. The wind had picked up, buffeting the car. Despite the air conditioner, the atmosphere felt heavy. In the rearview mirror she saw thunderheads massing behind her. Ahead the road stretched to the horizon, houses and barns few and far between. Apprehensively, she glanced at her odometer, calculating she was well over a hundred miles from Salt Flats. And the storm was moving fast. Already dense clouds obliterated the sun and a strong wind pushed the car.

A cloudburst was all she needed on the most desolate stretch of highway on the entire trip, where even seeing another vehicle was an event. She cranked on the radio, trying to tune in a weather forecast. Static and more static. Frustrated, she flipped off the radio and increased her speed five miles per hour in the vain hope of out-running the storm. But already the sky had darkened alarmingly and taken on a sickly greenish-yellow cast. Then the wind died as suddenly as it had arisen. As if the earth had suspended its rotation, deathly calm lay suffocatingly over the fields. Tornado weather.

Then came the inevitable. First, large plops of rain dotted the windshield, streaking the dust and bug spots. Without further warning, a blast of wind rattled the windows, followed by such a downpour that even the high-speed wiper setting did little to clear the view. Giant pincers gripped Kate's shoulders as she leaned forward, squinting at the road. It was as if she'd driven into a maelstrom—water spewed across the highway, filling the drainage ditches, blinding streams gushed over the windows, and the gale wrapped the automobile in its tentacles, maniacally rocking.

Oh, God. Oh, God. Panic, numbing and insistent, filled her. Should she pull over? Should she keep going? Ed had always advised her not to stop unless she could get completely off the road. But she saw no driveways, no rest areas, and only fleeting glimpses of lines on the road helped her keep the car on the asphalt.

Her body was rigid with tension as she forced deep breaths. Relax. Relax. But fear—palpable and paralyzing—triumphed. She slowed to twenty miles per hour in the effort to hold steady against the surges of wind battering the countryside with unabated fury.

When she thought things couldn't possibly get any worse, the rain now drove horizontally across the barren land. Clunk. Accompanied by the banshee shrill of the tempest, hailstones the size of hardballs bombarded the car.

Helpless, Kate clutched the steering wheel, her throat constricting, tears rolling down her cheeks. Terror clawed at her. With a horrific crash, a hailstone the size of an orange broke a back window, landing with a dull thud on the floorboard and ushering in the roar of the storm.

Help me! Help me! Kate didn't know if she screamed the words aloud or only in the hell of her consciousness. Then, as if summoned by her fear, a vision of Sam loomed before her—his cocky grin encouraging her, his strong arms beckoning her, his eyes bathing her in warmth. "Sam?"

She shook her head. This couldn't be happening. But it was. Sam was as real a presence as if he sat beside her. And it was then she spotted something through the fog of her windshield—red lights. Two of them. And a

form defining itself against the pewter of the foreground. Thank God. A semi. Another human being. The
trucker would know where he was going. She could
follow him. Like beacons, the taillights led her through
the storm until, almost after the fact, she became aware
the hail had stopped and the torrent was slackening.

She followed the trucker for several miles, intoning
Sam's name over and over as if to ward off evil spirits.
Finally, miraculously, a sliver of blue—cerulean—
opened in the heavens. Just as suddenly, the rain
stopped.

Ahead of her, she spied an abandoned service station.
She pulled off the road, stopped the car and sagged,
trembling, against the steering wheel. The storm had
passed. The sun came out, highlighting the crystal rain-
drops clinging to the weeds growing along the highway.
Cautiously, Kate rolled down her window. The air was
cool and redolent with the scent of growing things. She
drew a shuddering breath, then stepped from the car.

Pockmarks covered the surface of the roof, hood and
trunk. The broken window gaped jaggedly. She braced
her hands on the hood and leaned forward, aware that
she should be upset. That she should be thinking about
insurance forms and body shops. But instead, she was
filled with overpowering relief.

She was safe.

A meadowlark's song caused her to look up. Across
the road a small herd of cattle moved single-file toward
a pond. A hawk swooped over the road. Business as
usual for them.

But it was going to take her longer to recover. She
had truly feared for her life. Gulping in mouthfuls of
clean air, she finally felt calm enough to resume her

trip. But as she crawled behind the wheel, a thought struck her with all the force of the tempest itself.

Sam. He had gotten her through the storm. She had needed him. Not someone else. Not Ed. Not her daughters. Not Jean and Paul. Her hands fell to her lap. She sat stunned. It was Sam's presence, Sam's love that had sustained her.

She'd had it figured out. Then.

But now?

She started up the car, pulled onto the highway and drove at the speed limit all the way home, pondering anew what she would say to Sam.

"The source of your light?" Lupe's words sounded bell-like in her memory. "Where is it, little one?"

A SQUALL PASSED Salt Flats just in time to cool the air in preparation for the grand opening of Lester Jakes's repair shop. Jenny wheeled Parker in his stroller toward the assembled onlookers. 4-H members distributing balloons handed Parker a bright blue one. Squealing delightedly, he waved it back and forth in front of his face. The high-school business-class students manned an ice-cream stand. Across the door of Lester's establishment, a fire-engine red ribbon was stretched ceremoniously.

As Lester's story had unfolded in the *Examiner,* Jenny had felt ashamed that she, along with others, had dismissed him and that no one, till now, had unearthed the root of his problem. Clearly he had Sam Gray to thank for his reversal of fortune. Because Sam had cared. Just as he had cared for Parker. And, reluctant though she was to admit it, just as he apparently cared for her mother. The devil unknown had been easy to resent. But the devil known? Especially when he was slowly but surely winning the respect and affection of many. Charlene couldn't say enough about "Dr. Sam's" positive influence on Amanda. And it took a pretty big man to submit with humor and grace to a public shearing.

Eula Phinster caught up with her on the fringes of the crowd. "Jenny, kiddo, welcome home. I've been so busy at the beauty shop I haven't had a chance to call you."

Since Jenny and Eula had never been confidantes, Jenny couldn't imagine why Eula would have phoned her anyway. But with the woman's next comment, Jenny discovered the source of the beautician's sudden interest.

"I'm sorry to hear about your divorce. But it hasn't taken you long to recover." She smiled knowingly, then cracked her chewing gum.

"Excuse me? I'm afraid I don't—"

"Why, Dr. Gray, of course." She gestured toward the dais where dignitaries, including Sam, were assembling. "It's all over town."

Jenny felt as if she'd suddenly swallowed Parker's balloon. "*What's* all over town?"

"Your, uh, relationship with Salt Flats's most eligible bachelor."

Jenny didn't know whether to laugh or vent her irritation. "Sam is Parker's doctor. That's the only 'relationship' we have."

Eula remained unfazed. "Say what you will, but I saw you myself. It looked pretty cozy to me and, God knows, he's gorgeous. Don't get me wrong, I'm not blaming you—"

Anger took over. "Saw us where?"

"At your house, dear. In the dead of night."

"Are you talking about the Friday night Parker was ill? Is that what's started this ridiculous rumor?"

"Ill baby or not, there you were in your nightclothes. All I can say is you didn't wait long after your mother's back was turned."

"Stop it. Right now." Parker tried to stand up in his stroller, but Jenny gently pushed him down, never taking her eyes off the determined busybody. "What you think you saw and what actually happened are two vastly different things. I'll thank you from now on, Eula, to mind your own business."

"Well, 'scuze me, hon." Eula shifted her gum from one side of her mouth to the other. "Didn't mean to stir up a hornet's nest."

Jenny ignored the bald-faced lie. "Do me a favor. Beginning now, stuff those hornets back in the nest, please." With that she maneuvered Parker's stroller to the front of the crowd, away from where Eula still stood, indignation etched into her features.

Just then Parker's balloon got away from him, floating on the breeze toward Sam, who captured it and left the platform to return it to Parker, whose face was contorted in disappointment. Sam scooped the boy into his arms. "Hey, guy, you gotta hold on tight. See?" He clamped Parker's fingers around the string. "Or maybe I could tie it to your wrist." He looked questioningly at Jenny. She nodded. While Sam secured the balloon, Jenny became uncomfortably aware that those around her were watching them with more than passing interest. Damn it, anyway. Another kindness. Additional fuel for the fire.

Then, to make matters worse, when Sam finished tying the balloon, he kissed Parker on the cheek before depositing him back in the stroller.

"Thanks," Jenny managed to say before Sam returned to the dais.

She could barely concentrate on the festivities. She'd created a mess for Kate and Sam by voicing such strong objections, by chasing her mother off to Santa Fe. It was almost as if some perverse god was punishing her now by setting loose these absurd rumors she hoped her mother would never hear. Kate would be home late this afternoon. A big apology was in order. Jenny just hoped she could carry through with her intention to free her mother. She ruffled Parker's hair. It wouldn't be easy, but it was the right thing to do.

"... And now for the ribbon cutting, ladies and gentlemen." Arnold Jackson, the mayor, presented a huge pair of scissors to the president of the Chamber of Commerce, who, with Lester at his side, snipped the ribbon.

A cheer went up from the crowd and Lester, flustered by the applause, smiled, doffed his cap, then hung his head in an "aw-shucks" manner.

"Don't you wanna say a few words, Lester?" the chamber president asked.

Lester hesitated, obviously thinking about the question. The mayor placed a hand on his back and urged him forward. "Go on. You've earned it."

Lester edged closer to the microphone. "I jus' wanna say one thing." He turned to Sam. "I couldn't a done it without ya, Doc." The sudden applause temporarily discombobulated Lester, but recovering himself, he offered one last thought to the audience. "And those engines? Those mixers and radios and lawn mowers? Don't you worry none. Lester can fix 'em, yessir."

Appreciative laughter greeted the speaker's hasty retreat from public scrutiny. Mayor Jackson surveyed the crowd. "If no one else has anything to say, I guess we're adjourned."

"Wait." A harsh voice sounded from somewhere behind Jenny. "I do." Folks stepped aside to make a path through which emerged—of all people—Julia Jakes. Her stern face was set and she strode boldly toward the platform.

Jenny heard the buzz of low conversation around her.

"What's she doing?"

"Damn, she'll spoil this for Sam and Lester."

"Somebody stop her."

Julia clumped up to the podium and spoke peremptorily to the mayor. "I'm talkin'." Before he could react, she grabbed the microphone as if she were choking a hen for Sunday dinner. Lester cowered behind Sam.

"Listen, people. I know what you're thinkin'. Old Julia's gonna ruin everything. Well, I reckon I already done that for Lester for a long time. But things're better now. You know why?" She turned and fixed her gaze on Sam. "The doc, here. He wouldn't leave it be." She cleared her throat noisily. "I done you wrong, Doc. And here in front of God'n ever'body, I wanna say I'm sorry." She looked at the microphone, as if unaware she'd had the instrument in her grasp. "That's it." She strode quickly from the dais.

Lester's jaw dropped. Sam turned and enveloped him in a bear hug. Stunned silence was replaced by enthusiastic cheering. Parker clapped his hands energetically in imitation of the adults. Jenny swallowed the lump in her throat. It was Sam's moment. And he deserved every bit of the affirmation he was being given. Every bit.

KATE, BONE-TIRED, pulled into the busy parking lot of the Salt Flats IGA. She'd have preferred to head straight for home, but she knew once she started unpacking, she'd never return to town for the needed milk, bread, eggs, juice, coffee and dog food.

With a resigned sigh, she trudged into the store, retrieved a grocery cart and headed for the dairy counter. She was delayed in her mission by several acquaintances welcoming her home. Finally, dazed, she stood in front of the orange juice case, too weary even to decide if she wanted pulp-free or not. A finger jabbed her shoulder with the authority of a drill sergeant. "Kate, I thought that was you!"

Kate turned, defeated. She was in for it now. The mayor's wife would have an entire month's worth of juicy tidbits. "Hello, Berta." She leaned around the woman and grabbed the first carton of juice she could lay her hands on. "It's nice to see you, but I'm in kind of a hurry."

"Did you just get home?"

"Yes, and I'm worn out."

"Then you missed Lester's grand opening?"

She had no idea what Berta was talking about, but it was easier just to say, "Yes."

"You should've been there. Quite a tribute to our handsome doctor." She paused, obviously waiting for Kate to take the bait.

"That's nice." Kate pushed her cart forward and picked up a pound of butter she had not the slightest notion whether she needed. Berta trailed after her.

"And speaking of Dr. Sam, he and Jenny make the cutest couple. You must be very pleased."

Couple? Jenny? Sam? Blood left the upper half of Kate's body. Dizzy, she gripped the handle of the cart, praying it would support her until she could flee the store and Berta's news. Without consciously finding the words, she blurted, "Yes, but you'll have to excuse me. I'm really in a rush."

Heedless of the other shoppers, Kate wheeled the cart to the checkout counter. She'd been stupid, stupid, stupid. Of course. It made sense. Perfect sense. Sam was lonely. Jenny was lonely. Kate had no claim on Sam. In fact, she had avoided commitment. Who could blame the man for looking elsewhere?

Frantically she scrabbled in her purse for her billfold. The checkout girl thankfully was preoccupied discussing with the bagger the timing of her next break and virtually ignored Kate, whose hand shook as she made out the check. Grabbing her receipt and the sack of groceries, she stumbled toward her car, squinting back tears of exhaustion and disappointment.

"Oh, Kate," Berta, followed by a carryout boy, chased after her. "One last thing. I understand the doctor took a date to Oklahoma City last night." She rolled her eyes suggestively. "And that they didn't come home till morning."

Kate threw her groceries on the back seat, then turned and faced Berta, her hands on her hips. "Is that all, Berta? Because if it isn't, I really don't want to hear another word. If you don't mind, I'll wait and size things up for myself."

"Land's sakes, you don't need to get huffy about it."

"Berta, I'm tired." She jerked the door open. "And I'm going home. Now."

"Well, I declare—"

Kate roared out of the lot, leaving Berta gasping like a fish on a dry bank. How could she have forgotten this town and its intrigues? Casa Santiago and her idyllic memory of it seemed far, far away.

As did her sense of Sam's presence.

Done in by a reality she'd never even considered. Jenny and Sam.

CHAPTER FIFTEEN

THE HOUSE, closed up for a month, smelled musty. Kate turned on the ceiling fans and adjusted the thermostat, relieved when cool air began pushing aside the trapped heat. Mastering the temptation to collapse, she made herself unload the car. "Letdown" didn't begin to describe what she was feeling. Exhausted. Disoriented. And, worst of all, displaced.

Mechanically she put away the groceries. The decision had been sharp and clear this afternoon on the storm-cleansed highway. She loved Sam. He would be waiting for her.

Before Berta. Before Jenny.

Garment bag in hand, she entered the bedroom. It looked the same as always. Everything did. Including her life. How had she ever dared to think anything would change? All the time she was unpacking, the bed mocked her with images of that night with Sam when he'd told her their lovemaking was for keeps. She sagged onto the mattress, clutching a denim jumper to her chest. At last she could admit what she'd never said aloud. She'd believed him. Even as she'd struggled with her feelings. Struggled with him out of her deepest fear—rejection.

God, what could she say to Jenny? To Sam? She sucked in an anguished breath. She had to steel herself to make it easy, natural for them. Above all, she must never betray what she'd come to know too late. Heaven help her, she loved him.

She stared at the phone. She had to dial the Manleys' number. Had to project warmth, enthusiasm, fulfillment. All the while feeling heartbroken and incredibly foolish.

Summoning every last shred of histrionic ability, she picked up the receiver. After only two rings, Jean answered, her voice mellowing as soon as she realized the caller was Kate. "You're home! Did you have a good time?"

"Fabulous. I learned so much." That, at least, was true.

"We've missed you and we'll want to hear all about it, from the very beginning. But—" Kate heard her grandson jabbering in the background "—Jenny's standing here on pins and needles waiting to talk to you."

Kate squeezed her eyes shut.

"Hi, Mom, glad you're back. I have so much to tell you."

Jenny sounded upbeat, happy. Kate prayed she'd find her voice. "Fill me in."

"Yesterday, at Lester's grand opening— Oh, that's right. You don't know about that. Sam helped him. But that can wait. Anyway, I ran into Doris Mayes. She runs Kinder Haus, the day-care center. I have an interview Tuesday. It's a full-time job, *with* benefits. I wouldn't even be charged for Parker."

Kate opened her eyes, fixing them on Jenny's graduation photograph displayed on the dresser. "That's wonderful. You'd be terrific."

"How was your workshop?"

"Relaxing. Helpful. One day soon I'll tell you and

Grandma and Grandpa all about it. Lupe Santiago was terrific.''

Jenny rattled on. The divorce suit was proceeding, amazingly trouble-free. Todd had an upcoming visit planned to see Parker, although Jenny wasn't holding her breath. Then she said something that captured Kate's full attention. ''…he had a convulsion. I was so scared.''

Kate's heart rate doubled. ''Is Parker all right?''

''He's fine. Sam came right over. He explained that febrile convulsions are fairly common and Parker will outgrow them.''

That was the second 'Sam.' No more Dr. Gray. ''I'm glad it's nothing serious.''

''Your grandson's fine, Mom. He and Sam are quite the buddies now.''

Kate tried to reassure herself. Parker needed a strong man in his life. Sam had experience with boys. And there was no escaping the lilt in Jenny's voice when she said Sam's name. For once, Berta had been right on target. ''How was your trip to Oklahoma City?''

''What trip?''

Kate's stomach flip-flopped. ''Didn't you and Sam go to the city yesterday?''

''I have no idea what you're talking about.''

Either Berta was lying or she wasn't one-hundred-percent accurate after all. ''Never mind, honey. I must have my facts wrong. I'm bushed.''

''You sound tired. Take a long, hot bath and go to bed. The chores will wait.''

''I think I will. I'll talk to you tomorrow. Good night.''

She hung up, puzzled. If Sam took a date to Oklahoma City and it wasn't Jenny, he was really making the rounds. Kate felt even more foolish than she had before. She was usually a good judge of character. But even as she indulged in these negative thoughts about him, a voice pecked away inside her head. *Don't rush to judge.*

Taking Jenny's suggestion, she tried a bath. It didn't help. Her thoughts continued to go in circles, each coil further fraying her nerves. This afternoon's thunderstorm had been only a precursor of the emotional storm seizing her now. When, at last, she crawled between the cool sheets, tears of hurt and exhaustion traced down her cheek. But no catharsis followed.

SAM RACED INTO THE HOUSE late Sunday evening, heading straight for the answering machine. He hated that he'd been gone—treating a farmer kicked in the chest by a mule—when Kate had undoubtedly phoned. The quick Oklahoma City trip and Lester's grand opening had helped pass these last long hours before he could hold her again. And then that damned call—one of the few times he'd resented an emergency.

He stared, stupefied, at the message light, ominously monochromatic. Not willing to believe the evidence of his senses, he reviewed his caller ID. Nothing.

Had she been delayed? Had there been an accident? Please, God. Surely there was a rational explanation. She had to know how eager he was to hear from her. It'd been hell being out of touch with her—literally and figuratively. But it was almost midnight. Too late to call.

As he turned away from the phone, he experienced an unnerving gust of cool air, lingering on the nape of his neck. Like a premonition. Was it not only too late to call her, but too late, period?

He grunted in self-disgust. He was letting his imagination run loose. She'd arrived exhausted, needing time to settle in. She'd call tomorrow morning. Everything would be fine. It had to be.

ALTHOUGH SHE FELT about as clearheaded as a scarecrow, Kate dressed hurriedly the next morning and was at the boarding kennel by eight, where she was greeted by an ecstatic Charger. She buried her face in his fur, reveling in his unconditional love.

From there she went to the post office to pick up the mail Minnie Odom had been holding for her. It would take her a full afternoon to go through it all. On top of the stack was a hand-printed envelope postmarked Santa Fe. In the car, Kate opened it and withdrew a miniature watercolor of an eagle soaring high above cliffs and crags. In the background light pastels washed the absorbent paper with the hint of a rainbow. The lower right hand corner bore the inked initials—LS—and the one-word title. *Kate*.

"Oh, Lupe," Kate sighed, carefully replacing the one-of-a-kind message in its envelope, "if only it were that simple."

Aware that, emotionally, this was no time to be alone, she set out for the Klingers' farm. Charlene's hearty laugh and warm embrace might prevent her from hitting bottom. For now.

Amanda and Charlene were in the kitchen rolling out cookie dough. Amanda jumped off her stool and threw her arms around Kate. "You're back!"

Kate held the girl by the shoulders, studying her. "You're walking. And your hair—what've you done?"

"I'm letting my bangs grow out."

Charlene nudged her daughter aside. "My turn."

Ironically, Charlene's bear hug did more to move Kate nearer tears than to chase the blues away. "Welcome home. I've missed you."

Misty-eyed, Kate whispered, "Me, too, you." She dug in her purse and retrieved a small box. "I hope you like your earrings."

While Charlene tried them on, Amanda resumed her cookie-making, chattering all about what her 4-H group and the high school business class were doing for Lester Jakes. She finished with a play-by-play description of the grand opening of his repair shop the day before.

"It was quite a do," Charlene chimed in. "Julia Jakes even got into the act."

"Jenny mentioned it. I'm glad Lester's coming into his own."

"Only because Dr. Sam helped him," Amanda pointed out. "He's the coolest."

Kate couldn't stop herself. "I understand he's been dating."

Charlene's head snapped up. "Dating? That's ridiculous."

Amanda set down her cookie cutter and observed the two women intently.

"Not according to Berta Jackson," Kate said.

"Honey?" Eyes filled with concern, Charlene reached for Kate's hand. "Are you all right?"

"Fine."

"Nobody believes that old windbag," Amanda volunteered.

"No name-calling, please," Charlene chided. Looking first at Kate and then at her daughter, she firmly suggested Amanda find something to do outside.

The girl rolled her eyes. "Oh, right. Just when things get interesting."

"Amanda—"

"Okay, okay." She slid from her stool and took her sweet time going to the door.

After the latch clicked, Charlene led Kate to a chair at the kitchen table. "What exactly did Berta say?"

Kate told her, trying desperately to sound dispassionate.

"So you think Jenny and Sam are an item?"

Kate sighed. "Makes a lot of sense when you think about it."

"Not to me."

Kate smiled ruefully. "That's because you're my friend. But haven't you heard the rumors, too?"

"Yes. But I don't believe them."

"Out of loyalty or—"

"Sam loves you, Kate. Or haven't you noticed?"

"Then what about the date he took to Oklahoma City just Saturday night?"

Charlene eyed her pointedly. "Why don't you ask Sam?"

"You know something, don't you?"

"This is between you and Sam. Talk to him, Kate."

"I-I can't."

"Bull. Do you think avoiding problems is the solution? Jeez!" She shook her head in bewilderment. Then her tone softened. "You're afraid."

Helpless, Kate nodded.

"You love him, don't you?"

"But—"

"For Pete's sake, girl. Get out of here and get on with your life." Charlene stood and propelled Kate to the door. There she put an arm around Kate's shoulder and with an affectionate smile, offered her parting remark. "And you're right. I *do* know something. About that Oklahoma City date? It wasn't Jenny, Kate."

"Then who—"

"That curvaceous, man-hunting siren Nellie Forester."

At first Kate couldn't process what her friend had just said. "Nellie?"

"None other. Sam decided she needed some musical education and took her to a rock concert at the Zoo Amphitheatre."

"You're kidding! Nellie at a rock concert?"

Charlene loosed a go-figure grin, leaned close and whispered in her ear. "Now quit worrying and talk to the man."

Kate hugged Charlene. But she made no promises.

"WERE YOU EVER going to call me?" Sam stood on Kate's back porch late Monday afternoon, a bouquet of yellow roses dangling from his hand, cursing himself for his bulldozer approach. Kate remained frozen in the doorway, her startled expression tacit proof she'd had no intention of phoning him. "Surely you knew I'd be waiting to hear from you. Wondering what you've decided."

"Sam, I've been home less than twenty-four hours and—"

"And I've cancelled two patients to get here as soon as I could." Belatedly, he remembered the flowers. "Here." He offered them to her. "These are for you." He wanted to take her in his arms, hold her tight, never let her go. But something in her stance let him know that would be the wrong move.

She took the roses, looking sadly at them before raising her eyes and saying, "I don't want your flowers."

His gut twisted. "What the hell's going on here?" He started toward her. "Will you at least let me come in?" When she didn't answer, he grew more agitated. "Talk to me, Kate."

A flicker of hesitation crossed her face, but then she said, "Not now. Please not now."

Damn. She was putting him off. "When, then?"

"I'll call you."

"Not good enough, Kate. We'll talk face-to-face. You set the time." This was crazy. The woman he loved, instead of looking thrilled to see him, regarded him with cool, sad eyes.

"Give me a couple of days," she said with a sigh. "Wednesday night?"

"I'll be here." He paused, his hands balled into fists. "Whatever it is that's changed, I promise I'll get to the bottom of it. I told you before and I'll tell you again. I don't give up easily."

With that, he turned and strode toward his Suburban, more frustrated than he'd ever been in his entire life.

AFTER CLOSING THE DOOR, Kate slumped against it, the fragrance of roses fracturing her composure. Sending Sam away was the most difficult thing she'd ever done. With all her heart she'd longed to throw herself into his arms, to believe any lame excuse for the rumors, to forget pride and...

He'd acted angry, defensive, his jaw muscles twitching, his eyes uncomprehending. And he'd looked different. Not older, exactly, but... Then she realized what it was. He'd cut his ponytail. It made him seem somehow more serious, more determined.

"Oh, hell," she muttered, gathering what was left of her dignity before tossing the bouquet into the trash.

There was only one antidote for her pain. She'd bury herself in work. After Wednesday Sam would be history. All the fantasies she'd woven were simply that. Fantasies. *Get used to it.*

But, Lord, it was hard.

"GRANDMA? WHERE ARE YOU?" Jenny raced through the Manleys' house and finally discovered Parker and Jean in the backyard. "Guess what?" she exploded. "I got the job."

Jean gave Parker's swing a healthy push. "That's wonderful. Tell me all about it."

Jenny dragged a lawn chair nearer the swing set and ushered her grandmother to the seat, taking over the pushing duties herself. To the rhythm of her shoves, she told Jean all about the day-care facility and staff, thrilled that at last her life was on track again.

"Sand. Pahkah want sand, now." Jenny slowed the swing to a stop, then lifted the boy to the ground, where he made a beeline for the sandbox and his yellow plastic tractor. Keeping her eyes on her son, Jenny sank onto the grass beside her grandmother.

"I'm proud of you, dear," Jean said. "Your mother will be, too."

"I hope so." Jenny didn't say anything for a while, trying to decide whether to confide in her grandmother. Yet she didn't know how to handle the situation on her own. "Grandma?"

"Yes?"

"When I was at the clinic, I saw Sam briefly. He said something strange."

"What was that?"

"He asked me what was wrong with Mother."

Jean cocked her head, as if she couldn't have heard

correctly. "What was 'wrong'? Why, I don't know what to make of that."

"I didn't either. So I asked him what he meant."

"And?"

"He said Mom hadn't called him when she got back. Furthermore, that she didn't appear happy to see him when he dropped by." Jenny watched Parker, who was making growling noises as he guided the tractor through the paths he'd made in the sand. "Sam seemed totally bummed about it. And now that I think about it," Jenny added, "she wasn't exactly herself when I went over there last night."

"Strange. Before she left, I could've sworn she had strong feelings for Sam. Even Paul thought so."

"Me, too. And since our talk about putting myself in her place and getting to know Sam better, I've even decided it's okay. I wonder what in the world could've happened?"

Jean leaned back in the lawn chair, deep in thought. Jenny waited, puzzling over her mother's strange behavior.

Jean finally spoke. "I can think of only one explanation."

"What, Grandma?"

Jean took Jenny's hand in hers. "The rumors."

At first Jenny didn't comprehend her grandmother's meaning. Then, like a revelation, it came to her. "Oh, my God. Sam and me."

Her grandmother smiled sadly. "Exactly. Kate must've heard them."

Jenny let the lunacy of the situation sink in before scrambling to her feet. "I've gotta go. Can you watch Parker for me?"

"It will be my pleasure." Then as Jenny hurried toward her car, her grandmother called after her, "Good luck, Cupid!"

HER MOTHER'S CAR was in plain sight, but no one answered Jenny's knock. Charger rounded the house, and when he saw Jenny, began barking excitedly. Jenny hunkered down and petted him. "Where's Mom? Painting?"

As if he understood the question, Charger cocked his head, then followed as Jenny crossed the yard to the studio.

She paused at the door, listening to the faint strains of an Enya CD. She rapped softly, then went inside. Her mother stood before the unfinished oil painting of her father, her head cocked quizzically. "Mom?"

Kate wheeled around, her face a mask of surprise.

"I'm sorry. I thought you heard me knock."

Kate set down the palette and brush. "It's all right." She studied the painting again. "The work isn't going well today." Gesturing at the broken-down sofa in the corner, Kate said, "Sit. I could use a break."

Her mother's words sounded stiff. Formal. Jenny sat.

Kate pulled a couple of bottles of spring water from the ancient refrigerator. "Join me?"

"Sure."

Kate perched on a stool, one foot wrapped around the leg, then took a swig from the bottle. "What brings you here?"

Jenny swallowed, reluctant to get to the point. "I got the job."

For the first time, Kate smiled. "That's super news. I'm so pleased for you."

Jenny bought time by giving her mother the replay of the interview. At last there was nothing left to say except what she'd come for. "Mom, why were you so rude to Sam yesterday?"

Her mother's eyes widened and a flush covered the skin at the neck of her work shirt. "Wh-what are you talking about?"

"I saw Sam this morning. He told me you hadn't called him when you got back."

"There was no need." Again that unnatural, prissy tone.

"And that you cut him dead when he stopped by yesterday."

"Jenny, I don't want to—"

"What? Talk about what's really going on? Are you happier burying your head in the sand?"

"I don't know what this is all about, but however I treated Sam, it's not any of your business."

"I think it is. You love Sam."

Kate jumped from the stool and paced to the other end of the room, her back to Jenny. She said nothing, but the iron rod where her spine used to be spoke volumes.

"You've heard the rumors." Jenny waited, her heart hammering.

Slowly her mother turned, her face anguished. "It's all right, Jenny. I understand. He's an attractive man. You're both lonely and—"

"Stop it. Right now." The staccato of Jenny's protest filled the room. She rose to her feet and approached her mother. "There's nothing to the rumors, Mom. You know how people are in this town. They'll seize on anything." Then she explained the scene with Ethel in the park, Eula's late-night reconnoitering and Sam's attention to Parker at Lester's grand opening. "That's all there is to it," she concluded. "Ask Sam."

Kate rubbed both palms through her hair. "It's not that simple."

"I think it is, Mom. You love him. What's more simple—and wonderful—than that?"

"'Wonderful'?" Kate slumped against the wall as if she couldn't have heard correctly. "But—" she gestured at the portrait "—what about your dad?"

Jenny put her arm around Kate and drew her back to the sofa. "You know, Mom, you just could be the luckiest of women—loved by two great men." She pulled her mother down beside her. "Nothing you could ever do will convince me you didn't love Daddy. And he loved you. But I've been thinking." She took in a breath before continuing. "You'd be a fool to pass up a future with Sam."

"But—"

"Listen. Please. He loves you. I can't imagine what it would be like to have a man love me the way Sam loves you. While you've been gone, he's done nothing but remain devoted to you. I'd give anything for a man like Sam. Hear me? *Like* Sam. Not Sam. He's yours, if you don't screw it up." She turned, grasping both of her mother's hands. "Answer me one question, Mom. Do you love him?"

"I-I…"

"Yes or no?"

Kate's eyes filled with tears. In a strangled voice, she uttered a "yes" just before Jenny pulled her into a hug.

"Then I'll say what Rachel already has. 'Go for it, Mom!'"

When Kate finally pulled away, extracting a tissue from her pocket and wiping away her tears, she said, "What made you change your mind?"

Jenny managed a self-deprecatory smile. "I took a

good look at the busybodies in this town and decided I
didn't want to be as judgmental as they are. And that's
exactly what I'd been doing. Judging you." She so-
bered. "I was wrong, Mom." She stood up. "That's
what I came to say. I'm going now so you can get back
to your painting."

Kate rose, too. "And back to some serious thinking,"
she said, her eyes no longer hooded, but glowing.
"Thank you, darling girl." Jenny felt peace come over
her as her mother wrapped her in a warm embrace.

Before she left, Jenny studied the portrait once more.
"You don't have him yet."

Kate put an arm around Jenny and stared at the rendering. "No. It's the strangest thing. Ed just refuses to
come to me."

"He will." Jenny continued her scrutiny. Then she
saw the flaw. "It's the way he's looking."

"What do you mean?"

"Straight at the viewer. It's too…confrontational.
Daddy wasn't like that. He was generous, loving, fun."
She shrugged. "You know."

"Yes, I think I do." Kate dropped her arm and faced
Jenny, her face alight. "Thank you, thank you. You've
been very helpful."

Jenny couldn't hide a smug smile. "In more ways
than one, I hope," she added pointedly.

"Oh, yes. In many more ways than one."

SAM HAD BARKED at Nellie, acted abrupt with Berta
Jackson, who was in for another appointment under the
guise of her recurring "female problems," and if he
wasn't careful, he'd start kicking stray dogs. Damn it,
why hadn't he just stormed into Kate's house Monday

and gotten to the bottom of whatever was making her act so indifferent to him?

He took off his lab coat and hung it in the closet, relieved as hell that one more day was over. Now only one remained before his appointed Wednesday visit. His instincts urged him to take matters into his own hands and go see her, but his head told him to wait.

His thoughts were interrupted by a blaring from the stereo system—the insistent, rhythmic sound of a bass guitar, a keyboard, a drum, and—

"Like it, Doctor?"

He whirled around. Nellie had entered the room and stood smirking at him. "Or is it too loud?"

He felt himself relax. "One thing's for sure. It isn't the Melanchrino Strings."

"I thought you might need a bit of cheering up."

"Are you mellowing, Nellie?"

She shrugged. "Well, it's not every day a handsome man invites me to a concert."

"Tell the truth. It wasn't too bad, was it?"

"No." She winked then, big as life. "Why else would I have bought the group's CD during intermission?" She watched the grin spread over his face, then added, "I'm not fully converted, though. This will never do during office hours."

He held up his hands in surrender. "Agreed."

No sooner had she departed, than his phone rang. He was surprised when Jenny Lanagan identified herself. And even more surprised by her message. He listened intently. Her explanation for Kate's aloofness made perfect sense. But it was her last comment that caused his hopes to soar. "Grandma says to tell you that when you see Mom, you go with her blessing." She paused. "And mine, too."

WHEN SAM ARRIVED at Kate's Wednesday evening, the house was dark, but there was a light in the studio. He parked the Suburban, then greeted Charger. "Whaddaya think, boy? Did she forget I was coming?" With his hands deep in his pockets, he followed the dog, who trotted companionably just ahead of him toward the studio.

Sam had intended to knock, but Charger nosed the door open. With her back to them, Kate, absorbed in her work, was unaware of their presence. Sam couldn't take his eyes off her. Her hair was drawn back in a loose ponytail and her thin shoulders were hunched in concentration as she worked rapidly, applying shading here, a burst of color there. Every so often she would stand back. Then, as if finding a solution, she would add another decisive stroke.

The painting itself was remarkable. It was of a tanned, broad-shouldered man in work clothes, turning away from the fence post on which one gloved hand rested. In the body, Kate had caught an earthy strength. But it was the glance the subject was throwing over his shoulder that arrested Sam's attention—it was full of laughter, warmth, love. This was a man Sam would like to know. It was in the final subtlety, though, that the power of the painting lived. The man seemed to be inclining his head, as if giving permission to someone or maybe saying goodbye. Sam choked up. No wonder Lupe Santiago had wanted Kate. She was remarkably talented.

With a dab of dark green, Kate stepped back again, standing motionless for what seemed a long time. Then, as if satisfied, she knelt before the canvas to sign her name.

Sam walked up behind her and gently laid his hands on her shoulder. "Kate?"

She rose to her feet and turned toward him, flustered. Then she checked her wristwatch. "Oh, Sam. I-I completely lost track. I'm sorry."

Lost track? Only the most important meeting of his life. "You're operating on artist's time, I guess," he suggested wryly. He nodded toward the portrait. "It's a great piece of work, Kate." He took a guess. "Your husband?"

"Yes." Then as if scrambling for something to say, she added, "I've been working on it a long time. But until now, it just wasn't right."

"And now?"

Her glance drifted over the canvas. "I'm satisfied."

"What was wrong before?"

"I-I think I was holding on too tightly."

He was aware of the charged atmosphere, of the profound silence. "To what?"

"Ed. His memory." Her eyes pleaded with him for understanding. "As long as I could cling to his memory, he protected me."

Sam made no move, though he desperately wanted to enfold her in his embrace. If she needed protecting, he wanted to be the one. "From what?" Then, with a flash of insight, he answered his own question. "From me?"

She lowered her eyes, shifting her weight from one foot to the other. "Yes."

He framed her face with his hands, forcing her to look at him. "Couldn't you trust me not to hurt you? I love you, Kate."

Her lips trembled. "I know that now. But I wouldn't let myself believe it. I thought you and Jenny—"

"Believe it." He drew her into his arms, burying his face in her silky hair. "Today, tomorrow, always."

She gave a tiny gasp, before entwining her arms around his neck. "I have to apologize," she said breathily. "I never should have doubted you."

"Just don't do it again," he murmured, then kissed her with all the pent-up emotion of a long month without her.

When he finally released her lips, she smiled up at him. "You know Ed's portrait?"

"What about it?"

"Lupe told me it would come. But only when I was ready."

"And now?"

"I'm ready. And it came. The reason I'm ready?" She moved her fingers through his newly shorn hair, as if discovering him all over again. "I love you, Sam." Her eyes were luminous.

"And I love you. I'll try very hard to make you happy, Kate."

"You already do." When he tried to kiss her again, she drew back. "Wait. I want to tell you the title of the painting. It makes everything perfect."

He nuzzled her neck. "And what might that be?"

Her answer was strong and sure. "Freedom."

EPILOGUE

BART AND BLAKE SPRAWLED on the Manleys' living room floor helping Parker build a tower of wooden blocks. Sam and Paul sat on the front porch discussing whatever men discussed after church on a lazy summer Sunday. In the kitchen Jenny was putting finishing touches on the flower arrangement she was creating out of cuttings from Jean's garden. Jean, with all the artistry of a master chef, was garnishing the glazed ham with maraschino cherries and orange slices.

Kate put the last serving spoon on the dining-room table, then stood back checking to be sure she'd set the table properly. She knew she shouldn't be this nervous. She and Sam already had Jenny's approval. And Rachel's. Sam, who seemed to know something she didn't, had assured her Jean wouldn't pose a problem. But still. There was Paul, a father who had doted on his only son. And Bart and Blake, who would be nothing if not outspoken about the matter.

Kate wiped her hands nervously on her skirt. She had no idea how she'd be able to ingest a morsel of food until it was over. How Sam could be so darned nonchalant mystified her.

"Watch out, Mom." Jenny, carrying the centerpiece, edged around her and carefully set the flowers in the middle of the table.

Jean followed. "The table looks lovely." Her eyes darted from place to place. "Are we ready?"

Kate couldn't find her voice. She nodded.

Jean stepped to the living room door. "Boys, go get the men. It's time to eat.

"Pahkah go, too," the toddler said, trailing after his heroes.

Kate couldn't look at Sam or Paul when they gathered with the boys in the dining room. Jean nodded to her husband, who asked them all to join hands. On one side, Kate felt Jean's warm grasp; on the other, Blake's sticky fingers squeezed hers tightly.

"Heavenly father, bless this family gathered here today…"

Family? Kate focused on the word. Could she dare to hope?

"…and bless this food to the nourishment of our bodies. Amen."

Out of the corner of her eye, she saw Sam hold up his hands. "Before we sit down…"

It was happening.

"…I have something I'd like to say." He stepped around the end of the table and took his place beside Kate. "As I look around, I see people who are very special to me. The Manleys who've welcomed me here today. Parker, who's helped me feel like a successful doctor. Jenny, who straightened me out. Bart and Blake, the finest sons a man could have. And Kate." Smiling down at her, he put his arm around her and pulled her closer. "Kate," he repeated her name fondly, "who has done me the honor of accepting my proposal of marriage."

Kate waited, her heart pounding. The reactions

weren't slow in coming. "Dad," Bart shouted, "that's awesome."

"I figured it out first," Blake told his brother.

Kate found herself engulfed by Jenny's and Jean's hugs, but over their heads, she saw Paul step back, then draw a handkerchief from his pocket, remove his glasses and wipe his eyes.

Jean clapped her hands. "Glorious news. Just glorious. Sit down, everybody."

Jenny went to her accustomed place. Jean waited by her usual chair. The three children found their seats at the card table set up for them. Kate hesitated, unsure where to sit.

Then Paul laid a hand on Sam's shoulder, steering him to the place vacant for so many painful months. "Have a seat, son."

Kate's heart melted, and a lone tear trickled down her cheek. She found her father-in-law's eyes and held them, silently thanking him for the gift he'd just given her and Sam.

"Thank you, sir," Sam said holding out his hand to Kate, who joined him at the table. "I only hope I'll be able to do justice to this wonderful meal."

"Why wouldn't you?" Kate asked.

Sam chuckled. "Ask Millie at the café. I told her when I had something to celebrate I'd have the cholesterol special for breakfast." He leaned over and in front of everybody, kissed her. "And today I had something to celebrate."

"Yuck! He's doing it again," Blake said.

"What?" Jenny asked.

"Kissing her!" Then the twins, joined by Parker, broke into delighted, contagious giggles.

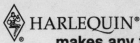